MW00588215

THE MOSCOW PROTOCOL

A UNIVERSITY ESPIONAGE THRILLER BOOK FOUR

TERRENCE MCCAULEY

ROUGH
EDGES
PRESS

The Moscow Protocol
Paperback Edition
© Copyright 2022 (As Revised) Terrence McCauley

Rough Edges Press
An Imprint of Wolfpack Publishing
5130 S. Fort Apache Rd. 215-380
Las Vegas, NV 89148

roughedgespress.com

This book is a work of fiction. Any references to historical events, real people or real places are used fictitiously. Other names, characters, places and events are products of the author's imagination, and any resemblance to actual events, places or persons, living or dead, is entirely coincidental.

All rights reserved. No part of this book may be reproduced by any means without the prior written consent of the publisher, other than brief quotes for reviews.

eBook ISBN 978-1-68549-018-8
Paperback ISBN 978-1-68549-019-5

THE MOSCOW PROTOCOL

CHAPTER 1

SOMEWHERE

THE MAN CALLING himself James Hicks felt his handheld vibrate in his shirt pocket.

He moved out of the heavy flow of foot traffic on the sidewalk and ducked into an alcove of an office building. He already stuck out in this city. No reason to play the ugly American who checked his phone in the middle of a busy street.

He removed his handheld from his shirt pocket and checked his phone. Just like any other office worker on a break.

But James Hicks didn't work in an office. And his handheld was no ordinary phone.

He was disappointed to see Rahul Patel was calling him directly. He may have only been with the University for a short time, but he should've known better than violate the organization's Moscow Protocol.

After the University had struck its first blow against The Vanguard in Berlin and China, Hicks enacted the emergency protocol to put the covert organization on a war-time footing. The protocol had been designed to protect the organization. All communications between Department Heads, Faculty Members, Teacher's Assistants and Assets were kept to a minimum. Only texts to Jonathan, the organization's Dutchman, were allowed through their secure internal network. Further contact was allowed only during an op or an emergency.

Rahul's phone call broke protocol. Hicks was not pleased. The call potentially put the rest of the organization at risk. The Vanguard had proven to be a capable and elusive enemy.

He let the call go to voicemail as the device scanned his thumbprint, face, and retina before granting him access to the Optimized Mechanical and Network Integration system on his phone. It was not only the university's internal communications platform. It was also one of the most advanced computer networks in the world.

But Hicks knew that no network was perfect. OMNI had never been hacked because, like the University, it had operated in obscurity for years. Taking on The Vanguard directly had changed that forever.

Hence his displeasure with Rahul's phone call.

Rahul's op was confirmed. All the details had been decided. Contingency plans finalized.

He tapped out a secure text message to Rahul.

Why are you calling me? You have your orders.

Rahul's reply was immediate.

Why won't you take my calls? Where are you?

Hicks decided to ignore the question about his location.

Moscow Protocol, Ace. Video and voice comms are minimal unless during an operation.

Hicks checked the street to see if he'd drawn any unwanted attention. So far, so good.

Patel typed out a reply.

Reviewed your target package. Your plan is difficult to execute. One month is not enough time to set a honey trap for this kind of target.

'Honey trap', Hicks thought. An old term for a love ploy against a target, but an accurate one.

The timeframe is adequate if you use it wisely.

Again, Rahul's reply was immediate.

This isn't some drunk convention attendee on the make. This is a very dangerous and crafty target.

Hicks didn't need Rahul Patel or anyone else to tell him Colonel Yeung was a dangerous man. That's why

Hicks had ordered Roger Cobb to break Tessmer so he could help them track down Colonel Yeung.

Now that they knew how to get him, it was up to Rahul Patel to bring the colonel in.

Hicks knew a month would be ideal for a couple of reasons. An agent of Rahul's skills would be sufficient for Patel. A month would also give Hicks enough time to heal from his procedure. By then he'd be ready to personally oversee the final stages of his plan to bring The Vanguard down.

For attacking his city. His country. And killing the woman he loved, Tali Saddon.

The plan he was ordering Rahul to launch was the masterwork of Hicks's career. He'd spent weeks refining it. Its perfection was in its simplicity. He knew things would go wrong. Mistakes would be made, and unexpected complications would arise. His plan already allowed for such things.

Hicks knew there was only one catch. Every step had to happen in precise order if his plan had any hope of succeeding.

That was why he'd selected Rahul Patel to conduct the first operation in the scheme. Colonel Yeung would be the first domino to fall that set his plan in motion.

None of his people knew the complexity of the plan or where it led. Only Hicks knew that. To tell anyone, even Jonathan or Roger or Rahul, could put the entire scheme in jeopardy. His faculty members couldn't know the details of his plan, only the specific role they played in causing each specific domino to fall when and how Hicks ordered it.

It would require a lot of oversight on Hicks's part, but by then, he'd be ready.

He quickly typed out a response to Rahul.

You have two weeks to select a Field Assistant, preferably one already in country. You have an additional two weeks to bait the hook and reel in the target. You have your orders. You have sufficient time to execute them. Plan accordingly. Keep Jonathan informed. Hicks out.

Hicks ended the conversation by closing out the discussion in OMNI. As dean, he had that unique technical privilege to shut down dialogue whenever he chose. The course had been set. Any further debate was pointless.

Hicks pocketed the handheld again and looked at the endless stream of people moving along the sidewalk. It was an oppressively hot and humid day by his standards, but none of them seemed to notice.

His mind drifted back to his plan. It would work. Rahul would see to that. Once they had Colonel Yeung in hand, he could know exactly where to focus his next attack on The Vanguard. He'd have a place to start and, if he was lucky, a bit more.

Hicks decided he'd been standing there long enough and continued walking to his destination. He didn't want to keep his surgeon waiting.

CHAPTER 2

VLADIVOSTOK, RUSSIA - ONE MONTH LATER

RAHUL PATEL's fingers drummed the steering wheel while he waited for his colleague to call.

The concrete parking garage seemed to only get smaller as each second ticked by. The lights grew more intense. He hated being closed in like this during an op. Exits were limited. The number of cars parked around him provided numerous spots for an ambush.

The trap should've been sprung already. They were still on schedule, but he wanted to be on the move *now*.

Waiting had always been the toughest part of the job for him. Patience was the most important skill he possessed.

He knew his Asset would call him as soon as the drug took effect. He wasn't worried about that part of the plan.

He was worried about all hell breaking loose in the minutes that followed. Colonel Yeung's security team would not be happy.

Rahul knew Colonel Kim Yeung, an army officer of The People's Democratic Republic of North Korea, had come to Vladivostok to indulge his carnal appetites, particularly his fondness for young Russian men. The university's surveillance of the colonel also showed Yeung's security team often gave their boss privacy during his frequent visits to the Russian city.

Their discretion and Yeung's indiscretion had given the university a prime opportunity to kidnap him. To make him confess all he knew about North Korea and The Vanguard's operations in the United States.

Patel knew grabbing Yeung was one thing. Escaping with him would be something else entirely.

Yeung was one of the most dangerous men in the world, though few outside the intelligence community knew his name. Officially, he was a colonel in the North Korean State Security Department (SSD). As was the case with most people in such positions, his influence extended far beyond the definition of a title.

Yeung had been a driving force behind the SSD for decades. Publicly, he swore allegiance to his party and its leader. Quietly, he began to question the decadent young man's commitment to the cause. To Communism.

Intelligence reports revealed the colonel to be a hardline Communist who considered himself closer to Stalin than Gorbachev. He resented the new regime's overtures to the West, wishing instead for a more hostile, provocative stance with the sworn enemies of Communism. He thought his leader's repeated saber rattling quelled soon after by concessions from the Americans made The Hermit Kingdom look like a beggar nation.

His frustrations explained why Yeung had quietly allied himself with a group of former Russian and Chinese intelligence operatives who shared his world view. A group known as The Vanguard.

In doing so, Yeung had found a way to support the spread of Communism while he lined his own pockets as well. Communism might be the best way to rule a country, but Yeung believed himself to be exempt from such limitations. He had been a peasant before joining the army. He enjoyed being wealthy much better.

When Roger Cobb broke the prisoner named Tessmer, the University learned that Yeung had become wealthy by allowing The Vanguard to use North Korea's loose infrastructure of spies in the United States to infiltrate his country's most hated enemy.

The intelligence infrastructure was so loose, in fact, that most American intelligence organizations paid the North Korean network little mind. What's more, few of Yeung's operatives in America knew they occasionally served the aims of The Vanguard, not their country.

But now the University had Yeung's network in its sights. Not because of the threat it posed, but because of a man Tessmer had said was hiding in a North Korean safe house somewhere in California.

Someone Hicks wanted captured. And Yeung could provide the information they needed to get him.

If Rahul could get him out of the building alive, of course.

Rahul sat up straight when he heard his Asset's voice in his hidden earpiece. "Base, this is Hammer. Do you copy?"

In compliance with the University's communications protocol, Rahul kept his radio chatter simple. "I copy, Hammer. Sit rep."

"Target is down," the Asset reported, "but I don't know for how long. Hurry."

Rahul was already out of the car and on his way to the elevator. "Prep him and get him ready to move. Any guards outside your apartment?"

"No," the Asset said. "He forbids them from even entering the building, though they're usually stationed in the lobby. He's afraid they might get the right idea."

Rahul got into the elevator and hit the button for the eleventh floor. He hoped the elevator wouldn't open in the lobby. Yeung's bodyguards might see him, and that could present a problem later. An Indian man in a diverse city like Vladivostok wasn't as rare a sight these days. But seeing him so soon on a return trip with their boss bound and gagged would make him memorable.

He wasn't worried about the doorman seeing anything on the security cameras at the desk. OMNI had been playing a looping feed for the cameras in the garage, on the eleventh floor and inside the empty elevator for the past ten minutes. If all went well, there'd be no trace of him when this was all over.

Rahul breathed a bit easier when the elevator skipped the lobby and ran directly to the eleventh floor. He made sure his jacket was open in case he needed to grab the nine-millimeter Glock holstered under his arm.

The elevator doors opened, and the hallway was clear. Fortunately, the Asset's apartment was directly across from the elevator. That had been Patel's idea when he'd arranged to lease the apartment a month before.

The apartment door was already ajar as per their plan, and Rahul pushed his way in.

He found his Asset, Dusan Petrov, in the bedroom, struggling to get Colonel Kim Yeung's pants back on.

Colonel Yeung's preference for pale, blond Russian men was an open secret among North Korea's military and intelligence apparatus. But since Yeung was the keeper of many secrets, including those of his government's ministers, his superiors turned a blind eye to Yeung's proclivities. There was no reason to risk the colonel bringing their own shortcomings to light. Kim Jong Un was not known for being broad minded.

Rahul rushed to help Dusan get the colonel dressed.

"You dirty dog," Rahul chided. "You boys usually don't get down to business this quickly."

"He said he was in a hurry this time," Dusan told him. "He was worked up about something and drank his champagne faster than normal." He nodded at the bottle on the bedside table. "He never tasted the drug I used to coat the glass. Whatever was bothering him must've been big. I've never seen him like that."

Rahul knew what that something was. He may not have known the details of Hicks's greater plan, but his objective was obvious.

The University had already taken a healthy bite out of the Vanguard's European operations. It had also coordinated an airstrike on The Vanguard base in Xianyang. OMNI's intelligence showed Yeung's masters at The Vanguard were pushing him to help safeguard their remaining interests in Asia against further University attacks.

The Vanguard had no idea that the one man they'd

relied on to save them was literally in bed with a University Asset. At least not yet.

With Yeung's pants on and hastily buckled, Rahul held the colonel by the collar, keeping him upright while Dusan pulled Yeung's arms into his jacket.

Together, they carried Yeung out of the apartment and into the hallway. Rahul bore most of the unconscious colonel's dead weight while Dusan rang for the elevator. If one of the tenants happened to see them, they looked like they were taking care of a friend who'd had too much to drink.

The colonel's security detail would see things differently.

When the elevator doors separated, Dusan held them open with his foot while he helped Rahul haul Yeung inside. Rahul let the apartment door shut locked behind him.

As the elevator doors closed, Rahul said, "Sorry about that. Hope you have a key to get back in."

"I won't be going back after tonight," Dusan said as the elevator began to descend to the basement garage. "Too dangerous. Besides, they're promoting me to Teaching Assistant after tonight. I'm on my way to Istanbul after this. Just got word of it this morning."

Rahul would have congratulated the young man if he wasn't concentrating on the electronic numbers counting down the floors to the garage. Once again, he willed the elevator to not stop in the lobby. The security cameras might be on a loop, but he'd have no way of hiding Yeung from his bodyguards if they happened to be looking at the elevator at the wrong time.

His stomach sank as he felt the elevator begin to

slow as they approached the lobby. The damned thing was going to stop after all.

"I've planned for this," Dusan said as he shoved the unconscious Yeung into the corner of the elevator and propped him up as he pushed the much larger Rahul in front of him. "Lean back to keep him from falling over. He'll be tougher to see if he's behind you."

Rahul did as he was told and Dusan pulled Rahul's jacket all the way open, further concealing the colonel from view. He placed his head on Rahul's chest and began rubbing his shoulder as the elevator doors opened.

Rahul spotted a stocky Asian man in a black trench coat standing guard in the lobby. He glanced at the open elevator, but quickly turned away when he saw two men embracing.

Dusan sighed and cursed in Russian as he hit the button to close the doors and shot the security man a dirty look as the doors shut. The elevator continued down to the basement.

As soon as the elevator began to move, Dusan helped Rahul pull the colonel out of the corner. "Public displays of affection make people uncomfortable. A dash of homophobia doesn't hurt."

Rahul liked the young Russian's style. "Let's hope he didn't recognize you as Yeung's boyfriend."

"The colonel always kept me his dirty secret," Dusan said. "But that goon probably knows what apartment I live in. We've only got a few moments before they realize we're gone."

Rahul began to pat down his prisoner while keeping him propped up. "I take it you checked him for tracking devices?"

"Always. I made sure his phone is still in the bathroom. That's all he ever brings with him when he comes to see me."

All that he knows about, Rahul thought as the elevator doors opened again and the two men began dragging the North Korean into the garage.

"Which car is yours?" Dusan asked, grunting under Yeung's dead weight.

"The black Lada Granta over there," Rahul said as he steered them in the direction of his car. It was at the end of the row closest to the elevator.

Dusan was already out of breath. "The garage is full of black Lada Grantas."

"So is most of Russia," Rahul said. "Best way to blend in."

Rahul hit a button on the key fob, and the trunk of his car popped open. He kept hold of the North Korean's shoulders as Dusan took his legs and they dumped him into the trunk.

Rahul slammed the trunk shut as Dusan scrambled around to the passenger's side.

Rahul got behind the wheel and was glad the rental started up immediately.

"How well do you know the city?" Dusan asked as he buckled in beside him. "Some of these streets can be—"

Rahul ducked as automatic gunfire raked the passenger side of the car. Round after round punched through the door and the side window. The windshield became a web of cracks and gaping holes.

Rahul stayed low as he hit the gas and sped the length of the underground garage, trying to put as much distance as possible between him and the shooter. He peered through the shattered windshield as he sped through the garage, looking for other threats to avoid.

He didn't risk taking his eyes off the aisle to check on Dusan. He knew by the way the operator was slumped that Dusan was dead. Only the seatbelt kept him reasonably upright.

At the end of the aisle, Rahul was forced to take a hard left as a black SUV screeched to a halt, blocking his exit.

His only exit.

Patel rounded the corner and slammed on the brake before throwing the car into park as he dove out of the vehicle. He heard men shouting in Korean as they got out of the SUV and began to spread out.

Rahul rolled behind the cover of a parked car and drew his Glock. He hoped the thought of their boss in the trunk might keep them from firing in his direction. But he quickly remembered the first gunman hadn't cared, so he doubted these men would, either.

Rahul knew Yeung had a four-man security team. He counted three men as they began to move toward him.

The first shooter was still out there. Probably hiding, just like him.

One of the men from the SUV was continuing to shout in Korean when Rahul popped up from behind the car, ready to fire.

His first target had just taken cover across the aisle behind a parked car on his left. Rahul fired once, hitting him in the throat.

Another gunman on the left side of the aisle cut loose with a full blast in his direction as Rahul dove flat on the garage floor. Bullets tore through the windows and doors of the cars on either side of him, but the angle of the wild firing was too high to reach him.

Rahul heard the man from the SUV continue to shout orders above the gunfire, though Patel had no idea what he said.

As soon as the gunman's rifle clicked empty, Rahul popped up on a knee and took him with a single shot to the head as he began to reload.

Two down. Two to go.

The man from the SUV kept shouting and Rahul moved through the line of parked cars at a crouch. He'd fired from the same location twice. With one shooter in front and another somewhere behind him, staying in the same place would be suicide.

He checked the driving lane in both directions before rounding the corner and moving up three aisles closer to the SUV and the leader still crouched there.

Rahul paused. Listened. The man was no longer barking orders, but Rahul could hear him panting in the heavy silence.

He was close.

Maybe one row ahead.

Rahul checked the aisle again, saw it was still clear, and inched around the corner of the next row of cars.

He found the leader crouched behind a car at the end of the row. His back was to Rahul as he whispered into a microphone clipped to his sleeve. His rifle hung from a sling across his body.

He was an older Korean man with close-cropped gray hair on a square head. He looked like a capable man, one who had been chosen for his post due to his bravery, skill and loyalty.

But security posts tended to make even the best

soldiers soft, hence the reason why he was crouched with his back to his target.

Knowing the SUV was his best, quickest route of escape, Rahul decided stealth was more important than firepower now.

He tucked his Glock back in its holster and pulled the small blade concealed in his buckle.

He moved silently at a crouch toward his target. In one practiced movement, he slipped his hand over the leader's mouth as he drove the blade deep into the side of his neck. Patel quickly withdrew the blade and wrapped both arms around the man's head as he pulled him backward with him into a sitting position.

Patel's knees kept the dying man from reaching for the rifle slung across his body as his lifeblood escaped him with every heartbeat. Patel spread his legs to pin the dying man's arms against the sides of the cars around them. There was still one shooter out there who may not know his position. No reason to make himself an easy target.

He squeezed the man's mouth and nose harder as his death throes worsened, muting his gasps as blood continued to shoot out from the severed artery in his neck.

The guard's body reluctantly went slack as he continued to bleed to death.

When the man went limp, Rahul slipped the automatic rifle from his body as he gently eased himself backward. The guard's head hit the garage floor with a muted thud as his left leg began to tremble.

Rahul recognized the weapon as a QBZ-191 Assault Rifle. The same kind of hardware he had seen Yeung's men carry during surveillance. He checked the chamber and the magazine. The gun hadn't been fired. He quietly slapped the magazine back in as he moved back to the end of the aisle.

Only one shooter left. The first one. The one who'd killed Dusan.

He remained crouched at the end of the aisle and listened.

He heard something but couldn't identify it at first. The harder he listened, the more he was sure it was someone crying.

A woman. He was sure of it. She was crying somewhere deep in the garage behind his current position.

If he could hear her, the shooter would be able to hear her, too. He might be heading in that direction right now, seeking to use her as a hostage.

Rahul knew better than to break cover and give the last gunman an easy shot, so he crept slowly toward the sound of the crying.

He swept each row he passed with his rifle before moving on. So far, all of them had been empty.

When he reached the row where the crying sounded the loudest, he paused. Another sob confirmed this was definitely the row.

Was the woman wounded? Being held as a prisoner? Or just a resident caught in the crossfire, scared out of her mind?

Rahul kept his rifle at his shoulder as he stole a quick glance around the car. It was a woman with blonde, curly hair pulled back in a high ponytail. She had big blue eyes and was crouched between two cars. She was dressed in all black.

Just like the men he had just killed.

And a black skull cap was on the ground beside her.

Rahul decided to see if she passed a test. He squeezed the rifle's trigger.

The empty chamber clicked.

The woman's head snapped around at the sound. There were no tears in her eyes.

Only a pistol in her right hand.

Rahul cut loose with a short burst.

Her nine-millimeter skidded across the garage as she fell. It was one of the sweetest sounds Rahul had ever heard. *The sound of victory.*

Confident he had cleared the garage; Rahul stood and removed his handheld from his pocket. He took a picture of the dead woman and took a quick scan of her fingerprints. OMNI would automatically begin searching for her identity as soon as he got a signal. It might come in handy sometime in the future.

He knew he should do the same with the rest of the guards but knew he didn't have that kind of time. Someone must've heard the shooting and called the police. He had to get himself – and Colonel Yeung – out of there. Fast.

He slung the rifle over his shoulder as he stepped over the dead woman and ran back to his ruined rental car. He popped the trunk and found Colonel Yeung still unconscious. He pulled him up by the collar and hauled him onto his shoulder.

He carried him over to the SUV, dumped him in the back seat and shut the door. The vehicle hadn't been hit by rifle fire and the engine was still running.

He got behind the wheel and placed the assault rifle on the passenger seat. He wanted to keep it close in case he needed it again. He backed up the vehicle, then cut the wheel left and sped up the ramp out into the night.

He palmed his handheld and tapped the screen for the device to emit a signal that would block any tracking device that might be embedded somewhere in the SUV.

He didn't like leaving Dusan behind, but Rahul could already hear the wail of approaching sirens. He didn't have much of a choice.

Now that he was in the open, he activated the handheld's secure features that gave him access to OMNI. The mission screen appeared, and he tapped the contact icon with his thumb.

When the man answered, Rahul gave the all-clear sign. "This is Dr. Kumar speaking."

Jonathan asked, "Do you have the item?"

Jonathan was quiet for a moment.

"I have him. Proceeding to the extraction point. Dusan is dead."

"Damn," Jonathan swore. "I'd just promoted him, too."

Rahul knew that but had more immediate concerns. "I've got cops closing in on my position. I need you to find me a safe way out of here."

He heard Jonathan's fingers on the keyboard. "Christ, you're in a North Korean state security vehicle?"

"My handheld is blocking the tracking device."

"Barely," Jonathan said. "Dump it and steal something else."

Sometimes, the Dutchman's lack of field experience frustrated him. "Easier said than done with an unconscious North Korean colonel in my back seat, old man. Besides, hot wiring cars has never been my specialty."

Jonathan swore again as Rahul heard his hands work the keyboard. "Follow the route I've just sent to your phone. You'll be intercepted along the way by another vehicle that will flash their lights at you in two three-set bursts. Do not shoot. They're the flight crew to our aircraft. Follow their lead and we'll get you out of there."

Sometimes, Rahul missed his old job as the chief counterterrorist with India's Security Service. He would've had an entire team and backups in place for a mission like this.

But the University was different. OMNI gave them an incredible technological edge, but their field operations were often barebones at best.

"We lost a good man tonight," Rahul told him, ignoring University communications protocol. "Roger damned well better be able to get this one to talk."

"Is he alive?"

Rahul glanced back at the colonel as he navigated traffic. He was snoring lightly. "He's alive."

"Then Roger will get him to talk. Until then, have a safe flight. We'll touch base when you land."

"Wait," Rahul said before Jonathan could kill the connection. "I want to talk to the Dean."

He knew better than to say James Hicks's name over the air. Even one of the most secure communications networks in the world like OMNI was safe until it wasn't. Too many capable people were hunting the man to risk saying his name.

"That's not possible at the moment," Jonathan said. "He's in the field. You know that."

That wasn't good enough for Rahul. Not on a night like tonight. "Damn it, mate, he hasn't been reachable for weeks. I just won a pretty big prize for him tonight and I think I'm entitled to tell him about it personally."

But Jonathan wouldn't be moved. "As you know, we are currently operating under The Moscow Protocol. I suggest you review those protocols on the plane to explain why you can't talk to him. You and I will connect when you deliver the prisoner safely to Roger. Until then, we're over and out."

The line went dead, but the map remained on his handheld's screen.

Rahul punched the steering wheel as he stopped at a red light. He knew damned well what The Moscow bloody Protocols were. The University had been on a war footing since blowing up The Vanguard base in Xinjiang several weeks before.

He might've known what The Moscow Protocol was, but he didn't have to like it. And he liked the idea of Hicks being out of communication even less. He knew his assignment to grab Colonel Yeung played a part in a much larger plan. He wanted to know what that larger plan was. He was operating in the dark, and in this business, what you couldn't see could kill you.

But he'd already known about Hicks's methods when he'd agreed to join up with the University almost a year before. He always had a good reason for whatever he did, even if he didn't explain himself clearly.

Rahul decided the best he could do was follow the blue line on the map on his handheld and hope it didn't lead to a dead end.

CHAPTER 3

WASHINGTON, D.C

THE NEW DIRECTOR of National Intelligence looked up from his screen when his aide knocked on his office door.

"Excuse me, Director Demarest," the young man said. "Your visitor has arrived."

Charles Demarest had been so deep into approving the president's Daily Intelligence Briefing that it took him a moment to remember what visitor his assistant was talking about.

But when he did remember, it was like remembering an upcoming colonoscopy appointment. "Where is he?"

"In the second-floor conference room as per your previous instructions, sir."

Demarest turned off his monitor, automatically locking the computer from prying eyes. He took his suit coat from the back of his chair as he stood. "Thank you, Norman. I'm on my way."

A stickler for detail, Demarest normally would have chastised the young aide for not providing him a quick synopsis of the meeting on his calendar. For not reminding him about the agenda and details of the people waiting for him.

But this meeting was not on Demarest's official calendar and Norman had not been asked to provide briefing materials. Neither had anyone else on his staff.

Demarest had scheduled this meeting personally. And the fewer people who knew about it, the better.

Demarest's four-man security detail surrounded him as soon as he stepped out of his office and cleared a path for him through the crowded hallway. Having been a field man for the early part of his intelligence career, Demarest hated making such a scene, but the security came with the job. It could only be altered by a direct order from the president.

Demarest hated the fact that he couldn't even walk down the hall without armed men at his side. He was grateful he had a private bathroom, or else he wouldn't have any privacy at all.

The hallway was full of office workers and uniformed personnel from various branches of the military going about the important business of protecting the country they served. Demarest usually tried to take the sting out of the disruption his presence caused by returning the few smiles and nods they directed his way. He knew each of them dealt with enough threats in their inboxes and on their monitors every moment of the day. They should at least be spared from the sight of armed guards clearing a path whenever their boss decided to leave his office.

But that day was not a day for smiling. There was

too much at stake and there were too many questions that only one man could answer. The man who now waited for him on the second floor.

ANOTHER SECURITY MAN greeted Demarest and his team when he stepped off the elevator on the second floor, bringing the total number of men guarding his life to five.

The second floor had no windows and was often used as swing space for departments whose floors were undergoing refurbishment or the replacement of old equipment. It was where contractors on short-term assignments parked themselves while they did their work in-house.

The security detail followed Demarest as he walked toward the largely forgotten conference room once known as the Bubble.

"I've been told my guest is already here," Demarest said to the fifth security man.

"Yes, sir," he said as he tapped his keycard to release an electronic door lock. "We wheeled him inside about half an hour ago."

Demarest remembered his guest was now an old man confined to a wheelchair. It was a fact that would take some getting used to. He'd once roamed these very halls with the ferocity of a caged lion and was feared accordingly. "What's his disposition?"

"Frankly, sir, he's a nasty old bastard."

Demarest grinned. "Glad to see some things never change. I take it you searched him for devices. The wheelchair, too. Just because he's old doesn't make him any less crafty."

"We gave him and the chair and the conference room a thorough search," the guard assured him. "Magnetometer and the full spectrum of scans, too. We even searched the paper files he brought with him. Everything came up clean. Said he knew enough to leave everything electronic in his car."

Demarest had expected no less from his old nemesis. After working for the Agency for more than thirty years, John Meager knew the drill.

"I want you to have someone search his car while we're meeting," Demarest told him. "If you find anything, interrupt us. I want to know right away."

"Consider it done, sir," the guard said as he led him down the hall. "Should we be looking for anything in particular?"

"When it comes to John Meager," Demarest said, "I've learned it's best to keep an open mind."

Demarest waited for one of the security men to open the hatch before he entered the oldest and most secure room on the entire campus.

The relic from the Cold War known as 'The Bubble' was more bunker than conference room. It was a simple rectangle that had been constructed of steel repurposed from a decommissioned battleship. Its sole purpose was to serve as a secure place to discuss secret matters in person. It had no phone lines and no electrical outlets.

The only furniture was a long wooden table, and ancient metal chairs so uncomfortable that Demarest thought they had been part of a medieval torture chamber.

Upon being confirmed Director of National Intelligence a few weeks before, he had ordered chairs with more padding and ergonomic support to be placed in the Bubble. The Security Department politely reminded him that padding presented a ripe environment for listening devices in the cushions, thus posing a risk to the room's only purpose: absolute assured privacy. His request was conveniently forgotten.

A powerful magnetometer had been built into the bulkhead to ensure that all tapes or electrical devices would be erased on their way into and out of the room. Bitter experience over the years showed the same happened to SIM cards, floppy disks, credit cards and memory boards of laptops. Thick steel walls lined with lead made it difficult, if not impossible, for anyone to listen in on what happened inside the Bubble.

The only power in the room came from a bank of overhead lights installed high overhead. The vents that circulated air into and out of the room led straight up to the roof. A tiny device just above the grill emitted a powerful scrambling signal that made eavesdropping from above impossible. The entire duct was also monitored for movement and blocked every few feet by rebar. If a mouse somehow found its way into the vent, security immediately knew about it.

The room had been overbuilt for the time it was constructed and was completely impractical in the modern age of tablets and cellular technology. But Charles Demarest and his predecessors had decided to keep the room exactly as it was because, every once in a while, a lack of technology was exactly what a situation required.

With his security detail standing guard, Demarest

pulled the hatch door shut and activated the magnetic lock that sealed them in.

"Seems like a hell of a lot of bother for a talk between two old men like us," a familiar voice growled from the table.

The voice may have been familiar to Demarest, but the figure seated at the far end of the table was not. The John Meager he had known all those years ago had been a balding, paunchy man with a penchant for white short-sleeved shirts, a pocket protector and thick, black-framed glasses. He'd looked like a rumpled accountant or an absent-minded academic instead of an unsung pioneer of modern computer networks.

Meager's accomplishments had been nothing short of genius. Had he decided to work in the private sector instead of serving his country, Demarest had no doubt that John Meager's name would've been mentioned alongside those of Bill Gates and Steve Jobs.

But the man in the Bubble with him now was a shrunken, arthritic husk of his former self. Pale, wrinkled skin now hung loosely from his face. Hands that had typed out innumerable amounts of code upon which most of the current world now functioned were gnarled things perched on the worn armrests of his wheelchair. The leather case on the table in front of him appeared even older than its owner.

Anyone who saw John Meager in his present condition could be forgiven for thinking he was just another retired bureaucrat living on a government pension. But Charles Demarest knew that neither age nor infirmity had dulled the man's sense or abilities.

Which was why Demarest had summoned him here.

Demarest attempted to break the ice with flattery. "It's good to see you, John. You're looking well."

"And you're still full of crap," Meager sneered, showing teeth yellowed from age and black coffee. "You only brought me here because you needed me. And only you would be dumb enough to ask for a report from a computer engineer in a black room. In the Bubble no less." The old man laughed. "I never thought much of you, Charlie. Glad to see the years haven't proven me wrong."

Demarest had prepared himself to absorb the old man's anger when he scheduled the meeting. "And I'm glad to see you're still the same cantankerous old bastard I remember."

Meager grunted his approval as he pulled his cracked leather case to him. "What you should be glad about is that I printed out my findings for you." He flipped open the flap and removed two thick folders bound by rubber bands. He struggled to push one along the table in Demarest's direction, but given the old man's weakness, the folder only made it halfway down the table.

Demarest left it where it was. "Why the hurry? It's not like you have someplace to be. You're retired, remember?"

"*Forcibly* retired, thanks to you," Meager corrected him. "And don't let this wheelchair fool you. If I could, I'd walk over there right now and backhand you for what you did to me. Your thugs out there wouldn't do you much good."

"Yet you accepted my offer when I contacted you last month," Demarest observed. "You set aside your hate for the sake of your bank account."

"I already have all the money I need," Meager said. "I only agreed to work for you because I still love the Game. I wasn't ready to leave when you pushed me out, Charlie. I still had plenty left to give. You knew that."

"Perhaps," Demarest allowed, "but it was time, John. I had just been assigned to take over your department and you made no secret of your dislike of me. Shouldn't I have the right to choose the people who work for me?"

"Transfer me, yes, but to force me out into the street like that?" Meager countered. "Under armed guard? That was unnecessary and just plain mean."

Demarest had never been accused of being a kind man. His ex-wives could attest to that.

Meager had once been Langley's technical genius. He'd been the cock of the walk at headquarters for years and was never shy about sharing his low opinion of field agents like Demarest. He was of that post-war school of thought that believed technology had made human intelligence obsolete. Listening devices and computer systems were the new ways to gather information. *Toss the cloak in the dustbin and melt down the dagger for scrap. We have computers now.*

Meager and his generation saw themselves as a new type of warrior, where programmers were generals and people like Demarest were mere cannon fodder at best. Their orders delivered via printouts. Their instincts and knowledge replaced by algorithms and databases.

Demarest distinctly remembered a wooden sign Meager used to have on his desk: 'And the Geeks Shall Inherit the Earth'.

Demarest hadn't allowed Meager to take the sign with him when he'd had him thrown out of the building. He had taken great pleasure in watching the damned thing burn in his fireplace that evening.

The geeks may inherit the earth, he remembered thinking as he enjoyed a glass of scotch by the fire, *but the ones with the guns still get things done.*

But Demarest decided he had enjoyed his decades-long victory over Meager long enough. He saw no reason why he couldn't eat a little crow in the assured privacy of the Bubble.

"That was a different time, John. A different era. We were just beginning to understand how technology and fieldwork could benefit each other. God, fax machines and beepers were still miracles of the age, much less the Internet."

Meager brought a frail hand down on the armrest of his wheelchair. "Don't you dare tell me about the Internet, you ignorant pup. I built the damned thing, remember?"

No matter how much Demarest disliked Meager's cockiness, there was no arguing his credentials. Men like Cerf and Kahn may have received credit and awards for building what had become the Internet, but Meager and his team of programmers had toiled in the shadows nearly a decade earlier. If any single person could lay claim to creating it, John Meager could.

"No one is challenging your bona fides, John." Demarest finally took a seat. "I was talking about the bureaucratic philosophy at the time. No one has ever questioned your ability. Not even me."

"Just my loyalty," Meager spat, "which is even worse."

"Your loyalty to me, yes, but never your patriotism,"

Demarest countered, "which is why I brought you in on this particular project."

Demarest cleared his throat and forced a smile, as if he was struggling to put his thoughts into words. "You're the only one who can help me find this man, John. Not for me or my benefit, but for the good of your country."

Meager slowly shook his head. "Good God. You're still the same insincere bastard you were thirty years ago. The vocabulary might've gotten better, the suit might be a little more expensive, but it's just as empty now as it was then."

Demarest wasn't surprised Meager had been able to see through his façade. And he was glad his frail condition hadn't dulled the fire in his belly. He'd need that fire now.

He gestured at the file on the table halfway between them. "Let's skip the pleasantries and tell me what you found."

"I found out a hell of a lot just by you asking me to work for you again."

Demarest furrowed his brow. "I'm not sure I follow you."

Meager sat back in his wheelchair. "You wouldn't ask me to work on something as easy as tracking down someone unless you needed them found soon and fast." He raised a crooked thumb to the ceiling. "You've got a building full of clickers and coders who can do that for you if that's all you wanted. But you put me on it instead." He smiled. "That means you've got something to hide, Charlie boy. Something off-book."

Demarest glanced at the ceiling. "I only put you on it after *they* failed to find him." That was a lie, but he wouldn't give the old man the pleasure of being right. He appealed to his ego instead. "I brought you in to succeed where they could not."

Meager lowered his weathered hands and folded them across his lap. "This James Hicks fellow really has you scared, doesn't he?"

Demarest bristled. "Hicks is an Asset. Nothing more. If I were afraid of him, I wouldn't need you to take care of him. He'd be dead already."

"If you could find him, which you can't," Meager mocked. "All these years and you've never grown up, have you? Never met a problem a bullet couldn't solve. Men like you write off Assets like Hicks all the time. What's so special about this one?"

The old programmer sat a little further forward in his wheelchair. "I've got my opinions, of course. Like maybe he's your long-lost son. The result of an illicit rendezvous you had with a stewardess one snowy weekend in Minsk or some other God-awful place. I'd like to think you have cancer and want to meet the boy one last time before you wind up roasting in the fires of Hell." He shook his head. "But I wouldn't be that lucky, now, would I?"

Meager's mouth was quickly becoming an annoyance. No one had ever been able to get under his skin quite like John Meager. Except, perhaps, for James Hicks.

"Sounds to me like you're justifying your failure in being able to find him."

"We'll get to that," Meager assured him, "but not before I get some answers."

Demarest didn't like being questioned, especially

by the likes of John Meager. "I gave you sufficient parameters by which you could conduct your search."

"You gave me an alias, some blurry ATM footage and some possible last known locations. A bunch of blown-up brownstones in Manhattan. A shooting in Toronto. A cemetery in Berlin. A destroyed base in the Mongolian desert. That's not a hell of a lot to go on, Charlie, so I had to do some digging on my own."

Demarest dropped his head into his hand. He knew what Meager's digging often led to. "Christ, John. Tell me you didn't."

"Damned right I did," Meager boasted. "Was easy, too. You boys managed to close a lot of my backdoors into the network, but not all of them. I found out that James Hicks is giving you actionable intelligence that's helped you break the backbone of some Russo-Asian syndicate your people are calling The Vanguard. He's identified dozens of operatives you can either interrogate or put behind bars for decades. You've seized almost a billion dollars in assets and virtually crippled The Vanguard organization in Europe. As far as I can tell, this 'Asset' of yours is feeding you the best information of your miserable career right when you needed it most, yet you hired me to find him for you. Why?"

Demarest was beyond annoyed but dared not give him the satisfaction of showing it. But he also needed to tell Meager something to break down the stonewall he had erected. "Hicks is a renegade, and I can't trust a renegade. I can't rely on his good will to keep feeding me actionable intelligence. Like you, he has forgotten his place in the order of things and, like you, I need to bring him to heel." He threw open his hands. "That thorough enough an explanation for you?"

Meager frowned and gestured toward his files on the table. "I cleaned up that image you gave me and ran it through every facial recognition program in the world, including a few programs I'd designed myself. Nothing came up. Every single lead you've given me, which wasn't a hell of a lot, has led to a dead end. I can't find anything on this man anywhere in the world. I didn't even bother with social media. I mean no references anywhere, no military or criminal history, no licenses of any kind, no diplomas, nothing."

Demarest's own people had confirmed that, but Meager had forgotten more about systems than most of them could ever know. "I take it you found a way to check the databases of our allies, particularly in Europe?"

Meager looked insulted. "You know damned well I did. There are no fewer than twelve official images of James Hicks across the entire intelligence community. None of them are of the same man and no two descriptions of him are alike. That face in the ATM footage doesn't appear on any network anywhere except yours."

Demarest watched the years seem to peel away from Meager as he continued.

"That left me with two possibilities. Either this guy has been trained to stay completely off the grid, or someone has gone through a hell of a lot of trouble to erase his past. I checked traffic footage from the time and date the ATM footage was shot. The system was hacked at the time, but all traces were scrubbed so clean that I almost missed it. That means he's got friends who are technologically proficient."

Meager went on. "The Manhattan address you gave me is to a brownstone owned by an off-shore dummy corporation. It was destroyed in a gas leak several months ago and the Berlin cemetery was the site of a shootout a few days later. The Mongolian Desert location you gave me was a complete waste of time. Just a ruined base that the Chinese military used for target practice."

Demarest knew the base had been The Vanguard's main center of operations but saw no reason to share that information with Meager. His patience with the old man's grandstanding was growing thinner by the second.

"Why do I think this is a long-winded way of you telling me you couldn't find him? Still covering your incompetence after all these years."

Meager seemed to take the rebuke as a challenge. "Don't be so sure. I did something neither you nor that kindergarten class you call an operations center could do with all of your resources. For starters, I found out who James Hicks really is."

Demarest dropped his hand. His true identity could give him leverage he could use to make Hicks come forward. Family to threaten. Anything. "Tell me."

Meager shook his head. "Not until you tell me why you want to gut the goose who has done nothing but lay golden eggs for you."

Demarest hesitated, but he needed answers. He decided to give him one that would get his attention. "Because I have every reason to believe that James Hicks is the Dean of the University."

Meager unlocked the wheels of his chair and turned it so he faced him head on. "You're not serious."

"I didn't have a sense of humor when we worked together," Demarest said. "I still don't."

"The University?" Meager repeated, as if hearing the word for the first time. "They're a joke. A bunch of eggheads who eavesdrop on conversations at UN cocktail parties. They're policy geeks, not field men, assuming they ever existed in the first place."

"They exist, alright." Demarest decided to feed him a little information. "That brownstone explosion in Manhattan? A drone strike on what we believe was their headquarters. Those shootouts in Toronto and at the Berlin cemetery? Their people put that together." He conveniently left out his personal intervention with the Germans about the Berlin operation. "Those policy geeks, as you call them, have built themselves one hell of a tactical operation. And the technology you think they have scares the hell out of me. All of it is completely off-book. Not one penny in government funding. No congressional oversight, either."

Meager looked like he would've had to sit down if he wasn't already in a wheelchair. "How the hell do they get their money? How do they communicate? Surely you've got a line on them."

"That's what I needed you to find out," Demarest admitted. "You're right that Hicks has never fed us a single shred of wrong information. Want to know why? Because the people they've given us are either already dead or in jail by the time we get to them."

"What about the money you've seized based on his intel?" Meager asked. "It's about a billion by my count."

Demarest was reluctant to admit, "That was all Hicks's doing. Though we have reason to believe he's skimmed some of it to fund his operation. Maybe as much as half."

"Sounds like an enterprising young man," Meager

said. "Can't blame him for that. You've done the same thing in your time, Charlie."

Demarest knew better than to deny it. "The information Hicks is giving me is too big to hide and too good to be lumped in with all of our other intelligence. People on the Hill and at the White House are beginning to ask questions about where all of these golden eggs are coming from. It's just like math class. They're asking me to show my work and I can't exactly tell them it's coming from some mad monk intelligence group that might not even be allowed to exist. Those who don't laugh me out of the room will be angry I've allowed them to exist for so long without bringing them under control. I need Hicks to work with me on a strategy, especially now, and I have no way to reach him."

Demarest had walked into the meeting prepared to eat a certain amount of crow, but he'd finally had his fill. "Hicks is capable and deadly and knows how to cover his tracks. His information has brought a lot of attention his way and I don't know how long I can protect him unless I can coordinate with him."

He spared Meager the details about the congressional investigations he believed Hicks had triggered. The aftermath of 'Black Site-gate' still haunted the Community. Half a dozen agencies wanted Hicks's head on a pike even though they didn't know who he was. And they were good enough to get it if Demarest couldn't run interference for him.

He wasn't worried they'd find him. He was worried they'd miss him, and Hicks would respond in kind.

Meager tapped his finger absentmindedly on his briefcase. "I need to know what you'd do if you found him, Charlie. Level with me. Would you kill him?"

"Have you been listening to everything I just said?" Demarest asked. "He's too valuable to kill. I just need to get him to work with me before somebody finds him and stops him. Now tell me who he really is."

Meager let out a long, slow breath. "I suppose that's as close to an honest answer as I can expect from you." He winced as he continued to mindlessly tap his files. "You know, this job has taught me that sometimes you can only understand something by its outline, not by looking at it head on."

Demarest could feel the weight in his words. Meager was working up to something, so he let him talk.

"Sometimes, you can only identify it by the shadow it casts instead of seeing it directly."

Meager glanced at Demarest, who realized his expression undoubtedly told him he was lost, so he went on. "Since the information you gave me was useless, I read through the action reports in the Berlin police records about the shooting at the cemetery. My German's a little rusty, but I was able to tell that one of the graves had a fair amount of blood on the grass. The gravestone was completely destroyed. I accessed the cemetery records for who owned the grave where the blood was found. I came up with two interesting pieces of information."

Demarest didn't realize he was sitting on the edge of his seat until Meager stopped talking. "Well? Go on, damn it."

"The grave is owned by the Von Hayek family. That might not mean much to you, but a man named Tessmer—"

"Is one of the Vanguard agents Hicks captured,"

Demarest said. "He's been missing since the cemetery in Berlin and is presumed dead, though I think Hicks may still have him."

"I have no idea if he's dead or not," Meager admitted, "but I traced the records of the mason who laid the gravestone and what it said. The records show the stone had only three odd lines engraved on it. 'Stephen Henry Bumgarner. Lieutenant, United States Coast Guard. Semper Paratus'. Since Hicks was at the cemetery and someone went to the trouble of destroying the stone, I think the name meant something to him. Probably his real name."

Demarest sat back in his chair. Outside of meeting Hicks on that park bench in Washington all those months before, this was as close as he had come to discovering who the man was.

Stephen Henry Bumgarner, a lieutenant from the Coast Guard. "What did you find on Bumgarner?"

"His file has been redacted. Everything. No photos, not even a single slip of paper on him except for a Stephen Bumgarner signing in at a Coast Guard base in New Orleans twenty years ago. I think he was assigned to their intelligence unit, but I can't swear to it. I traced his background and the best I came up with was two possible parents, both deceased. His old man was with in the army. Airborne. Saw action in Korea and Vietnam. A real bad ass. Got a couple of purple hearts and a bronze star. Ran a skydiving school in Idaho. Mother was named Mary. She was a schoolteacher. Stephen was the only son. The rest of his life is a blank."

Demarest's hopes sank. If someone of Meager's skill couldn't find anything on Bumgarner, none of his people would. "That's all?"

"That's a lot," Meager told him. "It means someone worked hard to erase his past. Knew what they were doing, too. It means he's been smart enough to stay off your radar and remain untraceable for more than twenty years. It means he's been able to tie up some of the best intelligence agencies in the world into knots looking for him. That shootout in the cemetery? Not one trace of him or his people on any of the traffic cameras in the area. All of them swept clean or put on loops during the time in question. Same with that Toronto shooting, too. There's no way this University could exist without some means of communication, especially in today's world. So, if you can't find him with all the tools you've got, it's because his University pals are communicating over a bandwidth you know nothing about and have no hope of cracking, which means you're right about one thing. You should be scared of him."

Unfortunately, Meager hadn't told Demarest anything he didn't already know or hadn't already considered. At least he had a name to look up. Files to search for, but that was all.

"Recommendations?" he asked.

"A great big one." The old man leaned forward in his wheelchair. "Leave this guy alone, Charlie. He's every bit as capable and smart as he thinks he is. You can't afford to tangle with a man like that, especially given your new position. Keep taking the intelligence he's giving you. Ignore it if it's too good to cover, but don't try to pin him down and definitely don't try to corner him. He'll hurt you if you try."

Demarest felt a bead of sweat run down his back

and commanded himself to remain calm. "I need to find him, John. And I need you to do it. Can you do it?"

Meager gestured toward his bundle of files. "I think I already have. But God help both of us, because I don't think we'll like what we find."

CHAPTER 4

OUTSIDE GJIROKASTER, ALBANIA

WHEN COLONEL YEUNG AWOKE, he felt himself
floating in fire and darkness.

As absurd as that sounded to him, it was the only
description his mind could find for his current state.

He knew his eyes were open, but he could not see
anything. He sensed a space above him but all he saw
was absolute darkness. He tried to move his head, but it
was being held in place by some unseen force. He felt
something might be stuck to his head but couldn't be
sure.

He tried to feel for it but found he could not move
his hands. They would not budge, though he tried his
best to move them. His legs were equally useless. He
felt water slosh around his body as he struggled. He was
splayed like a starfish.

He cried out in frustration but couldn't hear his
own voice, not even in his head. All he heard was an
echo of infinite silence.

The water was warm, and he was naked. This was all he knew.

This was how he had woken up.

Someone had captured him.

He decided to stop screaming and accept his fate. Conserve energy for the battle that surely lay ahead. He knew he would need it.

He knew Dusan must have betrayed him. The champagne must have been drugged. His security team had been loyal to him for years. None of them would have dared to allow him to be captured, much less in Russia. It had to be Dusan. He would see to it that the miserable cur paid a dear price for his treachery.

But for the moment, Colonel Yeung reminded himself that calm was his only weapon. He had been trained to stand the rigors of interrogation. He knew how the game was played. The best he could do is wait for his captors to make the next move.

He tried to keep his mind a blank as he floated weightless in the water, but the memory of fire kept returning to him. Where had his memory of fire come from? Had it been part of a dream?

The memory quickly became reality as a current of electricity coursed through him. His body tensed, straining to arch against whatever restraints bound his limbs in place. His inability to move only made his agony more vivid.

The torment had lasted only for a second but had felt like years. He knew from experience that electricity was a wicked tool when applied properly.

His body went as limp as his bonds would allow when the current stopped flowing. Every cell in his body felt like a burning ember beneath his skin.

"Good. You're awake," a voice said in English. Anglo, Yeung decided as his pain subsided. The accent was difficult to place, but it wasn't British. Perhaps an American with a strange accent?

"Who are you?" Yeung shouted into the silent darkness. His own words lost to him. "What do you want with me?"

"Me?" the voice repeated. "I'm not important. Think of me as a friend. If you do, it'll only make this endeavor easier for both of us. Think of the time we'll spend together as an investment in that friendship. Because, by the time we're through here, Colonel, you and I will be close friends indeed."

Yeung tried once more to struggle against his restraints, but it was useless. He couldn't even see what was holding him down. He yelled once more into the darkness. "Why am I here? What do you want?"

"A small dose of electricity has made you quite the philosopher, hasn't it?" the voice said. "You've just asked the eternal questions humanity has been asking since that first night we crawled out of the cave and looked at the stars. Fortunately, we can narrow down your question to a specific topic. But first, some ground rules."

Yeung felt a surge of strength and struggled again, but his bindings were solid.

"If you tell me the truth, you will remain as comfortable as you are now," the voice explained. "You will even be rewarded for your cooperation. But, if you lie to me, I'll know it and I'll hurt you worse than I did just now. The water you're floating in is an excellent conductor of electricity and will serve to enhance your agony. The more you lie, the more pain you'll feel."

Yeung felt several sensations across his back. It wasn't pain, but something else. Contact.

Something was in the water with him.

His fear spiked.

He did his best to flail around to see what it might be, but his head remained immobile in the terrible darkness.

"Don't worry about them," the voice said. "As long as you don't bleed, they're harmless, though I assure you they're quite hungry. They haven't been fed since we brought them from the Ligjang River a few days ago. But we won't let it come to that, will we, Colonel?"

He was familiar with the Ligjang River. And what lived in its waters.

Piranhas. I'm in a pool filled with flesh-eating piranhas. I'm in the clutches of a madman.

He cried out again when he felt their fins and teeth scrape against his spine.

The voice filed his mind once more, drowning out his growing terror. "Now, I know you're an accomplished interrogator in your own right and that you've been trained to withstand all sorts of tactics and techniques. You may rest assured that no one has trained you for me. For instance, I know a German colleague of yours named Tessmer. He's a rough customer, as you know well, but I eventually managed to win his cooperation. In fact, he was instrumental in our efforts to find you. If you're truthful, you will come out of this in one piece. If not, you'll find out just how hungry your new neighbors are."

Tessmer, Yeung thought. The Vanguard's man in Europe. General Zhou had told him he had gone missing and was believed dead. Yeung believed so, too.

Tessmer was not the type of man who would allow himself to be taken alive.

Yeung wanted to believe this man was lying about breaking Tessmer, yet he knew it was true. There was something about his voice that made Yeung believe. It was not the language, for Yeung spoke English fluently. It was not the accent or the threats he had made, either. Yeung had been threatened before.

It was way he spoke. With certainty. A cold finality. He was not looking to simply making him talk. He was enjoying this.

Yeung felt his bladder go, warming the water around him.

"That's it, Colonel," the voice filling his mind once again. "Let it all out. Whatever comes naturally to you is perfectly fine. We have no decorum here. No formality. All your secrets will soon be my secrets. The burdens you have carried alone for so long will now be shared by me. This is as assured as the sun rising in the east each morning. The only question is how much pain you are willing to endure before we reach that place of peace together. So let us begin. Tell me about The Vanguard's operations in the United States. And remember what will happen if you lie."

The fins and teeth scraping across his back made Yeung scream.

Two HOURS LATER, Roger Cobb muted Yeung's sobs through the control room speakers. He looked back at Rahul, who stood against the door, arms folded.

"Well?" Roger beamed. "I think that was rather productive, don't you?"

Rahul had never been one to endorse brutality, but Roger had done his job. "I've used sensory deprivation before, but never on such a grand scale."

Roger was the picture of modesty. "I've always found it quite effective. I perfected it on Bajjah back in New York. The lack of stimuli forces the subject's mind to work against itself, making breakage much easier to attain. Quicker, too. It requires constant monitoring lest the subject go mad, but when applied properly, it works wonders."

He smiled. "The electrodes along his back are a recent invention of mine. They exceeded my expectations."

"The bit about piranhas was a nice touch," Rahul admitted. "I think that's what really broke him, though I didn't know they had them in China."

"Neither did I until I Googled it," Roger said. "Just one river, but it was enough to convince our friend in there. Have you ever encountered piranhas?"

"Never had the pleasure," Rahul said.

"I did in Paraguay a few years back. Nasty little things."

He sighed as he looked up at the infrared image of Yeung held suspended in the pool. His mouth was open, and he appeared to still be screaming. "Granted, it's not as rewarding as beating him with a telephone book, but it works."

He picked up a pen and began writing down some notes. "I still have a few kinks to work out, but all in all, I'm pleased with the results. I only hope our Dean concurs."

Rahul felt himself shiver despite the heat of the humid room. Roger was so casual about inflicting pain. Terror. He supposed that's what made him so effective.

He removed his handheld from his pocket and contacted Jonathan. When the Dutchman picked up, Rahul put him on speaker.

"I've been tracking your session via OMNI," Jonathan said. "Excellent work, gentlemen. Now we know the extent of The Vanguard's operations in the United States. The Dean is already putting the next phase of the plan in action."

"About our beloved Dean," Roger said without looking up from his notes. "I need to speak to him. Right now."

"Like I told Mr. Patel earlier, that's not possible."

"And as you've undoubtedly seen during the course of my interrogation of Colonel Yeung, nothing is impossible. You're in communication with him. Put me through to him. Immediately."

Rahul knew what Jonathan would say and set the handheld on the table. This was between Cobb and the Dutchman. Rahul wanted nothing to do with it.

"I only communicate with him through text and email," Jonathan said. "Moscow Protocols, remember?"

Roger set his pen aside. "I know all that. I've tried that. He's not responding. To say I'm concerned would be an understatement."

"I understand," Jonathan said, "but—"

"Something's wrong with him, Jonathan," Roger said. "He's cut himself off from everyone except you. He's never done that before. He's out there somewhere on his own planning God knows what." He glanced at Patel, as if reaching some sort of decision, before saying,

"I don't think he's in his right mind. He's not thinking clearly."

Jonathan's silence spoke volumes before saying, "I don't disagree with you, Roger, but I'm as much in the dark as you are. I don't know where he is or what he's working up to and that's the truth."

"And if you did know, you'd never say."

"At least I could assure you he was safe. But I don't even know where he is. I can't track his handheld or laptop. All I get are terse orders via email and text that I pass along to whomever he tells me to. I haven't actually spoken to him since shortly after China."

Rahul had been through all of this with Jonathan before and believed him. He only hoped Roger believed him. If he didn't, things could get complicated.

Roger looked down at the handheld as if he wanted to smash it – and the man on the other end of it – to pieces. "Then in your next communication with him, be it by text or email or smoke signal, please be kind enough to tell him I'm done interrogating people for him until he calls me. I'm not demanding this as his agent or his employee but as his friend. I've seen what he's capable of when he withdraws like this and it's not pretty. Convey that to him and let me know what he says."

"You have my word I'll pass along your message," Jonathan said. "And, for what it's worth, I'm worried, too. But I can't make him do anything. All I can say is that his orders are lucid, and all of this seems to be part of a grander plan he has in mind. You've just succeeded in giving him a handle on The Vanguard's network in the United States. What he plans on doing with that information is anyone's guess."

"Just do as you're told," Roger said. "You're good at that."

Roger killed the connection and gave the handheld back to Rahul. "The insolent little shit. He's useless."

Their conversation had gone better than Rahul had expected. He hoped if anything could reach Hicks, it would be Roger's demand. If he couldn't get answers from him, no one could. And if he didn't, they would continue to operate in darkness, just like the North Korean colonel they now had suspended in the pool.

Rahul pocketed the handheld. "What do we do next?"

Roger returned to his notes. "You get to take a break for a few minutes while I finish here. Once we know what they want us to do with Yeung, we'll act accordingly. We may have to move quickly, so be ready."

As Rahul stepped out into the hallway of the abandoned pool house, he heard Roger unmute the audio feed from the pool.

Yeung was still screaming.

CHAPTER 5

KOREATOWN, SAN FRANCISCO

"Damn it, Base. This is Tango Alpha. I say again, I need a response!" Mary Foster's frustration filled the inside of her minivan. She continued to act as though she was checking her look in the visor mirror. "I'm not walking in there without keyword verification."

To anyone who happened to be walking, Mary Foster looked like a soccer mom on the phone with one of her friends as she touched up her makeup before heading into the Gateway Korean Market. Their affordable produce was a closely guarded secret within a select group of parents in the local soccer-playing community.

Except Mary Foster did not have any children. She didn't have any friends. And she certainly didn't know how to cook, either.

She wasn't there to take advantage of the Gateway Market's great prices. She was there to infiltrate North Korea's intelligence network in the United States. The facility in the basement was one of the Hermit King-dom's most important intelligence hubs on the West Coast. And everyone who worked in the market was a North Korean spy.

OMNI scans of the building showed the twenty-four-hour market was guarded by no fewer than six personnel at all times. Every one of them was armed.

She flicked a strand of long black hair over her shoulder as she appeared to dab mascara on her eyelashes. The hair was a wig, and the application brush was dry. She never wore makeup during an operation.

She was anxious to get started with this one, but not before she had verification on one very important detail.

"I need confirmation on the keyword before I go in," she said. "Is it Colonel Kim *Young* or Colonel Kim *Yeung*?"

The difference in pronunciation might be lost on Anglo ears. But considering she was about to meet one of the highest ranking North Korean intelligence offi-cers on the west coast, Mary knew the correct pronunci-ation would be the difference between her walking out of the market alive or spending the next several days being interrogated in the market's basement before being shot in the back of the head and dumped with the rest of the garbage.

She hadn't been briefed about the role her mission played in the greater scheme of things, but that was how the University worked. Each operative was only told as much as they needed to know to complete a specific mission. The organization didn't use trite phrases like 'need-to-know', but that's what it boiled down to.

Mary's assignment was as simple as it was dangerous. Pose as a Russian operative needing access to the North Korean safe house somewhere in California. Convince the North Korean agent posing as a cashier in the market to take her in or give her the address of the safe house. OMNI would then track Mary remotely while she reached her destination.

Once she was situated, Base would give her further instructions.

But none of that would happen until Base confirmed the right keyword. And Base wasn't responding.

She was glad when she finally got a response in her earbud. "Copy, Tango Alpha," the electronic voice said. Tango Alpha was University-speak for her current title of Teacher's Assistant. The flat, metallic tone told her the professor's voice was being electronically altered.

A Teacher's Assistant was one step below Faculty Member, a Professor. A designation she desperately wanted. "Hold for a moment."

At least she'd finally gotten a response from Base. Not much of one, but any response before an op was more comforting than dead air.

She touched the dry brush to her lashes as she waited for a response from her Professor. She had no idea what his name was, but anonymity was another common practice in the University.

All she could hear was the sound of the professor breathing. It wasn't heavy breathing, but loud enough to tell her someone was on the line.

His silence didn't help calm her nerves.

She checked her handheld to make sure the connection to Base was still live. *Why the delay? And why the voice-altering software? What was wrong with her handler?*

These were not questions she wanted to be asking herself in the moments before walking into a building filled with suspicious, armed personnel from a belligerent nation.

When she had been elevated from an Asset to a Teaching Assistant a year ago, Mary's handler had told her she'd have a chance to continue making a difference in the world. She had been working for the University as a Consulting Asset for almost five years by then and had been impressed by how efficient the organization was.

This was the biggest assignment she had ever been given. She was at the top of her game and ready for the challenge. She was beginning to believe that her Professor was not.

That was a problem.

Under ordinary circumstances, she would have written it off as a technical glitch and aborted the mission by driving away. But these weren't ordinary circumstances. The University was operating under Moscow Protocol, which meant no assignment could be refused or aborted without a handler's permission. Doing so meant immediate termination from the organization. She imagined it also meant termination from living, too.

She could accept the danger, but not the silence. "Are you still there, Base? Come in!"

Still nothing, except for the breathing.

Her worry ticked up a notch. This was all too similar to when her Apache had been shot down behind enemy lines after a *jihadi* nailed her helicopter with a lucky shot from a TOW missile in Mosul. Her crew-mate had been killed immediately and her comms were dead.

After a hard landing, it had taken more than an hour for the rescue team to reach her position. Despite a fractured leg and a severe concussion, the Apache's weapons systems had remained functional, and Foster had managed to single-handedly fend off several attacks from ISIS raiders anxious to reach the downed chopper and take the American crew hostage.

After some time in the hospital, her leg and brain eventually healed, but not well enough for her to ever get behind the stick again. Her aptitude for languages had landed her a spot with Army Intelligence in Seoul, studying troop movements in North Korea.

Despite glowing reports from her superiors, she didn't re-enlist when her hitch was up. She'd joined the Army to fly one of the deadliest helicopters in the world, not ride a desk. The same government that had trained her to fight wouldn't let her back in the field. She took her Purple Heart and went home. No harm, no foul.

Once a civilian, she didn't find many employers who were eager to hire a grounded helicopter pilot who hated office work and seemed to have a problem with authority.

Somehow, the University had found her. A series of mysterious texts were followed up by several phone calls designed to gauge her interest in continuing a different kind of intelligence work. The kind of work where she could serve her country her way.

After a meeting in New York with an odd man who'd called himself Roger Cobb, she'd been given a smart phone linked to OMNI and access to a numbered online bank account. He gave her the rank of Consulting Asset and said she'd receive details about her assignments via the handheld. The line about still making a difference had hooked her.

She'd told Roger that she hated deskwork, and could still remember the chill that ran up her spine when the strange little man laughed. 'Oh, I don't think that will be a problem.'

Her assignments had mostly been rough stuff and gun play, which was fine by her. It wasn't flying, but it beat reading reports all day.

The money was more than she'd made in the Army and more than enough to keep her from asking too many questions. Her assignments eventually became more varied and interesting. All of them had prepared her to walk into that Korean market now.

But she wouldn't commit suicide just because her Professor was having a bad day. She was beginning to consider putting the minivan in drive and taking off.

She finished miming the application of mascara to her lashes and screwed the brush into the container. She could practically feel every camera outside of the market focus on her. The longer she sat there without getting out, the more attention she would draw from the North Koreans inside the market. They hadn't kept this facility intact for twenty years without having a healthy level of suspicion. She needed to move soon. Any longer and their guard would be up.

"We're short on time here, Base," she said, "and my cover is about to be compromised. I either move in now or I drive away. Please acknowledge."

"Stay on mission, Tango Alpha," the electronic

voice came back. "The keyword verification is Colonel Kim *Yeung*, not Young. Repeat, keyword is Kim *Yeung*. Yankee Echo Uniform November Golf. Do you copy?"

Finally. "Copy, Base."

"You are clear to proceed. I have video and audio on your position. Good luck."

Mary dropped the empty mascara bottle in the minivan's cup holder. "Copy, Base. Tango Alpha is on the move."

She tied her wig into a high ponytail and hit the sidewalk. *Just make sure you cover my ass, you bastard.*

MARY IGNORED the looks she drew from the Korean women on the street as she walked to the market. She was more concerned about the four security cameras in front of the store currently tracking her every move.

Despite her sunglasses, she knew her face was undoubtedly being run through a variety of databases attempting to identify her before she entered the store. Base had assured her that her phony cover was already uploaded into the appropriate systems. She only hoped Base hadn't blanked on that detail, or her mission was over before it even started.

Her black wig and black windbreaker were plain enough to make her blend in as well as any Anglo could hope to blend into Koreatown.

The black yoga pants were tight and left nothing below the waist to the imagination. She knew she would attract attention from men stationed at the market, which was the idea. Even trained spies were known to admire the female form. She hoped they would dismiss her as nothing more than eye candy. To them, she was just another barbarian westerner who looked like a whore.

A fat old man sitting on a cheap plastic stool at the front door of the market leered at her as she approached. He stopped her when she tried to go inside, and motioned for her to open her bag for examination.

She complied and watched him pay more attention to the triangle gap of her thighs as he probed the contents of her bag with an old wooden spoon handle. She could practically feel his eyes on her backside as he waved her into the market.

Fat Man called out something in his native tongue to the rest of the men in the store and, judging by their laughter, she was glad she didn't understand the North Korean dialect of *Chosono*.

Four Korean women Mary pegged for civilians were pushing shopping baskets through the aisles. They were dressed conservatively and, judging by how they looked at her, didn't approve of a white woman in such immodest dress. She bet their daughters probably dressed the same way, making them hate her by proxy.

In her earpiece, Base said, "The four women are civilians. One stock boy in the back. Your target is behind the counter. There are three more downstairs. The old man at the door is packing, so you're up against six. Stay on target. You're doing fine."

Of course I'm doing fine, she thought. *I just walked into the place. I haven't done anything yet except draw attention.*

Mary recognized her target behind the counter from the target package Base had sent her. A plump

Korean lady of indeterminate age perched atop a stool behind the cash register. She was Colonel Ye-rin Pak and ran her country's counter-intelligence operation on America's west coast.

She looked up from a notebook when she saw the Anglo woman approaching. But unlike her customers, her expression was inscrutable.

From the corner of her eye, Mary saw the stock boy's head pop up over the shelves. His eyes moved up and down over her body. It was as much a leer as it was part of his training. Like the rest of the market's employees, he was assigned to Bureau 225, North Korea's counter-intelligence group trained to infiltrate the Bay Area's Korean community.

But the agent playing stock boy wasn't looking at her as a threat. He was looking at her as a scantily-clad diversion from his cover. And he was enjoying the view. She knew the bulge in his pants wasn't entirely due to her, but to the nine-millimeter he had tucked under his shirt.

Mary hefted her black, oversized bag on the counter and folded her hands across it. She leaned closer to the woman and whispered in Russian, "My uncle told me you might be able to help me a young woman in need of a favor."

The woman's blank expression didn't change.

Mary repeated the script she had rehearsed a hundred times in front of a mirror until her tone and look were perfect. She continued in Russian, "He said I should pay you a visit the next time I was here in San Francisco."

The woman's expression didn't change. She replied in English, "And your uncle's name?"

"Uncle Yeung."

The woman's eyes barely flickered. "Never heard of him. Go away now."

Mary had been told the first response would be a rebuke. She took off her sunglasses and laid them on her bag. "That's a shame because he speaks very highly of you and your store. He said this market is the backbone of your community. He told me you were most generous to strangers in need."

The woman shifted on her stool and kept speaking in English. "I don't know anyone by that name. Buy something or go away."

But Mary offered the last piece of the puzzle instead. "He asked me to speak to you personally. He said you had a very special gift."

The woman's eyes narrowed. "What gift? Nothing's free here. You pay or go."

Mary leaned in closer and continued to speak in Russian. "A gift for magic. A gift that allowed you to hide something in plain sight no matter who was watching."

The woman slowly raised her head. Her eyes moved to the four customers scattered throughout the store, going about their shopping. She glanced at the ancient security monitors next to the register. Mary knew she had state of the art equipment in the basement below her, so the monitors were merely a ruse. She wondered if the facial recognition scans had already identified her. She hoped her false identity had been uploaded to the appropriate places.

But when the cashier was satisfied no one was listening to them, the woman asked in Russian, "When did you speak to your uncle?"

Mary stuck to the script Base had given her the day before. "A week ago in Shanghai. We often met there."

The older woman's eyes narrowed. "Where are you from?"

Mary was encouraged. "I was born in Kiev, but my family moved here when I was young. I have visited my homeland many times since. My parents never forgot the traditions of our forefathers."

Mary had been told the woman would take that to mean they had remained loyal Communists after democracy came to Russia.

Colonel Pak responded in Russian. "You didn't come here directly, did you?"

Mary shook her head. "Of course not. I entered through Canada and drove down here in a minivan provided by friends." She patted her bag on the counter. "I can show you my passport if you'd like to see it."

The cashier clutched Mary's bag and looked to the fat old man at the door. He nodded that he had checked it and she pulled Mary's bag toward her. She unzipped it and examined it herself. Mary knew she would only find the fake passport and wallet she had inside. All the information within would back up her story.

The cashier swept the passport off the counter and held it low, out of view of the other customers.

While the woman thumbed through the document, Mary caught the phony stock boy looking at her backside. He smiled when she caught him looking. Mary smiled back.

If things went sideways, she decided he would die first.

The woman's hand slowly moved out of sight

beneath the counter. Mary shifted to her right as if she was uncomfortable. It was because she remembered the intelligence report she had read on OMNI. Colonel Pak kept a sawed-off shotgun behind the thin paneling of her register to deter robbers. Even spies had to protect themselves against common thieves.

Base spoke in her ear. "Careful, Tango. Something's wrong."

Mary didn't have to fake her pensive expression as she nervously patted her bag on the counter. *No shit.*

She tried selling her nervousness by continuing to speak in Russian, "I trust everything is in order, Auntie?" She hoped the common phrase of respect would show she knew how to address her betters.

The woman looked at her over her glasses. It was impossible to tell if Colonel Pak was impressed or if she believed her.

When Colonel Pak smiled, Mary knew she was in trouble.

"Your passport is genuine, as are the stamps. But your uncle would've told you to say you were from Moscow, not Kiev, even though this passport says you are, indeed, from Kiev."

Mary hoped that was her only reason for her mistrust. She had been ready for this. "He didn't tell me to say that. He was very drunk when he told me about you. We were working together on a project."

"Were you?" Her hands remained below the counter, out of sight. "What kind of project?"

"The kind I can't discuss with strangers." She put a bit of iron in her voice. "Are you a stranger, Auntie? Perhaps I made a mistake. Perhaps you can't really help me at all."

Mary held out her hand for the passport, but the colonel put Mary's passport in the fold of her smock. Her right hand stayed out of view. Near the shotgun.

"Where was this project located?"

"Leningrad," she said, using the old Soviet name for St. Petersburg. Her passport had been stamped to verify that.

"Was the project successful?"

Mary smiled. "Of course."

The colonel cocked an eyebrow. "You must have reported your progress to him. Your uncle is a most fastidious man. When did you last speak to him?"

She remained on script. "Earlier this week."

The colonel raised her head. "When?"

Mary had no idea what to say but knew the slightest delay would blow her chance at finding the safe house. She tried to sound confident as she said, "Monday."

"Of this week?"

She heard her Professor begin to speak in her ear, but said, "Of course."

"Last week," Base said. "Last week."

Mary shook her head quickly as if to correct herself. "I'm sorry. I meant last Monday. My apologies. My Russian is a bit rusty."

"But how could that be?" the colonel asked. "You were just there last week, weren't you?"

Busted.

She tried to recover by feigning a sudden weariness. "Yes, of course I was. Forgive me, Auntie, but it has been a long and difficult journey. I haven't slept in days, and I've been hunted ever since I boarded the plane to Vancouver."

She held up her hands before the colonel could

protest. "No, I didn't lead anyone here, but I'm tired and scared. If you don't help me, I don't know who will. Please."

The colonel's expression remained inscrutable as she looked silently at Mary. She couldn't tell if the older woman was making up her mind or already had.

Base spoke in her ear. "Thermals show three men scrambling up from the basement. The old bitch must've hit a silent alarm. Get out of there. Now."

"Forget it," Mary said in English as she grabbed her bag. "I'll go somewhere else."

But the woman gripped her arm with surprising strength and speed. "Your uncle told you that I can hide some things in plain sight, did he not?"

Mary acted relieved. Maybe she could salvage the op after all? "Yes, that's it. That's exactly what he told me to tell you. Now do you believe me?"

The woman's grip on her left arm tightened. "That's what he was trained to say under duress, you imperialist bitch."

Base: "Damn it, Tango. Get out of there now!"

Mary fired a straight right hand that shattered the colonel's nose, rocking her back off her stool.

The customers screamed as Mary reached over the counter and snatched the shotgun just as Stock Boy pulled a pistol from under his shirt.

Mary dropped to a knee as Stock Boy fired twice. Both rounds hit the counter where she had been standing.

Mary racked in a load and squeezed the trigger. The gun kicked like a mule, but a blast of buckshot obliterated Stock Boy's right side.

She tried to swipe her bag off the counter, but Fat

Man began firing at her from his post at the door. She hit the deck in an aisle stocked with Korean candies.

Pistol fire hit the racks on either side of her as Fat Man tried to get a good angle on her position. She elbow-crawled toward dying Stock Boy and the pistol he had dropped when he fell.

Mary dove for the pistol as several more rounds bit into the floor around her. She grabbed the pistol with her left hand and brought it up to fire as she rolled onto her back.

Fat Man was crouched at the end of the aisle, feeding another clip into his pistol.

Mary fired once, striking him in the forehead. His head snapped back as he fell.

"Tango," came the voice in her ear. "The clerk is up!"

From the sitting position, Mary shifted her aim to the cashier's area in time to see the colonel on her feet. Blood poured from her broken nose, staining her blue frock.

Mary fired until the gun locked open. Each round struck the woman center mass. She stumbled backward against the wall but didn't fall. She didn't bleed, either.

Mary knew. *The bitch is wearing a vest.*

Fortunately, she had a gat for that.

She tossed the empty pistol aside as she leapt to her feet and swept the shotgun with her. She racked in another load as she leveled the weapon at the gasping intelligence officer and fired. She didn't have to look to know the woman was dead.

Mary racked another round and grabbed her bag off the counter as she ran for the door. "Three bogies down. Market is clear."

Again, the voice in her ear said, "Three rats in the basement closing in, Tango. Get out of there!"

Mary ran for the door, ignoring the continuing screams of the customers as they ran shrieking into the street. She held the black shotgun close to her leg as she exited the market. She knew she already stood out. No point in drawing even more attention by running. Maybe the three rats in the basement didn't know what she looked like.

She checked behind her and eyed the street. She expected the three surveillance men from the market's basement to be closing in on her position by now, but so far, it was just civilians gawking and pointing at her from a safe distance. No danger there.

She walked quickly toward her van but still did not run. She knew it would only be a matter of time before the customers who'd fled the store called the cops if they hadn't already. She didn't want them trying to prevent her from getting away. If they did, she had the shotgun to convince them otherwise.

Out of the corner of her eye, she saw a side door of the market burst open.

She raised the shotgun to fire; intent on blasting the first man through the door.

But the man launched himself at her midsection as she fired. The man behind him fell back into the stairway in a spray of blood.

The impact made Mary drop the shotgun as the first man tackled her against a parked delivery van. The shotgun skidded away.

Mary managed to hook her left hand under the chin of her assailant and pull him down with her as she fell. He was squirming to raise his pistol, but her bag got in his way. She reached over and wrenched it from his right hand. She dug the pistol into his left side and fired twice. The man went limp as she got to her feet, keeping the bag on her shoulder.

Her ribs hurt as she began running toward her mini-van. A heavy blow to her back sent her to the pavement as automatic rifle fire filled the street. Her jacket was Kevlar-lined, but the impact knocked the air out of her lungs.

Training made her roll onto her back as she brought up her pistol and saw another man in the basement stairwell firing an AK-47 in her general direction.

Mary ignored the pain coursing through her body and fired once, hitting the man in belly. The man dropped to his knees before falling face forward on the sidewalk.

"Are you hit?" Base asked as she gasped for air.

Finally, a full breath. "No. The Kevlar stopped it."

"Good. Police are inbound and less than five minutes away," Base said in her ear. "Get moving, Tango."

But Mary realized she couldn't go and began running back to the market. "The colonel still has the passport. I can't leave that behind."

"It's fake," Base said. "It's worthless unless the cops have you. They're closing in on your position fast. Get out of there while you still have time."

But Mary had already made up her mind that leaving any evidence behind was dangerous. OMNI and Base could scrub the video footage clean – if North Korean Intelligence didn't do that already. But Base's photo wasn't on that passport. Her photo was.

She hadn't infiltrated the safe house. Her mission

had failed. She had to salvage something. She had to get that passport back.

She got to her feet and began walking back to the market. Her entire torso ached. She almost lost her footing when the man she had just shot grabbed her leg.

She aimed the pistol down at him, ready to fire.

"Please," he said in English as he held up bloodied hands. He made no attempt at the AK-47 next to him. "Kill me. Don't leave me for the police."

Mary heard the distant sounds of sirens grow louder.

Base was in her ear again. "Tango, you've got maybe a minute. Move!"

Mary pried her leg from his grip. She had been in his position once. The last survivor of a failed mission. Enemies closing in fast. Options running out even faster, leaving her only one real choice that wasn't a choice at all.

She had put her gun under her chin in the desert outside of Mosul just as she heard the rescue team close in on her position.

But this man bleeding out on the sidewalk outside a phony market knew there would be no rescue team coming for him. Only a long stay in a hospital and inter- rogation before he ultimately died from the belly wound.

She had come for information on the safe house. She didn't want to leave without it.

Now, she might not have to.

She rested her foot against the dying man's side. "Tell me the address of the safe house."

Base yelled, "What the hell are you doing?"

"Completing the mission." In English, she asked the man, "You want to die?"

The sirens grew louder.

The man nodded quickly.

Mary aimed the pistol down at his head. "Give me the address and I'll kill you."

The man spoke quickly, in Korean first, then remembering himself, slower and in English.

He gave her the address she had hoped to get from the colonel. A building in Koreatown down in Los Angeles.

Mary looked away. "Base, did you copy that address?"

"I've already got people moving on it," Base replied, "and you have about thirty seconds before the cops grab you."

The wounded man looked up at her. Eyes wide. Expectant. Pleading. "You do as you say? You..."

Mary fired, fulfilling her promise.

She dropped the gun in her bag and bolted for the van. As she got behind the wheel and saw people pointing at her, watching her. One looked to be filming the whole thing from his cell phone. Her wig was crooked by then, but she kept it on as she turned the ignition key.

"We've got a Spielberg on our hands," she said to Base. "Some clown is filming me."

"OMNI's already in his phone," Base assured her. "The footage is being erased as we speak. Just drive."

She pulled away from the curb just as two of San Francisco's finest turned the corner and almost ran her off the street.

She watched her speed as she took the first right,

waiting until she was halfway down the block before flooring it. By the time the locals swarmed the cops, peppering them with broken English about the woman who'd just driven away, she was already pulling into a municipal garage with unreliable security cameras.

She ignored the pain gripping her body as she pulled off her black wig and stuffed it in her bag. She wound the van up the ramp, and quickly rubbed her fingers through her natural, close-cropped blonde hair.

The cops might start searching for her eventually, but not before they cleared the building and tagged all the dead bodies she had left behind.

Finding the operations center of a foreign government in the basement of the market would only complicate matters.

She stopped on the middle deck and pulled into a space next to a late model Volvo. She climbed down from the van, pulled her bag with her and threw it all into the trunk of the Volvo. She climbed in, checked her look in the mirror and fluffed out her hair. She'd never been big on fashion, but fieldwork played hell with her hair.

She drove down the ramp. Just another California blonde in a sedan.

She took the pre-paid parking card from the visor and slipped it into the machine, causing the mechanical arm to rise.

She decided it was time to check in with Base as she pulled into traffic. "I am on the street and in the clear, awaiting orders."

"Proceed home and await further instructions. Do you need medical attention?"

She was sure the man who'd tackled her had busted

a couple of her ribs. The impact from the AK set her back on fire. It could be a strained muscle or spinal damage. She'd take a long hot shower first and see if that did the trick. "I'm operational for the moment. No wounds but I'm sore as hell."

"Check in again after you get home," Base told her. "I'll make arrangements for a doctor if you need one. Might be a good idea to get yourself checked out. You took a couple of blows to the head. You might have a concussion, too."

She blinked away the double vision and rolled her neck until it cracked. It made her feel better. "I'll keep you apprised."

"Sorry the op went sideways," Base said. "Yeung played us. He'll pay for that. Good work on getting the address. Check in when you can. Base out."

She glanced down at her handheld and saw the line had gone dead.

The pride she felt numbed some of the pain as she drove. The op *had* gone sideways, but she had still managed to fulfill part of her mission. She'd gotten the address of the safe house. Her job was done. The bad guys were dead, and she was still alive.

It wasn't much, but it was good enough. Sometimes, good enough was the best she could hope for in this line of work.

She took her sunglasses from the center console and slid them on as she drove home.

Sometimes, anonymity had its privileges.

CHAPTER 6

JAMES HICKS DROPPED the headset on the desk and slowly ran his hands over his bandaged face.

He knew his surgery must have been a success because the pain was intense. The implants were still knitting to his bone structure. Sometimes he thought he might black out from the pain.

I need to snap out of it. I almost got her killed.

He held his hands against his bandages, which caused the throbbing to cease a little. He'd always done his best to avoid doctors, but the reconstruction surgery had been necessary. His old face was known to the intelligence community now. Extensive plastic surgery was the only way Hicks could regain the anonymity he needed from his own intelligence agencies and The Vanguard.

Hicks had traveled far to find one of the best plastic surgeons in the world. In fact, her location had helped shape his plan to strike at The Vanguard.

He knew the doctor's work was solid because she had used her skills to help several people elude him for years.

She didn't work out of a hospital, keep records, or take insurance. Complete anonymity was assured. She didn't know the identity of her clients and didn't ask questions. The ability to find her was the only referral she required.

She only accepted payment in cash and offered her clients two months of pain pills and antibiotics to help with the healing process. The operation was guaranteed to render him unrecognizable and would fool every facial recognition program in existence.

No follow up visits. No further contact. Any complications from the surgery and you were on your own.

He knew the pain medication was partially to blame for his fog, but not entirely. His mind had wandered often since Berlin. He sometimes found himself sitting in complete silence for hours before coming back to his senses. In the days after his surgery, while he was finalizing his plan, he only had himself to worry about. Lost time hadn't mattered much.

But this time, it had almost ruined an essential part of his plan. And it had almost cost Mary Foster her life.

The pain medication and antibiotics for his extensive facial reconstruction surgery had made him groggy. He kept use of painkillers to a minimum but needed them to sleep at night. He was usually able to fight through the sluggishness in the morning, but today, he had spaced out when Mary needed him most. That was unacceptable.

He knew part of it was because he had not allowed

himself to mourn the loss of Tali Saddon. There hadn't been time for the luxury of loss.

In fact, except for his surgery, Hicks hadn't had a moment's peace since China. That had been by design. The strike he'd arranged on The Vanguard base in the Mongolian desert had sent the organization reeling. Hicks knew he had to keep pressing the attack if he had any hope of cutting off the head of the dragon.

His plan was not only in place. It had been put into motion. The dominos were beginning to fall, but they wouldn't fall on their own. Not the way he wanted them to fall. The way he *needed* them to fall if he was going to spring his trap at exactly the right place and moment.

Timing meant everything now. Another episode of brain fog might not only threaten his plan. It would put his people at risk.

He had lost too many already. Tali. Dusan. And now, Mary. Almost.

He was the Dean of the University and 'almost' wouldn't cut it anymore. He couldn't afford failure. He'd committed too much to this fight to allow his own weakness to ruin it.

Coming up with a good plan wasn't enough. Executing the plan wasn't good enough. Results were all that mattered now.

He unscrewed the thermos beside his laptop and poured the last of his instant coffee into a plastic mug. His surgeon had told him caffeine and tobacco would hinder his recovery. He'd given up smoking cigars for the moment, but coffee was the one indulgence he'd allowed himself. His only comfort.

Hicks's current base of operations had been chosen

for its location, not its luxury. Before his surgery, he had assumed the remainder of a lease of a gaming company that had gone bankrupt in a high-rise building. The landlord was more than happy with the arrangement. He'd doubled his money and asked no questions once the check cleared.

Although the company had once occupied the entire top floor of the building, Hicks had sequestered himself in an interior office without windows. He'd spent his recovery from surgery in a sleeping bag atop a crate next to the desk. The contents of that crate would be the fruition of his plans unless he made another mistake. The time for its use would come.

A kitchen across the narrow hall stored his medicine, the MREs and dozens of cans of instant coffee he'd gathered in advance of his surgery. He hadn't stepped outside that defined area in weeks, especially during the day. He hadn't gone near the windows.

He'd also disabled the elevator so it couldn't stop on his floor until he was ready to use it. And he wasn't ready. Not even close.

But soon his scars would heal, and once the last domino was set to fall, he would inflict pain on The Vanguard who had hurt him and the University so dearly.

He had chosen this location to lure the dragon into his trap. But first he had to flush The Man out of hiding. Whoever he was. Wherever he was.

Hicks sipped the instant coffee from the plastic mug. It was far from the quality of Roger's civet blend, but he'd grown used to it out of necessity.

Even now, as he took time to have coffee, his plan was foremost in his mind. He saw it every time he closed his eyes. Like a line of dominos carefully arranged to fall in a specific order and pattern. A pattern Hicks had arranged personally.

Domino One: Roger had broken Tessmer, also known as Von Hayek, who'd given them information on how to capture Colonel Yeung.

Domino Two: Roger succeeded in getting Colonel Yeung to tell them about the joint North Korea/Vanguard operation in the United States. The colonel had been a gold mine of information. Hicks decided the West Coast targets would help him flush out the dragon quicker. Yeung had told them about the Korean market in San Francisco, which would lead them to the safe house and the target taking shelter there.

Domino Three: Hicks had personally chosen Mary Foster to go to the market and infiltrate the safe house according to a script Yeung had given them. Her Russian was excellent, and her cover had been solid. But Yeung had slipped a poison pill into the plan. Roger would make him pay for that.

Domino Four: Currently teetering, but not knocked over yet. Scott and his Varsity team was already conducting remote surveillance on the safe house via OMNI's satellite. By the time they reached the address, Scott would have a plan to hit the building immediately.

The staff at the safe house may already know what had happened at the market in San Francisco. Every moment gave them a chance to fortify their position and increase the risk to Scott's team. Time, as always, was against them.

The safe house itself was of little interest to Hicks. But a guest Yeung had told them would be there, was a high value target.

Victor Resnick. The Vanguard's chief financier and arms dealer in the United States. The fourth domino. Grabbing Resnick would bring Hicks one step closer to the person in charge of The Vanguard's United States operation and help cripple their organization. That person was the fifth domino in line.

But until Scott gave him his initial report of the safe house, Hicks had nothing but time.

Waiting had always been the hardest part of the job for him. It allowed him to over-think his plan. His decisions. His strategy. To question himself and his decision to handle this alone. To wonder if all of this was necessary or just vengeance for losing Tali. To wonder if he was just Ahab chasing a white whale.

Hicks didn't allow himself to dwell on this. He knew The Vanguard was already seeking revenge against the University for its losses in Europe and its base in Mongolia. In fact, he was counting on it. Because the more resources The Vanguard dedicated to fighting the University, the fewer resources it could use in its proxy war against the West.

Hicks drained the rest of his coffee, hoping the caffeine would kick in soon. He needed clarity right now and so did his people in the field.

He accessed OMNI's tactical screen and tracked the movements of Scott's Bravo Team. They were one of several Varsity tactical squads Hicks had positioned throughout California when Yeung had told them about the Korean market in San Francisco. He knew there was a safe house, but not the location. Fortunately, Bravo Team was the best in the University, led by Scott.

A window popped up on Hicks's screen. The Dutchman was calling. Jonathan Hammond was the University's second in command. The position had been known as the Dutchman after the old tale of the little Dutch boy who tried to plug holes in a dam.

They hadn't always had the best relationship, but since Hicks had become Dean, Jonathan had proven himself invaluable.

Hicks watched Bravo Team's progress through Los Angeles as he allowed the call to come through. He activated the voice-altering program to make himself sound stronger than he was.

"Scott and his group are headed to the safe house," Hicks said. "They're less than thirty minutes out."

"I'm surprised you answered," Jonathan said. "You haven't been taking calls as of late."

"I've had my reasons." Hicks bit off another spasm of pain. It hurt to talk. "None of them concern you."

"I'm afraid they do, sir," Jonathan said. "But we'll get to that in a moment. What do you want me to do about Mary? She was reckless and came too close to getting caught, for my taste. I think we should rethink her promotion."

"The op went sideways," Hicks said. "It happens. Her promotion to Faculty Member is approved as of now." His voice sounded off and knew Jonathan would pick up on it, despite the electronic enhancement. "Give her the good news when we're done here. Then send Doctor Oliveira to check her out. She got pretty banged up at the market, and I want her checked out.

Mary won't like it but tell her it's an order. I need her operational. We're going to put her back into action soon."

"As you wish," Jonathan said. "You realize she left her passport behind."

Hicks watched the tactical screen to track Bravo Team's progress. They were still thirty minutes out from the safe house address. Los Angeles traffic was its usual nightmare. "I told her not to go back for it. That's on me."

"Fortunately, someone took it upon themselves to remotely detonate a series of incendiary devices they had placed throughout the basement. The entire building has become a four-alarm fire, so the passport and all traces of Ms. Foster have most likely been destroyed."

Hicks was impressed. "The Vanguard isn't taking any chances. Send word to the remaining Varsity squads in California to stand down and head back to their various home bases. Let's just hope the address the dead guy gave Mary is accurate."

Hicks heard keyboard clicks on Jonathan's end. He considered himself a fast typist, but the Dutchman's fingers moved in a blur. "OMNI shows the address of the safe house is the Hotel Cedric, a former mid-level hotel that was converted into an SRO by the city a few decades ago. It was recently purchased at auction and turned into a boutique hotel. Private investor, of course. North Korean shell corporation set up by Victor Resnick. You know the drill."

Yes, Hicks knew the drill. And so did Scott and his Varsity team. He hoped the North Koreans hadn't made too many improvements to the building to make extracting the target difficult.

"I'm switching off to tactical," Hicks told him. "I want to track Scott's canvas of that safe house."

"Before you go," Jonathan said, "we have to talk about Charles Demarest."

Hicks shut his eyes. As if hunting The Vanguard wasn't enough, he still had to worry about taking fire from his own people.

Demarest may be an ally, but he was an uneasy one at best. They still didn't trust each other and the new DNI still hunted him. Hicks knew why. He still had Tessmer and Colonel Yeung. Demarest wouldn't rest until Hicks handed them over to him for proper questioning.

"What about him?"

"John Meager met with him today," Jonathan said. "That old fool is still poking around for information about you."

"Meager is no fool," Hicks said. "And he won't stop until he finds me. Or thinks he has."

"How can he find you when I don't even know where you are?"

And that's how it's going to stay, too. The Vanguard will know where I am when it's too late. "Any idea what they talked about?"

"No, but it was probably about locating you. Demarest has been peppered with questions about the source of the intelligence we've been giving him. The anonymous tip routine will only go so far and people in the Community are already growing suspicious."

"That's his problem," Hicks said. "He's the Director of National Intelligence now. If he can't get his own people to quit asking questions, he's the wrong man for the job."

"Being DNI only comes with more scrutiny," Jonathan argued. "I think it may be wise to consider giving him a timeframe on handing over the prisoners, sir. Tessmer and Yeung. He won't be expecting Yeung and it'll be a nice bonus, not to mention it'll get Demarest off your back."

Hicks knew Demarest had wanted Tessmer immediately after Hicks had captured him in Berlin. But Hicks had no intention of handing him over before he had drained the man of every bit of information he could.

According to Roger's latest reports, Tessmer had finally run dry.

Maybe it was finally time to give Demarest what he wanted. In exchange for something else, of course.

He checked Scott's status. Still thirty minutes away from the safe house. "We've got time. Get me a secure connection to Demarest."

He couldn't hear Jonathan's fingers on the keyboard this time. "Are you sure that's a good idea, sir? You don't sound right. You're altering your voice to make it sound stronger, aren't you? I need to know why. People are asking questions here, too. Roger is being especially difficult. You need to talk to him and soon."

Hicks knew from Roger's emails and texts that he was growing frustrated with his silence. He'd reach out to him in time. For now, he had to find a way to call off Demarest before he risked screwing up his plans. "Just connect me to Demarest. I'll worry about Roger."

Hicks watched the tactical screen while Jonathan put through the call. Bravo Team was now twenty-five minutes out from the safe house. He was currently reviewing a thermal scan of the building. That was good. Scott was as thorough as he was tough. He'd have a plan ready to go by the time they reached the Hotel Cedric.

Plenty of time to squeeze in a call with his uneasy ally.

Hicks watched his monitor as Jonathan directed OMNI to bounce the call off dozens of locations and satellites around the globe.

Demarest answered on the third ring. "Well, if it isn't the prodigal spy? Long time, no hear, Lieutenant Bumgarner. You don't call. You don't write. We were beginning to get concerned. I was even thinking about sending a team to Savannah to check on you."

Hicks's pain dulled as he bristled at the mention of his real name. And Savannah had been where his predecessor lived.

"Look at you doing your homework," Hicks said. "Sounds like Meager's earning his money. Congratulations."

Demarest cursed. "How the hell did you know about him?"

"I've got my resources, same as you, Ace," Hicks said. "Forget you heard that name. It'll get you nowhere. And if you use it again, it'll piss me off. Remember what happened the last time?"

"You've got to allow me a little fun," Demarest chided. "What did they call you? Steve? Gunny? I haven't been able to track down your file yet, so I don't know which."

Hicks's parents and friends had always called him

Hank, but Demarest was neither. "Let's stick to Hicks while you tell me what you want."

"Fine by me. What are you doing in Istanbul?"

Hicks's face began to throb. Istanbul had been one of the many stops he'd made before coming to his destination. "I wouldn't know. I'm not there anymore. Quit wasting time tracking me down and get to the point. What do you want?"

"I need Tessmer," Demarest said. "My people need a source for all this information you've fed me, and he would check a lot of boxes. Preferably alive, of course. How about you hand them over to me at dinner tomorrow night? Le Diplomate in D.C. Seven o'clock work for you? My treat on behalf of a grateful nation."

"With dessert at a black site in the Balkans?" Hicks forced a laugh. "No, thanks."

"I'll take that as a raincheck on dinner," Demarest said, "but I need Tessmer now. Those hearings you forced have caused a lot of ill will in the Community, James. A lot of very committed and capable people are burning the midnight oil hunting you. For now, they only have a face, but if they ever get more than that, you'll have problems."

"So will they," Hicks said.

"It only takes one of them to get lucky," Demarest said. "Feeding them a big fish like Tessmer will help refocus their efforts elsewhere. I can't protect you forever and you know I'm right."

Hicks wouldn't give in that easy. *Something for something.* "Let's trade, then. Tell me what the Chinese gave from the base in Xinyang? I know they must've given you a report."

"You were there," Demarest reminded him. "The

Chinese practically vaporized the place. What little tech that survived was useless. But they found two bodies in a safe room in the deepest part of the rubble. They ran DNA on what was left of their corpses and found a match to someone already in the Chinese military's system. A general, in fact. The name Li Jun Zhou mean anything to you?"

Hicks's hands began to shake as he gently cradled his aching head. *Could this be the head of the dragon I've been hunting?* "No."

"He was a general from China's Ministry of State Security. Bureau Nine. It's their counter-intelligence group charged with coming up with ways to destroy China's enemies from within. They're a think tank, mostly. Spend their time coming up with covert tactics to disrupt capitalist societies. They were mostly harmless until General Zhou decided to take his group operational."

Hicks's anticipation had made him anxious. "Explain."

"Remember that blackout that took down England's power grid ten years ago? That was Bureau Nine. So was the emergency shutdown of the Penly nuclear power plant in France. A few hacks and data breaches in the U.S., too, though various administrations chose to keep it secret. Don't ask me why."

Hicks didn't care why. He cared about Zhou. "Go on."

"Our Chinese friends don't mind tweaking the noses of the West, but they don't like it when their generals decide to do it without permission. They sent a kill squad to take Zhou out, but the general is popular with the war hawks in the Chinese military. Zhou managed to skip the country and take about ten million dollars of his bureau's money with him. The Vanguard started operations about a year after he disappeared. I'd say that makes him a likely candidate for the head of their Asian operations."

For once, Hicks agreed with Demarest. He felt hope spark in his belly. "Do they have any idea where he is?"

"No one has seen or heard from the son of a bitch in over a decade," Demarest said. "Believe me, they've looked. The Chinese want him even more than we do. Seems a few generals and colonels have disappeared since The Vanguard started up. The government told the rank-and-file they had been executed for disloyalty. Our contact admits they all disappeared to parts unknown. We don't have them and neither does anyone in Europe. We think they've been working with Zhou in The Vanguard, but we can't confirm that. No one knows where Zhou is."

Hicks knew Zhou had to be running The Vanguard's Asian operation. Tessmer's Chinese counterpart. The Man. The head of the dragon.

Another domino appeared in his mind. The last one to fall.

Demarest filled in the silence. "Which brings us back to Tessmer, James. I need him."

Hicks massaged his temples through his bandages. He knew Demarest was right. He'd held on to Tessmer long enough. Though he'd never given up Zhou's name. Was it because he didn't know it or because that was his last chip to play?

No, Hicks decided. Roger was too thorough. Tessmer didn't know Zhou's name. The Vanguard compartmentalized like the University did. Like most intelligence operations.

Tessmer had given him the key to destroying The Vanguard, but never counted on him finding the lock. Knowing Zhou's name put him one step closer in that direction.

Hicks decided to throw Demarest a bone. "Have your people monitor San Francisco PD calls. They'll find out about a shooting in a Korean marketplace and subsequent fire."

He heard Demarest's pen scrawling across paper. "Is Tessmer there?"

Hicks continued. "You'll want to get the FBI involved. The cops will investigate it as a robbery gone wrong, but it's not. The market was a front for The Vanguard and North Korean intelligence on the West Coast."

"A fire?" Demarest repeated. "Your people light the match?"

"No," Hicks admitted. "We were operating on intelligence Tessmer gave us about The Vanguard in the U.S., but the op went bad. Have your people examine the corpses in the building and the dead man on the street. You'll probably find something on them in your files."

In fact, OMNI had already confirmed they had files on them, but Demarest didn't need to know that. Let him do his own leg work for once.

"We've heard rumors about that market over the years, but never found anything solid. What intel did you acquire?"

But Hicks wasn't ready to share that much. He toggled to the tactical screen. Scott and his team were now ten minutes out from the safe house and Victor Resnick. "We have a lead, but I'll tell you more when I have it."

"Fine, but the FBI is going to want to know where the lead came from. You're a victim of your own success, James. Now I need Tessmer more than ever."

Hicks closed his eyes again. Demarest might be the head of America's intelligence operations, but he was still a relentless field man at heart. He never gave up.

Hicks saw no reason to hold it back from him any longer. "You'll have him within the week." He heard the director begin to bargain but cut him off. "It'll be sooner than that, but there are logistics to sort out. To make it up to you, I'll throw in a bonus. Colonel Kim Yeung of North Korea."

"Yeung." He heard Demarest swallow hard. "Jesus. We just got word the North Koreans think he was kidnapped. You really have been busy."

"You have no idea," Hicks continued. "But I want something in return. I'm going after Zhou. If any of your people get in my way, they won't be there for long."

Demarest was silent while he considered it. "You're in Asia, aren't you?"

With Jonathan listening, he wouldn't confirm or deny it. "I'm nowhere and everywhere. If your people track anything about Zhou or Yeung's disappearance, I want to know about it so I can plan accordingly. That's only fair."

"Agreed. Having Tessmer and Yeung in hand will be a big help to both of us." Demarest cleared his throat before saying, "We haven't talked much since Berlin. I know you lost an operative there. Tali Saddon. For what it's worth, I'm sorry."

Hicks killed the connection.

He was sorry, too. For a lot of things. But sorry didn't count for much in their world. Only bodies did.

General Zhou's body in particular.

He had OMNI begin a full spectrum search on Zhou. Now that he had a name, he wanted a face to place on that last domino set to fall.

As the system went to work, he checked the tactical screen again and saw Scott was still about ten minutes out from the safe house. California traffic.

He decided to put the delay to good use.

He called Roger Cobb.

CHAPTER 7

GJIROKASTER, ALBANIA

As THE CALL WENT THROUGH, Hicks toggled to the live camera feed from the University safe house outside Gjirokaster, Albania where Roger Cobb was holding Tessmer and Yeung.

Hicks could see Roger was alone, thumbing through his notes in the house's sitting room on the first floor. The front of his white cable sweater bore a thin dark stripe across the front of it that wasn't part of the design.

It was blood and probably not Roger's.

Roger Cobb was keeping the prisoners two levels below in the old farmhouse's basement. The space was deep enough to dampen their screams, and the dirt floor did a good job of absorbing the bodily fluids that tended to flow during Roger's sessions. The lack of windows made it impossible for his prisoners to know anything of the outside world, assuming they still cared to know. Subjects of Roger's interrogations usually lost interest in living and found the prospect of death more inviting.

Roger had been working Tessmer steadily for three months. Colonel Yeung had cracked after an hour or so of Roger's hydro-sensory deprivation treatment.

"I see the Dutchman delivered my message," Roger said as he answered the phone. He looked directly into the camera in upper corner of the sitting room. "How are you?"

"That's it?" Hicks asked as he searched the camera feeds of the rest of the farmhouse. Everything seemed to be secure, and Roger was alone. "No quips? No pithy remarks? You're losing your touch."

"I'm not losing anything except my mind with worry about you," Roger said. "Where are you? And why are you disguising your voice?"

Hicks trusted few people more than Roger Cobb, but he had to keep his location a secret until he finally dealt with Zhou.

"I'm fine." Hicks knew that wouldn't be enough to satisfy him. And since he knew Jonathan couldn't listen in on this conversation, he added, "I got some work done. But that stays between us."

"You stupid bastard!" Roger swore as he threw his notebook across the room. "You damned fool. Why didn't you tell me?"

"You've been doing more important work."

"And you had major surgery," Roger argued. "No wonder you've sounded off the last few weeks. Who did you use? And it better not have been one of those butchers in Mexico City or the Philippines."

"It was someone reliable," Hicks said. "I'm fine."

"Like hell you are," Roger fumed. "You're enhancing your voice to compensate for the weakness and the slurring from the medication. And I bet you're all alone, aren't you? Like some bull elephant going off into the jungle to die alone."

Hicks had known Roger would react like this, which was why he hadn't told him.

"I have no intention of dying. I said I'm—"

Roger raved on. "What did that hack give you? Some aspirin and an ice pack? A couple of vials of oxy and some topical cream for the scarring? Do you have any idea the complications that can set in? What if you get an infection?"

"It was weeks ago and there've been no complications. Some pain, yes, but it's manageable. But I didn't call to talk about me. I called about the prisoners. How are they?"

Roger continued to glare up at the camera. "To use your phrase, they're fine. And don't change the subject. How bad is the pain? That's why you blacked out during the market op just now, isn't it?" He punched the arm of his chair. "Damn it. I knew you were off your game."

Roger was nothing if not perceptive. "It was a brain fart. I recovered. And the prisoners are the subject. I need you to get Tessmer and Yeung in Washington by tomorrow night."

He watched Roger's eyes narrow. "You're giving them up already? Yeung may have more to tell us."

"He can tell Demarest and his pals," Hicks said. "OMNI will trace anything else on the back end when they write their reports."

"But Yeung still won't give up the head of The Vanguard in Asia," Roger said. "Give me a few more days with him at least."

"Demarest already gave me a line on a General

Zhou," Hicks told him. "I've got OMNI running a check on him now. I'll give you access to whatever it finds."

He also stole a glance at the tactical screen. Scott's Bravo Team was less than ten minutes out.

He had to wrap things up with Roger quickly so he could provide overwatch for their op. The safe house wouldn't be like the Korean market in San Francisco. It would have armed guards and armed tenants, too. They'd need all the eyes in the sky they could get.

But Hicks had one final question for Roger. "Has Tessmer told you who killed Tali?"

"He says it wasn't him and I'm beginning to believe him. He's confirmed the names of the members of the team he sent after her. All of them dead now, so whoever stabbed her was probably killed at the cemetery. All I know for certain is that it wasn't Tessmer."

Hicks felt the anger course through him again. Not at Roger, but at everything else. He needed to know Tali's killer was dead. "I don't want probably. I want certainty."

"Well, you won't get it by handing him over to Demarest. He cares about more than just some dead Mossad agent." Roger held up a hand to the camera. "I know she's more than that, but Demarest doesn't."

Hicks didn't want to think Tali's killer was dead. He wanted to know. He wanted to know if they were still alive so he could tend to them personally.

But there would be another time for that. It would have to wait. "Just get both prisoners cleaned up as best you can and on a plane by tomorrow morning. They don't have to be pretty, just alive when Demarest gets them."

"Thy will be done." Roger looked up into the camera again. "I'm worried about you, James. And not just about the scars on your face, either. I'm very worried about you."

Hicks drank the last of his coffee. "Concentrate on preparing the prisoners for transport. I want them in a plane and wheels up tomorrow morning so they're in D.C. that evening. Plan on remaining in D.C. after you deliver the prisoners but be prepared to move out at a moment's notice. I'll need you mobile tomorrow night."

Roger looked as sad as he felt. "Okay, James. They'll be there."

Hicks killed the connection and switched his screen to track Scott's progress. Six minutes out. Every minute counted as the safe house was undoubtedly on alert following what had happened to the market in San Francisco. They wouldn't evacuate, but they'd be on guard. That was just as dangerous.

He pushed all thoughts of Tali from his mind. He decided to risk the trek across to the kitchen to brew up some more instant coffee. He'd need a clear head to help Scott and his men breach that hotel.

Failure was not an option.

CHAPTER 8

SOMEWHERE IN THE VIETNAMESE JUNGLE

GENERAL LI JUN ZHOU swatted a fly that had dared to land too close to his tea.

He hated this damnable place, with its perpetual humidity and predatory insects.

He had never understood his beloved Party's love affair with Vietnam. He understood the reasons why they had fought the war, of course. He supported any conflict that drained American resources and soldiers. And the Vietnamese had proven themselves to be excellent fighters, if fickle allies.

But they had become too comfortable with the West in recent years and Zhou knew it was only a matter of time before they cast off their Communist ideology in favor of McDonalds and sneakers and blue jeans. In many ways, they already had.

But following the destruction of his base in Mongolia and the capture of his German counterpart Tessmer, General Zhou saw no other alternative but to flee his comfortable office in Singapore for the humid jungle wilderness of Vietnam. Perhaps the ways of the West had corrupted him, too.

The Vanguard controlled enough money to put some European countries to shame. He smiled at the thought of that. He *controlled* money. He enjoyed the irony of using the currency the capitalist pigs valued so highly against them. Their money and their greed.

The only thing he enjoyed more than using their own tools of oppression against them was having others doing his fighting for him.

The Islamists who The Vanguard had funded for their bio-terror *jihad* against New York City had become every bit as corrupt as the people they sought to destroy. They were expendable. Where capitalism was greed of the wallet and bank account, Zhou saw religious zealotry as a greed of the soul. Righteousness was its own corruption.

Zhou had successfully used the weaknesses of both sides against them for years and hoped to continue to do so for years to come.

Not even the angry termite known as Hicks could stop their progress.

He sipped his tea and wondered what had become of Colonel Yeung. The loss of his entire protection detail meant someone had taken him against his will. His sources in American intelligence assured him that they had not taken Yeung. That meant it must have been the work of the University. Tessmer had undoubtedly told them how to find Yeung and used his weakness against them.

Yeung was more of a loss for the North Koreans than for The Vanguard. Hicks undoubtedly thought

Tessmer and Yeung would provide a treasure trove of information.

Zhou knew otherwise. Compartmentalization had been the cornerstone of The Vanguard's success. Together, Tessmer and Yeung could shed no further light on his organization than a single match could reveal the depths of a cavern.

Tessmer and his Russian thugs had served their purpose. Their network was already in the process of being replaced by more reliable, less corruptible people.

Yeung's network, however, was still viable and already on high alert. The North Koreans were a nation of followers. They did as they were told. Zhou would corrupt whomever they chose to succeed Yeung and bend him to his will. To the will of the true Cause.

The loss of his sons at the Mongolian base still ached, but Zhou did not allow himself to think of such things often. Regret and mourning were useless emotions. He refused to indulge them. He had other sons who would succeed him when the time came. They would carry on his work. Everyone could be replaced, including him. Pride was merely a capitalist notion.

He swatted another fly as the youngest of his remaining sons, a timid boy barely eighteen, appeared at the entrance of his hut. "Father, there is a call for you. Rather urgent."

Zhou looked at his son, waiting for him to realize his error.

The boy was the slowest witted of all his sons, but he eventually understood his error as the reason for his father's silence. When next he spoke, he bowed slightly and addressed him properly.

"Father, you have a video call from our contact in America on the secure line. All steps have been taken to ensure its integrity. The caller is one of our allies from the north. It is rather urgent."

Zhou waved the boy away and tapped on his computer screen window that showed the incoming call. The face of Kang, the second in command of Vanguard operations on America's west coast, filled his screen.

The general did not like the way his operative looked. Worried. Perhaps even scared.

Zhou tapped on the 'Voice Only' option of the program. There was no reason why they needed to see each other and every reason why they should not. He did not want to allow the man to see where he was.

"Why are you calling and not Colonel Pak?"

"Apologies for disturbing you, comrade, but I have just learned that our facility in San Francisco has been attacked. All of our agents are dead, including the colonel."

Zhou knew of this facility. It was North Korea's eyes and ears on America's western coastline. Its staff not only monitored the Korean community but was part of the pipeline that helped Russian; Asian and Vanguard operatives escape America safely.

Zhou had paid handsomely for their discretion in helping Vanguard agents, but in his experience, North Koreans were far more susceptible to corruption than his countrymen, as evidenced by Colonel Yeung's capture in Russia.

"Are you sure it wasn't simply a robbery?"

"Details are still coming in," Kang said, "but the assailant wasn't found at the scene despite evidence of a protracted gun battle. Our cameras were off-line during the attack, so we have no idea of what actually happened. Out of an abundance of caution, I remotely detonated the fail-safe systems in the facility, sir. All computers were electronically destroyed before the building was set aflame. I wanted to notify you of what has been done and to see if you recommended any further steps be taken."

Zhou knew the staff of the market had been well trained and were efficient, considering they were North Koreans. If all of them were dead, including the intelligence operatives in the basement, it was much more than a simple robbery.

"How quickly can you evacuate the safe house?" Zhou asked.

"We believe the threat is contained to the market," Kang said. "My staff has been put on the highest alert and reinforcements are on their way. We have not detected any irregular activities in our vicinity."

Zhou was not pleased. "The market and the safe house are intertwined. Interest in one means interest in the other. Begin evacuation procedures immediately."

"I am afraid that would be impossible at the moment, comrade," Kang said. "Many of our special guests are in various states of disability." Zhou knew that 'special guests' were North Korean spies and Vanguard operatives. "Some are too sick to be moved. Some are under the effects of opiates or alcohol or other substances. Others would be unwilling to leave unless they were provided with a secure place to go and safe means of reaching their next location. And despite our informal arrangement, any formal evacuation would need to be ordered directly from Pyongyang. Questions would be raised otherwise. Questions neither of us would like to see answered."

General Zhou knew Kang was right. He might make a fitting replacement for Pak on the west coast. "Are our friends Pyongyang aware of what happened at the market?"

"Undoubtedly," Kang said, "but they have not contacted me yet to take precautions. I contacted you due to our special relationship."

Zhou knew their special relationship extended as far as the five thousand dollars he sent to Kang's private account in the Cayman Islands each week. Another Communist seduced by Western charms. At this rate, the wisdom of Chairman Mao would be reduced to a face on a T-shirt at tourist shops in Hong Kong like that arrogant fool Guevara.

He had expected a more creative answer to the dilemma facing them but remembered Kang was Korean. North or south didn't matter. To him, they were a people born to be lead, not to think. That was what had made them such an effective bulwark against the West on the Korean peninsula.

Kang's lack of creativity aside, the events at the market presented General Zhou with a significant problem. A problem undoubtedly caused by James Hicks and his damnable University. Had it been the work of another intelligence agency, Zhou's spies would've informed them in advance.

Zhou pulled up the hotel's register on his screen. Among the regular guests of the hotel, seven Vanguard members were currently staying there. According to the reports kept by the clerk at the front desk, three were recovering from wounds they had suffered in separate altercations. Two were being treated for alcoholism. One appeared to be on the edge of a nervous breakdown. He cursed the lot of them. He should have each of them executed for their weakness.

Only one member was biding her time, waiting for new papers to be created so she could fly back to the East and rejoin the group.

Zhou asked, "What are the warehouse's present defensive capabilities?"

"Minimal, comrade," Kang said. "Our orders were to blend into the community since we are subject to inspection by local authorities. This is why we have been able to operate so successfully over the years. The basement contains our equipment, so it is reasonably secure, but it isn't large enough to house all our special guests, especially in their various current states of distress. But, as I said earlier, reinforcements are being assembled and should be here soon."

Just because Zhou understood the logic didn't mean he liked it. "How many men do you have to repel any attack that might come?"

Silence.

Zhou hated bad news, but he hated silence even more. "Answer me, damn you. I have people staying there, too. How many security staff do you have on hand? What are their capabilities?"

But the call was ended.

Zhou's son appeared in the doorway a moment later. "Father, I am afraid we have lost the feed. It happens sometimes on international connections."

The general knew such things were common, but to happen when in the middle of an important conversation was a coincidence. And he had never believed in coincidence.

"Make every effort to restore the connection as soon as possible," he ordered. "Contact whomever Kang might use for reinforcements and tell them to proceed to the safe house with all possible speed. Keep me informed of your progress."

His son bowed and went back to his desk.

Zhou looked at his teacup. His tea was cold now, but warmer than the feeling creeping through his belly.

He closed the window of the dead connection on his screen and opened another window he always kept open beneath the other programs he ran.

It was a picture The Vanguard had acquired by infiltrating a portion of the Central Intelligence Agency systems.

It was a photo of a man crossing a busy New York street near Grand Central Terminal. A shabby looking man in a hooded sweatshirt and faded blue jeans. A man who looked in desperate need of a bath and a shave.

The same man who had foiled the biological attack he had sponsored in New York. The same man who had brought down The Vanguard's stations in Berlin and China. The man who had orchestrated the Chinese military attack on his base in Mongolia and the murder of two of his most valuable sons.

The same man he knew must be behind was happening in California today.

James Hicks.

The man he intended to kill one day. He would see to his torture personally.

Zhou called for his son, who once again appeared in

the doorway. "Amend my earlier directive. I want every available resource we have in the area to swarm the Los Angeles safe house. Trouble is coming to that place. I can feel it in my bones."

The son bowed to his father and went about carrying out his task.

Zhou drank the tea. It warmed him despite its coolness.

Perhaps today would be the day he finally caught James Hicks.

CHAPTER 9

SOMEWHERE

HICKS ADJUSTED his headset over his bandages as he tracked the Varsity Squad's Bravo Team on his screen.

The team's van had finally reached the safe house. It was parked in the alley behind a dingy hotel in Koreatown in Los Angeles.

"Bravo Team, this is Base. Situation report."

Every member of the team was outfitted with a body camera, giving Hicks several views of what was going on inside the van. He saw four angles of Scott, the team leader.

Scott was ex-Marine Recon and looked the part. He wasn't much taller than Hicks, but broader and more muscular. He had short-cropped silver hair, a lopsided jaw that had been broken at least half a dozen times and a nose to match. His appearance made him a lousy clandestine operative, but he excelled as the leader of the University's tactical squad.

"Base, this is Bravo Team," Scott said. "Who the hell am I talking to?"

Since it was a direct channel to Scott, Hicks said, "We worked together in Berlin. Lots of other places, too."

Hicks watched Scott sit back, obviously taken by the news. "Haven't heard from you in months. Glad you're okay. But you sound different."

Although he felt alert, the pain medication was making him slur his words. The voice-altering program cleaned up his speech. "It's just the connection, Bravo. We're doing fine. Situation report, please."

"Glad to see you're as charming as ever," Scott said. Knowing he was on camera, he pointed to the man in the wheelchair at the back of the van. "Thermal scans of the building are complete. Rivas is ready to take out their comms on your order. The rest of my team is ready to go on your mark. Any idea about what we're walking into?"

Hicks toggled to the tactical view of the building from the OMNI satellite high above California. He saw a three-dimensional thermal scan of the hotel. Knowing Scott had the same feed, he repeated the obvious.

"The Hotel Cedric has nineteen-floors and seven-hundred rooms. Most guests are civilians, but there are hostiles on site. Basement reads black, so it's probably lined with something and most likely serves as their nerve center. It is not our objective. Sending target information on your objective to your device now."

Hicks sent the image of Victor Resnick, the man they were hunting. The reason why Mary had risked her life to get the address of the safe house in the first place.

Hicks had hoped she would've been taken directly to the safe house and grab the man herself, but Scott and his team were an excellent secondary plan.

The target was a man with hard Slavic features and thick black hair. "His name is Victor Resnick," Hicks explained, "but he's got enough aliases to fill a phone book. He's a part-time arms dealer and full-time financier for The Vanguard. He doesn't appear to be a shooter himself, but you should still proceed with caution."

"Caution's our middle name," Scott said. "What about the building? What are we walking into?"

"It's used as a safe house for North Korean and Russian spies looking to skip the country unnoticed. Our boy works for The Vanguard, so he knows how to blend in."

"Acknowledged," Scott said. "How do you want us to get him?"

"As quietly as you can," Hicks told him. "A blood-bath will alert the locals and we want to avoid that at all costs. We just want Resnick. According to the footage we were able to hack from the hotel, he came in drunk last night, so he's probably still sleeping it off. Grab him and get out of there as soon as possible. Five minutes flat. Some staff are North Korean intelligence, but not all. You are to engage only if necessary."

He watched Scott sit upright. "My boys don't need a chair jockey telling them how to bag a drunk. Just give us a room number and we're good to go."

Hicks would've smiled if the pain wouldn't have made him black out. Scott never changed. "Confirm receipt of the target package."

Scott checked his handheld. "Confirmed. Sharing it

with the team now. Switching to open channel, so watch what you say."

Scott tapped his phone and held the device up for his team to see. All five operators looked at their handhelds. In the back of the van, Mike Rivas kept working on the laptop.

"This is our objective, people. Victor Resnick. Some kind of Vanguard scumbag. This hotel is being used as a safe house by the North Koreans. While you might be tempted to flat line everyone inside, be mindful of civilians. There are hostiles, but Resnick is our only objective. You are not to engage unless engaged. You copy?"

The men answered as one. "Copy."

Hicks watched the team look at their handhelds as Scott spoke. "Each of you have his image on your devices and on the HUDs of your helmets. You find anyone matching his description, wait for OMNI to confirm his identity. The building's going to be dark, but that won't affect our feed."

"What room number is he in?" one of the team asked.

"Working on that information right now," Hicks told them.

As Scott continued his pre-op briefing with his men, Hicks concentrated on OMNI. It had already completed a review of the hotel's ledger and cross-referenced it with the feed from the security cameras.

A guest matching Resnick's description had returned at 04:00. He was barely able to stay on his feet and obviously drunk. A bellman helped him into the elevator and brought him up to his room. Hallway footage confirmed he was staying in room Three-zero-three.

Hicks interrupted Scott's briefing to tell them the room number.

"We like that number," Scott told his men. "Means we won't need the elevator. Cuts down on our risk of exposure. We grab him, bring him down to the van and get the hell out of here. I want the target and the rest of us back here and moving in five minutes flat."

"What are we up against, boss?" It was Dom, an operator who Hicks knew had been with Scott and the Varsity for years.

"Assume handguns and rifles at best," Scott told him. "No detectible defenses but they might be expecting us. Defend yourselves if you have to, kill if necessary but keep Resnick alive no matter what happens." He looked at each of the men in turn. "You copy?"

They responded in one voice again, "Copy."

Scott pulled on his Devtac Tactical Helmet and the three others in his go-team did the same. In addition to their body armor, the black anti-ballistic helmets and face shields covered their entire faces, making them look like giant grasshoppers. The helmets could stop a .44 caliber bullet and had been modified by University technicians to include night-vision and a heads up display in the goggles. The tech was tied in to OMNI's tactical program to help them identify and track targets as they entered a building.

Each of them was armed with a HK MP5 on a harness and a SIG Sauer P226 sidearm. Scott demanded uniformity among his men on his raids in all things, including weaponry.

When all the men were ready, Scott said, "Base,

Bravo Team is locked and loaded. Requesting permission to proceed."

"Permission granted," Hicks said. "Base will ride shotgun. Rivas runs things from the van. Neary stays behind the wheel no matter what happens. He has my matching feed on his computer."

Hicks watched Rivas's fingers move along the keyboard. "OMNI is ready to block all ingoing and outgoing cellular and Wi-Fi signals as soon as you breach."

"Showtime, gentlemen," Scott said, as he pulled open the van door and hurried out into the warm California sunshine. Three men spilled out after him.

As the van door slid shut, Hicks saw Rivas switch to a private channel. "That you, James?"

"It's me." Mike Rivas had been his best agent before a bullet missed his heart by inches and severed his spine instead. Hicks kept him on the University payroll through his healing process, trying to convert his immense skills as a field operator into a technical support role. He may have lost the use of his legs, but he still knew how to run an operation. If he had any doubts about his abilities, he found his confidence again in Berlin.

But Hicks knew that, just like Mary Foster, when you were used to being in the fight, it was tough to watch it from the sidelines.

"You're looking well," Hicks told him.

"For a guy in a wheelchair."

Hicks had promised Mike the University would pay for experimental stem cell treatment that might give him use of his legs again. But his current fight against

The Vanguard had taken priority. "We're working on that, remember?"

"That doesn't make the waiting any easier to take."

Hicks wasn't one to make promises. He liked to keep the few he made. But Mike's treatment would have to wait until his business with The Vanguard was settled. "Let's just stay focused on this op for now."

Rivas made the transition without missing a beat. "Bravo Team is in position. Switching back to tactical."

Rivas switched back to the team's tactical channel and tapped a button. "Bravo Team, building just went dark. Your path is clear. You've got five minutes and counting. The clock starts now."

———

SCOTT HIT the back door with a crowbar and snapped the lock. He went through first. The rest of the team filed in behind him.

Hicks tracked their feeds on his laptop.

He watched Scott move down the narrow hallway, ducking into the first door on his left. The staff office had three people inside. All Korean. All of them were too puzzled by their internet and phones going dark at the same time to notice the man in the black face mask and body armor pointing an assault rifle at them.

When they saw him, they threw up their hands and began to scream.

"Do as I say, and no one gets hurt," Scott yelled over them.

As the rest of the team moved to secure the lobby, Scott motioned toward the door that led to the front desk. "Everybody move that way. Now."

The three people did as they were told. Scott moved into the hallway to join the rest of his men in the lobby.

Dom and Thomas had already covered the two clerks at the front desk. Reardon locked the front doors of the hotel and pulled down the ratty shades. The lobby was clear.

The five hotel staffers were huddled together in the narrow space between the wall and the front desk.

Scott yelled to keep the panic going. "Who's in charge here?"

A Korean man in a green vest and matching tie said in perfect English, "Since you have the gun, I'd say you are."

Scott turned to Reardon and motioned for him to stay in the lobby. To Dom and Thomas, he gestured toward the stairs. "Get going."

The two operators moved quickly and began their ascent. Rifles leading the way.

Scott pointed at the manager. "Play it smart and we're gone in five minutes. Do anything stupid, you die."

The clerk held up his hands and his people followed his lead. "It doesn't matter. I'm dead after this anyway."

"After this isn't my problem."

Reardon tapped his shoulder, telling him he was in position, before Scott hit the stairs. He took them two at a time until he reached the third floor.

Hicks heard Rivas continue the countdown. "Four minutes left, Bravo Team."

Scott pulled open the fire door leading to the third floor and swept both sides of the hall with his rifle before moving in. He found Dom and Thomas already cued up on either side of the door labeled 'ROOM 303'.

Scott whispered to Rivas, "Bravo Team in position outside the target's room. Need verification that it's occupied."

Rivas responded, "OMNI's thermals are picking up two people inside. One walking around, the other in an inclined position, probably in bed."

Thomas, from the left side of the door, whispered, "Want me to kick it in?"

But in a building full of people on the run, most of them probably armed, Scott wanted to be as quiet as possible. "Let's try something else."

With his gloved hand, he knocked on the door and moved in front of Dom.

In their ear, Rivas said, "Someone is approaching the door."

"Finally!" said a female voice in Russian as he heard the door latch undone. "I was wondering when you'd get back."

The door had only opened a crack before Scott rushed in, slipping his hand over the woman's mouth. Dom and Thomas moved into the room behind him.

"Stay calm," Scott told her as his men checked the room, "and you'll be fine."

Thomas cleared the bathroom on the right while Dom moved toward the bed.

"Boss," Dom said. "You're gonna want to take a look at this."

Scott heeled the door shut and kept his hand over the woman's mouth as he moved her toward the bed.

He saw a man hooked up to an intravenous feed. He was shivering uncontrollably. The bed sheets looked wet.

Hicks saw Dom keep his goggles aimed at the man in the bed while OMNI verified his identity.

Scott spoke to the woman in Russian. "Do you speak English?"

She nodded quickly. Her eyes wide. Scott didn't blame her. She probably hadn't expected armed men in tactical gear to ruin her day.

"I'm going to take my hand away from your mouth. There's no reason to scream. Do you understand?"

She nodded again and Scott slowly withdrew his hand. The woman didn't scream.

"What are you doing here?" he asked her.

"I'm a nurse." Hicks pegged her thick accent as Georgian, but her English was more than passable. "Please, I don't want any trouble."

Scott pointed at the man shivering on the bed. "What's wrong with him?"

"He has acute alcohol poisoning. The DTs, you'd call it. He was shaking and heaving like that when I got here. I hooked him up to some fluids to help ease his pain, but it's only beginning to work."

Hicks saw the positive identification on his screen the same time Dom saw it on his HUD. The man in the bed was Victor Resnick.

"He's our boy, boss," Dom confirmed.

Scott looked at the nurse. "Do you know who he is?"

She quickly shook her head. "I work at a nail saloon on La Brea. Back in Russia, I was a nurse. I get called to do things like this sometimes. Quietly. The money is good. More than I make in a month at the salon for one patient."

In another time and another place, Hicks knew Scott would've asked who'd called her, who she worked for and what kind of people were her clients. But this wasn't an intelligence mission. It was a snatch-and-grab job. And he didn't have that kind of time.

"Is he fit for travel?"

"Yes, but he's still very sick," she said. "If you move him, he might go into shock."

Scott looked at Dom and Thomas. "Unhook him and get him downstairs."

Thomas, the bigger of the two, plucked the IV needle from Resnick's arm and slung him over his shoulder like a sack of flower.

Resnick gurgled and puked down his back.

"I live a charmed life," Thomas said.

Dom moved past them, opened the door, and checked the hallway. When it was all clear, he gave Thomas the signal to follow him.

While his men brought Resnick downstairs, Scott pulled his handheld device and took the Russian nurse's picture. She flinched when the flash went off.

"You don't know who we are or what we look like," he told her, "but soon, we'll know everything about you. After we leave, I want you to sit here nice and quiet. Don't move until someone comes for you. Tell them everything you saw and everything you can remember about us. If you lie, they'll kill you. Do you understand?"

She was shaking now. "I don't want trouble. For you or for me."

Hicks knew she didn't and needed Scott to get out

of there. Time was wasting, but this was Scott's mission. He wouldn't interfere.

Scott told her, "Do as I say, and I'll make sure you get some money in a couple of days. Maybe some more work like this in the future so you don't have to go back to the salon. That sound good to you?"

She sat in a chair next to the bed. "If you don't want him to die, get some B9 and glucose into him. I'd give you more, but he used everything I have. I sent my friend to get more. That man is in bad shape."

In Scott's ear, Rivas continued the countdown "Two minutes and counting."

Scott opened the door and checked the hallway. Still empty.

He was about to follow his men down the stairs when he felt someone watching him.

He spotted a woman at the far end of the hall, halfway out of her room. A lean blonde. Hair pulled back into a high ponytail. Tank top damp like she had just come back from a run.

Steady blue eyes locked on him.

No fear.

Hicks knew that look. The look of a pro.

Shit.

Don't do it.

But she dropped to a crouch and brought up a pistol.

Scott fired two suppressed rounds, striking her twice in the chest. She bounced off the doorframe before falling face first into the hallway. Hicks could tell by the blood she hadn't been wearing a vest.

But she wasn't dead yet. She squeezed off a shot and fired into a wall as she died.

The gunshot boomed through the narrow hallway, much louder than Scott's rifle had.

So much for a stealthy getaway.

Rivas was in his ear. "We heard that out here. Get the hell out of there, Bravo. Now!"

But Scott was already running down the stairs.

Hicks was glad he'd gotten more coffee. Things were about to get interesting.

OUT IN THE ALLEY, Dom and Thomas were already loading Resnick into the van with Reardon riding shotgun.

Scott jumped into the van before pulling the sliding door shut. "Go, go, go!"

Rivas locked the wheels of his chair in place as the van sped down the alley. Bullets fired from the safe house guests peppered the van's roof.

Reardon took a hard right onto the street; horns blaring as the van cut off several cars in traffic. The van's armor plating kept the bullets from getting through. The weighted undercarriage prevented the van's momentum from flipping it over.

Hicks's voice came over the air. "Sit rep, now."

"We have the package," Rivas answered. "Bravo Team is clear and healthy. One hostile down. We are on our way to the rendezvous point."

"Acknowledged," Hicks said. "Scott, OMNI just analyzed the woman you shot. She was a Vanguard merc. Nice shooting."

Scott pulled off his helmet. "She turned our op to shit."

"At least she wasn't a civilian and everyone made it out alive," Hicks said. "What's Resnick's condition?"

Scott deferred to Dom and Thomas who were treating him.

Dom said, "He's crashing hard, boss. Could be booze. Could be from drugs. He's going to need some serious TLC when we get back to the safe house."

Thomas punched the van wall over Resnick's head. "Bastard puked on me," the black man yelled.

"Stow that shit," Scott ordered. "Better puke than your own blood."

"You took fire as you left the alley," Hicks said. "Any casualties?"

"Negative," Scott told him. "The van is fine. None of the rounds pierced the armor. We're already blending in with traffic."

Neary kept his eyes on the road. "The bullet holes in the roof might draw attention from a police airship."

"We'll worry about that if we have to." To Hicks, Scott asked. "What are our orders?"

"Proceed to the garage as planned and switch to alternate vehicles. I'll provide overwatch to track anyone who might be following you. Rivas, recalibrate your search to immediate threats in your area. I'll monitor on a wider scope from here."

"Copy," Rivas said. "Scans show we're clear for now. Police channels don't know we're alive."

"Let's keep it that way." Scott said to the driver, "Neary, take the next left. Do not go directly to the garage. I want to make sure we didn't pick up a tail."

Neary followed Scott's orders.

To Dom, Scott said, "Give our guest a shot of

morphine from your kit. It'll keep him stable until we get him situated."

As Dom dug into his first aid bag, Scott said to Hicks, "If we knew we'd be traveling with a hospital case, we would've been better prepared."

"I didn't even have an address on him until thirty minutes ago," Hicks answered. "How could I know what kind of shape he was in? Besides, I thought you Marines were supposed to be resourceful."

Scott shook his head. Hicks could be a real asshole sometimes.

Hicks came over the radio again. "Bad news, boys. OMNI has eyes on four males exiting the hotel heading toward two black Suburbans that just pulled up out front. Including drivers, that makes three per vehicle. Six bad guys in total. The security camera across the street shows they're all carrying AKs."

Scott knew their luck had already held out longer than it should have. "You copy that, Neary?"

The driver responded it by flooring it through a yellow light. "I copy."

"Shit," Rivas said from his laptop in the back of the van. "I've got two more Suburbans that just moved in one block behind us and closing fast."

"Where the hell did they come from?" Reardon asked. "No way they could've gotten there so fast."

"Looks like someone called in the cavalry before we got there." Scott grabbed his rifle. "Nothing we can do about it now."

In the passenger's seat, Reardon readjusted the sideview mirror. "Looks like this milk run just got more interesting."

Scott turned to Rivas as the van slowed in traffic. "How many in the SUVs?"

"Can't tell from the traffic cameras," Rivas said. "I detect at least two in each. Brings the total number of targets to eight. Looks like all four Suburbans are in contact and closing in on our position." Rivas looked up from his laptop. "It's as if they know exactly where we are."

Scott knew they must be tracking them somehow.

The only answer was lying on the floor of the van.

Resnick.

"Dom, pat him down for devices."

Scott watched him search the shivering Resnick. Since he was only wearing a hospital gown, he didn't worry about a cellphone or a transmitter in the lining of his clothes to give away their position. He wasn't wearing any jewelry or even a smart watch, so that was out, too.

It wasn't until Dom reached Resnick's chest that he pulled off a circular sensor stuck to his skin. He held it up for the team to see.

"Are you seeing this, Base?" Scott asked Hicks.

"It's a biosensor," Hicks told him. "That nurse was probably using it to check his vitals via a tablet. How the hell did we miss that?"

Thomas turned on Rivas. "I thought you were jamming the damned signals."

"I was back at the hotel," Rivas said. "Not in here. I thought one of you guys would've searched him."

"We didn't pick up anything in his room," Thomas said.

Scott snatched the sensor away from Dom. "That's because we were jamming the signal." He gave the device to Reardon, who threw it out the window as the light changed and the van began to roll again.

Scott went back to Rivas. "Any place where we can hide along this route?"

"Nothing but driveways before they converge on us," Rivas reported. "And since they already know what the van looks like, hiding in plain sight isn't an option."

Scott didn't know Los Angeles very well, but he knew their present course was taking them further away from their rendezvous point at the garage. The North Koreans might know the van, but the helmets had kept them from being identified, so they didn't know what they looked like.

If it hadn't been for Resnick, they could've ditched the van and equipment and scattered. But since Resnick was the mission, that wasn't possible.

Scott knew they were stuck with the van whether they liked it or not. That narrowed his options and created some necessities.

"Neary, take a right on the next boulevard straight ahead. They can't track us anymore and they might lose us."

"Copy," Neary responded.

"Rivas, how close are our friends?"

"Too close." Rivas worked his laptop. "They're four cars behind us and closing fast."

Reardon held on as Neary took a hard right onto the busy boulevard. "Glad this thing's bulletproof."

"Yeah," Neary said, "but it ain't a Ferrari."

Scott looked in the side view mirror and saw a Suburban gaining ground fast.

Scott asked Rivas, "Still nowhere to hide? A garage, an old factory. Something."

Rivas shook his head. "Welcome to gentrification. All I've got are apartment houses and one-family homes. They knew exactly where to hit us."

Scott and the other men in the back shifted their weight as Neary floored it and sped through a red light. The Suburban followed right behind them.

Rivas delivered more bad news from his laptop. "Traffic's at a standstill ahead. We'll be boxed in."

"Fucking L.A. traffic." Scott leaned forward and checked the side-view mirror again. The Suburban was about a car-length away and closing fast.

Good, Scott thought. He'd just made his first mistake.

Nowhere to run. Nowhere to hide. Might as well fight.

"Helmets on and safeties off," he told his men. "Brace yourselves because this is gonna hurt."

The men barely had time to don their helmets before Scott yelled at Neary, "Hard brake. Now!"

Neary slammed on the brakes. The men pitched forward. Dom kept Rivas's chair from toppling over while protecting Resnick.

Scott slid open the side door and hit the roadway as the van skidded to a halt.

The Suburban tried to turn too late and slammed into the back of the van.

Scott ignored the blaring horns and curses from surrounding drivers as he moved to the back to find the Suburban's front end wedged atop the van's rear bumper. The SUV's airbags had deployed on impact, temporarily blinding the men inside.

Scott brought up his MP5 and raked the windshield with a short, controlled burst.

He walked wide of the vehicle and saw both men in the front seat were dead. The back seat was empty.

"Two down," Scott reported.

Instinct made him take a knee when he heard horns coming from down the street. He saw two gunmen in the intersection, raising AK-47s in his direction.

Bullets smacked into asphalt and the back of the ruined Suburban as panicked drivers fled their vehicles, running in all directions.

Cars in the intersection behind them crashed into each other as they tried to veer out of the way of the gunmen blocking their way.

Scott remained in position. *Let them come.*

The gunmen advanced to the cover behind one of the abandoned cars blocking the intersection. The OMNI interface with the HUD in Scott's helmet tracked their position, but he didn't need it.

Scott didn't flinch when he felt Reardon's hand on his left shoulder, telling him he was there. They had trained for this.

"Neary's on the port side looking for a target," Reardon told him. "Dom's climbed up behind the wheel. Thomas is covering us from the top of the Suburban."

The gunman to Scott's right popped up from behind the abandoned car and raked the area with AK fire. A round kicked off the asphalt and plinked off Scott's helmet.

Neary brought him down with a short burst.

"Target down," Rivas said over the headset in their helmets. "One left, but more inbound. Police scanner's heating up. We're getting popular."

Scott kept his rifle trained on the second shooter

still crouched behind the car. The cops would be a problem, but the shooter was the immediate threat. He knew he hadn't moved yet because his feet were still visible behind the car. And he'd just seen what happened to his friend, so he wasn't moving any time soon. He'd sit and wait until the other two Suburbans arrived.

"Thomas," Scott said through the open channel, "you bring your MRAD?"

A loud crack echoed above him. Scott saw the abandoned car's driver's side window shatter as the fifty-caliber round slammed through the door and the man crouched behind it. Scott saw his body drop to the street from beneath the car.

"I never leave home without it," Thomas answered.

"Both hostiles down," Rivas reported above the screaming civilians in the surrounding cars, "but more are inbound. Police, too."

Scott got to his feet as Thomas dropped from the roof of the Suburban.

Beside him, Reardon asked, "You got a plan, boss?"

"I'm working on it." Scott called to Dom. "Is the van operational?"

The van bucked forward and took the bumper of the Suburban with it. "We ain't pretty, but we're good to go."

"Everybody back in the van," Scott ordered his team. "Let's keep this pig flying."

Scott could hear the wail of approaching sirens as they piled back into the van. Dom hit the gas before Scott had slid the door shut.

The drivers who hadn't abandoned their vehicles when the shooting started had pulled away into uptown traffic, leaving the van exposed in the middle of the boulevard. They were out in the open, but at least now they had room to move.

"Take the next turn up ahead," Scott ordered. "We need to get lost fast."

As the van and its occupants tilted from Dom's sharp turn, Scott reported to Hicks. "Base, all present and accounted for. We have four targets down, but police and more hostiles are on our tail."

"I've got you, Bravo," Hicks responded. "The two hostiles from the hotel are closing in on your position a quarter of a mile out. There are three of them in each car, bringing the remaining target total to six."

"I can add, Base," Scott growled as he watched the street through the windshield.

"Now let's see if Dom can drive," Hicks answered.

Dom looked back at Scott. "Who is this asshole, anyway?"

"Shut up and drive," Scott told him.

Dom went back to keeping his eyes on the street as Hicks said, "Take the next right and proceed northbound toward the garage. Traffic is at a standstill behind you, so you might make it."

"What about the cops?" Scott asked.

"I'm working on that," Hicks said. "They have your van's description, so heads on a swivel."

Scott used the lull in the action to do a quick mental inventory of his team's gear. He still had half a clip left in the MP5 and two more clips in his vest. Neary had fired a short burst, so he was in the same boat as Scott. Reardon hadn't fired at all, and Thomas had used the MRAD, so he had a full tank. Dom and Rivas hadn't used their weapons. None of them had used the SIGs on their hips, so his team was still rolling plenty heavy.

The way his men could shoot, they should have more than enough ammo to survive another scrape with the Koreans.

But the cops would be a different matter.

"Just keep the PD off our asses, Base. I don't want to mix it up with the good guys."

"Understood," Hicks said, "but Dom better floor it because those two hostiles drove on the sidewalk and are now clear of traffic. They're converging on your position from the east right now."

Dom blew through another red light and took a right at the corner just as the two Suburbans from the hotel took a fast left turn and fell in behind them.

Scott grabbed his rifle. "We've got company, boys and girls."

Dom hit the gas as Rivas called out, "We're two blocks away from the garage.

"We'll make it," Dom said.

Scott stepped over his men as he moved to the back of the van to look out the rear window. Traffic behind them was sparse, and the SUVs were closing in. They had a visual but hadn't opened fire on them yet.

Scott weighed his options. *Maybe this is a good place to stop short and make a stand. Surprise them like I did the others.*

Next to him, Rivas seemed to read his mind. He pointed at his laptop screen. "Cops are right behind them and closing fast. Let's keep our powder dry, get to the garage and take them there."

Scott pulled off his helmet and whispered to Rivas. "We'll be boxing ourselves in. What if the cops get to us first?" He nodded back toward Resnick. "And what about him? Hicks can get the cops to let us go if they grab us, but there's no way we'll be able to get near him again."

"The garage gives us cover which gives us options," Rivas said. "It beats risking a firefight out in the open where the cops will have no choice but to get involved. We don't want that."

Hicks interrupted over their earpieces. "Mike's right. Get to the garage. That's an order."

Had it been Jonathan or anyone else from the University, Scott would've hit the brakes and thrown down with these guys right here.

But Hicks wasn't just the Dean. He'd fought his way out of countless situations like this. He had tactical experience. Scott would be a fool to ignore him.

Scott yelled to Dom, "Get us to the garage. Run the lights if you have to, just get us there in one piece."

"I'm on it." Dom floored it, weaving in and out of traffic as much as possible before reaching the garage on Kenmore.

Scott watched through the back window as the North Koreans got stuck in cross-town traffic half a block away. They had seen where the van was going, but they couldn't do anything but watch.

Dom and Reardon took their helmets off as the van turned fast into the parking structure, almost smashing through the automatic bar across the entrance lane.

The attendant popped out of his booth, more concerned about the condition of the plastic arm than about the van.

Scott placed a hand over Resnick's mouth to quell

his moaning while the attendant looked over the vehicle.

"Sorry about that," Dom said. "I'm in a hurry and forgot it was there."

The attendant took his time going back into his booth and handed him a printed ticket. "You bust that arm, I'll bust your head. Keep that ticket displayed on your dash so you don't get a ticket."

Scott sweated the view from the back of the van while the attendant raised the barrier.

After everything I've lived through, I'll probably get killed because of a parking guy.

Scott removed his hand from Resnick's mouth as Dom took the corners on the way to the roof level where their getaway cars were parked.

But Scott had no intention of going that far.

When they reached the second level, he decided it was time to make their stand.

"Dom, stop here and let me and Reardon out. We'll hide between the cars and ambush them as they come up the ramp. Neary and Thomas, take positions on the next level up in case they get past us. Be ready to come running if I call for you."

"Copy that," both men said.

Scott slipped his helmet back on and continued giving orders. "Dom, you and Mike keep going up to the top and get Resnick in the Honda. Rivas rides with you. Wait until the shooting dies down before you make your getaway down the exit ramp. Don't worry about us. We'll meet later at the safe house. Hicks will keep you apprised of our status. Understood?"

"Copy!" Bravo Team said in unison.

Reardon followed Scott out of the van. The two

men took up positions between two parked cars on the right side of the aisle as the van snaked its way up toward the roof.

Scott heard squealing tires echo through the garage below them. He wondered if the SUVs had stopped for the attendant or just barreled through the arm.

Scott was glad his goggles compensated for the poor lighting in the garage. It was one of the reasons why he had selected this place to switch cars. Separate entrance and exit ramps were part of it. An ancient security camera network was the other. OMNI could easily render any footage unusable.

"Base, Bravo Team is in position. We will ambush the Suburbans as they come up the ramp. I believe at least one target is in the garage."

"Copy. One Suburban just entered the structure."

Scott thought he'd heard him wrong. "And the second?"

"Circling the block," Hicks said. "Will advise if they enter the structure."

Scott knew Reardon and the rest of the team were on the same frequency, so he didn't bother relating the bad news. Bagging one fish wouldn't be a problem. But that shark out there could cause difficulties.

From the next level up, Thomas asked, "Want us to move down to your position?"

"Negative."

Scott got lower as he saw the front of the Suburban inch around the corner and come up the ramp.

Scott heard the Suburban's tires squeal as it took the turn too quickly. He moved his finger just above the trigger. He knew Reardon would wait to fire on his mark.

Wait.

Scott heard the SUV's engine begin to gear down as it crawled up the ramp. They'd grown cautious. They knew they could be rolling into a trap.

Wait.

Scott knew the vehicle was only two cars away.

Showtime.

Scott popped up, MP5 at his shoulder, and saw two men in the front. Both Korean. Back seat unclear.

Not civilians. The passenger's AK confirmed that.

Scott and Reardon opened fire at the same time.

Round after round poured into the open windows and windshield of the Suburban at nearly point-blank range.

Scott's rifle locked open just as Reardon reported, "Three targets down. Bravo Team is still a go."

With its driver dead, the Suburban began to slowly roll back down the ramp. Reardon quickly pulled out the dead passenger and scrambled to throw the vehicle in park.

Scott ejected and tucked away his spent clip before slapping a new one into his rifle. There was nothing they could do about the spent brass rolling around the ramp, but he had other concerns now.

He knew their suppressors had muffled the sound of gunfire, but not completely. No car alarms had gone off, but the attendant down at the booth had probably heard something.

"Base, is the attendant calling the cops?"

"Happy to report he's currently out front enjoying a smoke," Hicks said. "OMNI confirms he's been on the phone to his wife the entire time. He never even turned around."

Scott was glad his team had finally caught a break.

He pulled open the driver's side door and pulled the dead driver from the vehicle. "What about that second SUV?"

"Still circling the block," Hicks said as Scott dragged the driver to the trunk. "I've fed their license plate into the police system as a suspected vehicle from the Hotel Cedric shooting."

Reardon had already opened the trunk and put the passenger inside. He helped dump the driver on top of him. The dead man in the back seat could stay where he was.

"Good thinking, Base," Scott said. "Bravo Team in the process of clearing the vehicle. Please advise if the second group approaches the building."

Reardon pulled down the lid of the trunk and shut it.

"What do we do now, boss?" Reardon asked.

Scott headed up to the driver's side and got behind the wheel. "We park this thing on the roof and go our separate ways just like we planned." He knocked on his own helmet. "No one's seen us, and they won't be looking for our cars. We'll drive out of here just like a bunch of civilians."

Reardon stepped on the running board and hooked his arm inside Scott's window as Scott put the Suburban in drive. "I thought you'd want to stay and finish this."

Reardon, like the rest of his team, knew him all too well. "I do, but we've got civilians and cops to worry about. Best if we clear out and disappear now while we can. Hicks might be a prick, but he's usually right about these things."

"I heard that," Hicks said in his ear.

Scott grinned. That's why he'd said it. He switched his comms to talk to his team. "Bravo Team, I'm driving up in the SUV. Do not shoot. We are proceeding to the roof deck and will pick you up as we roll by."

Scott peered through the bullet holes and the blood in the windshield to see where he was going. He rounded the corner slowly and Thomas and Dom followed Reardon's lead by climbing on the running boards on both sides.

Scott hit his comms again. "Neary, we're headed your way. Got the patient stowed?"

Neary's response was immediate. "Ready to roll on your mark, boss."

"Outstanding," Scott said as he rolled through the final level before reaching the roof deck. "This day's beginning to look better all the time."

Leave it to Hicks to ruin it for him. "Bad news, Bravo. Second target has just parked directly across the street from the garage."

Damn it.

Hicks continued, "One man is on the street and two are inside the Suburban. They have eyes on the exit. I repeat, they have eyes on the exit."

Scott cursed himself for picking a garage with only one way out. But he'd traded flexibility for lax security. The attendant was a joke. He figured it would take the operators days to find the van if they found it at all. The cops would probably find it first if they canvassed the area.

He hadn't intended on being hunted, much less leading his team into a trap. Now, it was up to him to get them out of it.

THOMAS'S SNIPER RIFLE.

Scott reached the top level and saw Neary had already removed his tactical gear in favor of jeans and a loose camp shirt. He'd blend in easier that way.

But he was surprised to see Rivas in his wheelchair wearing a T-shirt and baggy shorts. He was supposed to have been loaded into the Honda by now.

"Any more good news?" Scott asked Hicks.

"Police are beginning to set up a grid search for your van and the Suburban," Hicks reported. "They'll probably find the Suburban first, but their proximity to you will box you in."

Scott knew they couldn't just stay there and wait for the cops. And the men outside would be taking pictures of every car that left the garage. If they all left at once, they'd know something was up. Even if they got away, they might decide to follow one or track the car later. If they tracked them to the safe house, they'd bring reinforcements. He didn't like the idea of playing Davy Crockett at the Alamo.

If they chose to go after one of the cars before they reached the safe house, it would be three-on-two. Not good odds. If the cops searched the garage, they'd be sealed off. Civilians might not notice all the spent brass on the floor, but the cops would.

The men had peeled off the running boards and began changing into their civilian clothes. Scott remained behind the wheel.

He said to Hicks, "Send me the location of the other car."

Through his goggles, he saw the Suburban was parked directly across the street from the parking garage. He saw only one option. "Base, my men are ready to roll in thirty seconds. I'm going to ram the car across the street and let the others get away."

"Negative," Hicks said. "The man on the street is a wild card."

Scott patted the rifle slung across his chest. "Not for long."

"Too many police in the area," Hicks said. "They'd close in on you and take you in. We can't have that."

Thomas doubled back to Scott. "I can take them down with my rifle, boss. From this distance, I can't miss if I tried."

Hicks answered for Scott. "That's a negative. Too many cops in the area. You'd risk being intercepted by them before you left the garage. Besides, Rivas and I already have a plan."

Scott watched Mike Rivas rolling down the ramp in his wheelchair. "Where the hell is he going?"

"To save your asses," Hicks said. "Just make sure you're ready to save his. Load up Resnick and get it in gear. You've got two minutes."

CHAPTER 10

LOS ANGELES, CA

MIKE RIVAS STRUGGLED to keep his wheelchair under control as it rolled down the steep incline of the parking garage. He'd acquired some fancy moves in the chair since losing the use of his legs, but this was no time to show off. One spill and he was done for.

He wasn't worried about how he'd handle the wheelchair on the street. He was worried about how he would handle himself in close quarters combat. That Guatemalan cop's bullet had taken more than his legs. It had taken his faith in his abilities.

He knew he wasn't the same man as he had been when he could walk. He was better. But he was untested in the field in his wheelchair and was about to go up against three Vanguard men with guns.

But experience had always been Mike Rivas's best teacher.

The voice of Hicks in his ear reminded him of what was at stake. "Watch for cops and pick your targets,

Mike. I'm feeding conflicting locations of the SUV to the police onboard computers, but the dispatcher is over-riding me on the radio. One or two cars might get there before—"

"I never liked knowing the odds," Rivas said as he controlled his chair. "Still don't."

The attendant looked at the man in the wheelchair who had just emerged from the garage. "Where the hell did you come from?"

"From God, *esse!*" He cackled wildly in Spanglish like a madman as he rolled by. "*De los cielos!*" From the sky.

He sped up as he pushed his way along the sidewalk, behind the cars parked along the sidewalk. From their vantage point across the street, he knew the two men in the Suburban had seen him leave the garage. The man on the street looked the other way. They were looking for a shot up van full of armed men in tactical gear, not some crazy Mexican cripple.

Only Mike Rivas wasn't Mexican. And he wasn't crazy, either.

Rivas saw an opening between two parked cars just wide enough for his chair to fit through and checked both ways for oncoming traffic. There was a rare break in the flow of cars, and he began to push himself across the street.

Horns blared as he cut across the lanes. A bus narrowly missed him as he bumped his chair up on the curb and brought it to a stop facing away from The Vanguard men.

Rivas turned and cursed at the bus in Spanish. Many of the drivers following the bus cursed back at him.

He turned his chair and jawed after a car full of teens that had slowed down long enough to give him the finger. They were driving in the same direction as where the North Koreans were parked. He couldn't have asked for a more perfect cover.

Rivas shouted a challenge to the boys to fight him, which only drew laughter as they sped away. What harm could a skinny cripple in a wheelchair do?

But by the time they drove away, Rivas had already coasted close to the two men in the Suburban and their lookout man on the street.

"*Senor!*" he called to the Korean gunman on the street. "*Tengas dinero?*" He held up his left hand and rubbed his fingers together. "You know, money?"

The man turned his back on him and walked toward the Suburban.

The sidewalk was wide enough for Rivas to get a good look up into the SUV. Even though the truck sat higher than his wheelchair, he had the element of surprise. They were focused on the garage. Not some crazy beggar.

With the third man blocking the Suburban's view of him, Rivas slowly turned his chair to face them and locked the wheels in place. "You don't gotta be rude about it, homes," he said in English. "I just need a little bit of money to help me. You look like you got plenty. How about you give me some? My mother is sick."

They refused to look his way, lest they encourage more begging.

That was the point.

Rivas drew the SIG Sauer P226 from the side pouch of his wheelchair and shot the man on the street once in the back of the head.

As he fell, the passenger was slow to react. Rivas shot him through the open window, nailing him in the temple.

The passenger sagged against the driver as he struggled to open his door.

From his angle, Rivas couldn't see much of his head, but saw enough. He shot him in the back of the head. His body fell against the door, opening it as he spilled into the street.

A city bus slammed on the brakes too late as it rolled over the dead driver and smashed through the open door.

Move.

Rivas had already slid the pistol back into the pouch and began wheeling himself away from the scene, ignoring the attention he was drawing from everyone who had just witnessed the shootings and subsequent accident.

People on foot and in cars looked at him, but no one tried to stop him. He was ready to grab the pistol if someone took hold of his wheelchair, but no one dared. They grabbed their cellphones and began to film him instead.

The twenty-first century version of the responsible citizen.

He hoped Hicks and OMNI were already blocking the footage. "Front door is wide open," Rivas said, hoping his handheld was picking up his voice. "You bastards better not be late. I'm exposed as hell out here."

Scott's voice came over his earpiece. "Stand down, Speed Buggy. We're on the way."

Just as he reached the corner, Rivas saw a blue Charger tap its card at the garage exit and wait until the automatic arm went up. That would be Thomas and Dom. They took a right and went in the opposite direction according to plan.

He put his head down and kept working his wheels. He'd drawn a small following of citizens trailing behind him with cellphones aimed his way and didn't dare look back.

But he looked up when a Ram pickup did a hard U-turn in the middle of the street and skidded to a halt at the curb beside him.

Scott, still wearing his ballistic helmet, hopped out of the passenger side of the truck, picked Rivas up out of the chair, and set him in the back seat of the truck's cab. He grabbed the wheelchair and tossed it in the flatbed before getting back into the passenger seat and ordering Reardon to move.

The people who were filming him were more brazen now, running after the truck to get the license plate.

"You're a popular man," Reardon drawled as he took the next right. "Ought to get you an agent while we're here in LA."

Rivas wasn't in a joking mood. He asked no one in particular, "OMNI tracking those phones?"

Scott pulled off his helmet and raised his handheld so Rivas could see it. A live satellite image showed yellow dots that represented every cell phone and wireless camera in their immediate area.

"Hicks is already erasing the footage as we speak. All the cops will get are pixilated images and a lot of shaky nonsense they can't use."

Rivas still wasn't satisfied. "What if they call in our license plate to the cops?"

"Hicks is on that," Scott assured him. "The dispatcher will say one thing, but the on-boards in the cop cars will say something else. In all the chaos we created at that intersection downtown, they won't notice. We'll switch the plates when we reach the safe house."

Rivas knew what OMNI could do, but he was still running on adrenaline. It had been a while since he'd seen action like this. He didn't count the incident in Berlin as fieldwork. He hadn't been there for Tali when she'd needed him, and now she was dead. He didn't blame himself for it, but he didn't feel good about it, either.

He kept his mind on his current situation. "Where's Neary and the prisoner?"

"In the trunk of Neary's Cadillac," Scott told him. Pulled out just as you went to work. They'll meet us back at the safe house. Then we wait for Hicks to tell us where to bring him next."

Rivas felt his hands begin to shake as the rush began to leave his body. That was what he had forgotten about the job. About the Life. *Hurry up and wait.* A few seconds of blood and gore followed by hours of waiting and watching for the right time to move.

He'd forgotten the feeling and realized just how much he'd missed this life. How much he'd lost when he lost the use of his legs.

Scott glanced back at him. "That was some real bad *hombre* shit you pulled back there, Mike. I'm mildly impressed."

Rivas gripped his hands tighter to fight the shakes. "Goddamned right."

Reardon cut loose with a rebel yell. "Pancho Villa's got nothing on you."

"My people are Guatemalan, shithead. We hate Mexicans."

"That so?" The Texan shrugged it off. "Then I guess the Mayans ain't got nothing on you, either."

That was more like it. "Goddamned right."

THEY HAD BEEN BACK at the safe house in Pomona for two hours when Hicks called Scott for a situation report.

He'd decided to let his team continue playing cards while he stepped into the kitchen to take the call in private.

"Sit rep," Hicks said.

"Resnick's stable," Scott told him. "The morphine we gave him earlier worked, but Dom's the closest thing we've got to a doctor. He's a medic, so take his diagnosis for what it's worth. We've all seen enough junkies and drunks in our time to know he'll probably live."

"Is he conscious?" Hicks asked.

"Nodding in and out. Groggy as hell. He must've had himself a real good time last night."

"It'll have to last him for the rest of his life. You think he's strong enough to stand some questioning?"

Scott didn't like the sound of that. "You're not sending that freak Roger here, are you? That sick bastard gives me the creeps."

"Not physically," Hicks said, "but I want him to have a crack at Resnick via your tablet."

Scott liked that idea better. "Let me check."

Scott walked down the hall to the back bedroom. He opened the door and saw Resnick was still in bed and sound asleep. He hadn't moved since they'd set him down two hours before. "He's sleeping but not restless. I'd say he's pliable."

"Good. Grab your tablet and prop him up. Keep your sidearm handy but for show purposes only. Follow Roger's lead."

Hicks killed the connection, leaving Scott to stare at a blank handheld screen.

As far as he was concerned, Roger Cobb was a maniac and dangerous. He liked his work a little too much. Just because he usually got results didn't mean Scott trusted him.

He went to his room, tucked his pistol behind his buckle and grabbed his tablet. He brought it into Resnick, who was lightly snoring when Scott flicked on the light, snapping him awake.

The prisoner blinked his eyes as he tried to focus. "What's going on?" He looked down at his filthy hospital gown. "Where are my clothes?" He looked up at Scott. "Who the hell are you?"

"I'm the tooth fairy." Scott shut the door and snatched Resnick by the neck, pulling him upright in the bed. "That means I'm going to knock out every tooth in your head unless you do exactly what I say."

Resnick flinched when the tablet began to chirp at an incoming call.

Scott handed him the tablet. "It's for you. Answer it."

Resnick's hands shook as he took the tablet and tapped the phone icon.

Scott didn't have to see the screen to know Roger was on the other end.

His voice confirmed that much. "Good evening, Victor. Nice to see you're awake."

"Who are you?" Resnick asked him. "What's going on here?"

"Easy, Victor, easy," Roger said. "I need you to listen to me very carefully. Listen to me as if your life depends on it because, in fact, it does."

Resnick twitched but didn't let go of the tablet.

Cobb continued. "You no longer enjoy the warm embrace of The Vanguard. The people you may be expecting to come to your rescue are dead. The men in the house you're in now killed them, a fact you'd do well to keep in mind as we proceed. You're all alone now, Victor. No one knows where you are. No one is coming to help you. Your fate rests firmly in the calloused hands of the frightening man in the room with you now. Don't let those robin's egg blue eyes fool you. He's not as gentle as he looks. So, unless you want to test his patience, you're going to answer every question I ask you. Your answers must be truthful and complete. I can't stress that enough."

Resnick looked up at Scott, then at the pistol now in his hand. "What happens then?"

"That depends entirely on you," Roger said. "You're a man of comfort. A man of excess and decadence as evidenced by your current state of overindulgence. I'm going to ask you a series of questions about The Vanguard."

"Oh God." Resnick began to tremble. "I...I don't know what you're talking about."

Scott could hear the smile in Roger's voice. "That lie is free. The next one will cost you a bullet to your knee."

Resnick yelped when Scott pressed the barrel of his pistol against his kneecap.

"Now that we all know the rules, let us begin."

AN HOUR after the interrogation session ended, Scott was back in his room. He was thinking about sleep but was looking at the picture of the blonde Russian nurse instead.

He'd taken her picture out of habit. She had skills that Hicks might find useful later. The University could always use someone with medical training. Someone who knew how to keep their mouth shut and not ask too many questions. Someone who could keep a target alive long enough for Roger Cobb and his ilk to go to work on them.

He'd expected to include her photo in his after-action report to Hicks but found himself looking at it instead. It wasn't the best photo of her. She'd looked prettier in person. But having a masked gunman looming over you didn't exactly make for a good picture.

There was something haunted about her and not just from the crazed situation of the moment. She looked concerned, but not scared. She'd held up well despite finding herself caught up in the middle of something she didn't understand. It was a feeling he knew well. He'd spent most his life that way. He didn't see that changing any time soon.

He remembered threatening her and regretted it. She hadn't deserved that, but the circumstances hadn't given him much time to think.

He also remembered promising to send her money for her trouble. He intended on making good on that promise. He sensed a toughness to her that he could admire. Maybe he'd swing by that nail salon she worked at and give the money to her in person. She didn't know what he looked like, so the sight of him wouldn't scare her.

Manis and pedis had never been his thing, but for her, maybe he'd make an exception.

His screen changed, showing an incoming call from Hicks. He always found a way to be the turd in the punchbowl.

"That went well, didn't it?" Hicks asked when Scott accepted the call.

"Even through a tablet, Cobb still gives me the creeps," Scott said. "But he's got a way of getting people to talk. I'll give him that. Sounded more like a job interview than an interrogation."

"Roger's got a lot of tools in his bag of tricks," Hicks said. "If you were paying attention to what Resnick said, you've probably figured out I'm going to need you and your team in Chicago tomorrow."

"I was paying attention," Scott said. Resnick had given up a lot about his business dealings. Most of it went over his head, but gist of it was that Resnick's boss was a lawyer in Chicago. "My team and I will be wheels up at zero-six-hundred."

"Good," Hicks said. "Roger's going to be joining

you at some point. I'm going to ask you to follow his lead again. He knows what he's doing, Scott."

"He'd better not expect my people to jump through hoops for him. I run a linear outfit, Hicks. We don't do well with nuance. It'll be better for all of us if Roger keeps that in mind."

"I've already reminded him of that," Hicks told him. "OMNI's pulling together everything we've got on what Resnick told us about his Chicago operation. I hope to have a complete target package ready for you and your team by the time you land in Illinois."

Scott hoped he did. "One more brick in the yellow brick road, right?"

Hicks was silent for a moment. "Excuse me."

"From the Wizard of Oz," Scott said. "Ever see it? Tin Man. The Lion. The Scarecrow. Dorothy and Toto?"

"What the hell are you talking about?"

Scott swung his feet out of bed and put them on the floor. "It means I know you're leading us down a path and only you know where it's going. If it was just me, I wouldn't care. But I've got a team to worry about here. They're not just my men. They're also my friends. Whatever grand scheme you're cooking up has something to do with losing Tali, doesn't it?"

"Careful," Hicks said. "You don't know what you're talking about."

"I've ridden the vengeance trail enough times to know it when I see it," Scott told him. "And I know it never ends well. So, the next time you order us to hit a place, you'd better make damned sure you've thought it through carefully. My men wound up in a meat grinder today that could've gone a completely different way. If the cops had cornered us, it would've gotten ugly. That would've been on your head, not mine."

"Quit wondering about what could've been," Hicks said. "Worry about tomorrow."

"What do you think I'm doing?" Scott gripped his handheld tightly. "That's the last time we rush an op, Hicks. If you can't do our thinking for us, step aside and give us the time to do it ourselves or it doesn't get done at all. Because if one of my men gets hurt as part of whatever revenge play you've got going on, you and me are going to have a major problem."

Scott heard Hicks breathing on the other end of the line, so he knew he hadn't hung up. He also knew he wasn't used to being spoken to that way, but Scott didn't care. Some things needed to be said. He didn't place a high value on his own life, but he wouldn't risk the lives of his team on one man's quest for vengeance.

When Hicks spoke, it was quietly. "Take heed how you awake our sleeping sword of war."

Scott didn't consider himself a learned man, but he recognized it as a line from Shakespeare. He decided to respond with a favorite line of his own. "Try this one on for size. 'No greater friend. No worse enemy.' Don't make me prove it to you. I'll call you from the plane."

Scott killed the connection and tossed the handheld on the table.

Maybe now he could get some sleep.

CHAPTER 11

SOMEWHERE IN THE VIETNAMESE JUNGLE

ZHOU FELT his face redden as his son told him about what had transpired in California. At the hotel and in the street and at the garage.

Resnick was gone and some of their best people in California were dead. He imagined the remnants of Tessmer's organization still had people in America, but he hesitated to use them. They were not Zhou's people.

"How many dead?" the general asked as he rubbed his sore hand.

"Eleven, father. Ten of our comrades and one of our guests. A Russian asset who attempted to stop Resnick's kidnapping was killed at the hotel. The others were killed while pursuing the assailants on the streets of Los Angeles."

Eleven dead in an embarrassing public display that would be next to impossible to cover up. When combined with the loss of the San Francisco facility, it amounted to a disastrous day for The Vanguard. "How many assailants were there?"

"The hotel staff reports four armed men, all wearing masks that made them look like giant grasshoppers."

The general slowly glared up at his son. The boy was disappointingly gullible at times. "Did you say grasshoppers?"

"They're only Koreans," his son pointed out. "Mere peasants given to superstitious exaggeration. We believe the men were wearing anti-ballistic tactical masks."

Zhou thought that made much more sense. "You said the hotel staff told you this. What has Kang told you?"

His son looked at the ground. "Comrade Kang seems to have disappeared, father. He most likely feared he would be held responsible for the assault."

Zhou was glad Kang was smart enough to know his own life was in peril.

Upon first hearing of the attack, Zhou had ordered his son to have their people access and review all the security footage from the hotel. Yet for all of Kang's boasting about his facility's state-of-the-art surveillance system, not a single camera was functioning anywhere in the building.

The assailants had obviously known how to block the system remotely, which proved they were both technically and tactically proficient.

With each battle, I learn more about you, James Hicks.

"And you are certain they only went after Resnick," Zhou asked his son. "None of our other people?"

"I am absolutely certain, father."

Interesting.

Zhou began to form a picture of Hicks's possible strategy in his mind. The attacks against the market and the hotel had been calculated. The fragments of footage his people had managed to retrieve from the market's security cameras before setting off the blaze showed the young Anglo woman hadn't gone into the market with guns blazing. She had tried to cajole information from Colonel Pak before the gunfight ensued.

Unfortunately, he could not hear what they had said, but something had gone awry, forcing the colonel to sound the alarm and for the young Anglo woman to defend herself. Quite capably, too. Bloodshed had clearly not been her primary objective. Hicks had sent her there to obtain information about the safe house.

She had sought to infiltrate, not assassinate. Her mission would have been a failure had it not been for the dying coward on the street who had given her information in exchange for an easy death.

Yes, the University's methods had told Zhou much about them. About Hicks.

This wasn't a continuation of the hostilities started between Hicks and Tessmer. By capturing Victor Resnick, Zhou knew Hicks was coming for him.

Zhou knew Resnick, of course. An arms dealer responsible for a substantial portfolio of The Vanguard holdings in the United States.

But grabbing him showed a remarkably shortsightedness on Hicks's part. There had been far more important Vanguard operatives staying at the hotel who could have given Hicks much more extensive information about The Vanguard, but he had not shown any interest in them. *Why Resnick?*

Zhou reached his conclusion quickly. *Time.* Tessmer had led him to Yeung who had led them to Resnick. His focus was myopic. He was following a trail he hoped would lead him to an ultimate prize. Zhou himself.

By knowing where Hicks had been, Zhou could see where he was going. And how to stop him.

The former general looked at his son. "Compile everything you can on Resnick's dealings. I want to know everything about him. You have one hour."

"Of course, father." His son bowed but paused before carrying out his order. "Father, forgive me, but in light of all that has happened recently, do you think it may be wise for us to move you to a safer location?"

Zhou laughed at the young man's ignorance. "Safer than a hut in the middle of a jungle? We are miles from any hint of civilization and our best people are guarding the perimeter. I have never even met this Resnick and there's nothing he can possibly tell our enemies that would lead them to me. I have no intention of scurrying around the world just because some angry American is nibbling at the fringes of our organization. When I find out where Hicks is, I will swat him like the pest he is."

His son bowed again. "Forgive me, father, but it was you who once told me: even the smallest mouse can consume the world if he is allowed to do so."

Zhou was as surprised as he was pleased to hear his own words repeated by his son. The boy had been listening after all. Perhaps he was not as simple-minded as he had believed.

"Those words are still true, my son. Only now we have an idea of where the mouse is headed. Let him nibble a little longer so we can listen and discover his true direction. When we find that," he slammed his hand on the desk, "we break his neck."

CHAPTER 12

SOMEWHERE

Hicks woke up on the floor.

It took him a minute to realize he had fallen out of his cot. He had landed on his back, not on his face, so his recovery hadn't been derailed by his clumsiness.

But his T-shirt and underwear were sopping wet from sweat. So were the sheet and the cot itself. Hicks made sure to keep the office space almost cold enough to hang meat in, so his sweating wasn't for lack of air conditioning.

It was due to the same nightmare he had every time he closed his eyes.

Not his plan, not his row of dominos, but the silent footage of Tali's death that played in a constant loop in his mind. No words, no sound. Just the slightest flinch before she collapsed to the street and died.

Hicks had seen far more gruesome deaths. He'd been responsible for dozens of them. He'd killed men with his bare hands and with knives and with rifles.

He'd killed with pistols at point blank range. He'd stood over them as he watched the last flicker of life leave their bodies so he could verify their death.

Tali wasn't even the first agent he had lost. His mistakes had gotten other agents killed in various parts of the world. Warning signs he'd missed. Situations he hadn't fully understood. Most had died from something beyond Hicks's control. A mistake they'd made that had made a target suspicious.

But the death of Tali Saddon death had been different. It haunted him in a way no other death had or could. Love had never been involved before. Love had been involved now, even though he knew it was wrong. Her death haunted him because it hadn't been avenged. Yet.

Yet. The biggest three letter word in the English language. He closed his eyes and spoke to her quietly in his mind, hoping she could hear him. *Not yet, my love. But soon. I promise to give you in death what I couldn't in life.*

His computer began to beep; telling him a call was coming in.

Hicks pulled himself off the floor and saw it was Roger. He pulled his headset on and activated the voice modulator to enhance his speech. He didn't want anyone knowing how weak he sounded. Not even Roger.

He allowed the call through, activating the camera in Roger's car. Roger was behind the wheel, driving at night.

His mind still foggy from sleep, Hicks asked, "Where the hell are you?"

"Where you told me to be," Roger said. "I dropped off our packages on time and per your instructions."

Hicks toggled his screen to OMNI's Global Positioning Satellite to show Roger's exact location on the planet.

He closed his eyes when he saw it. "You didn't."

"Why not? Demarest wanted Tessmer and Yeung as soon as possible and now he's got them. The green beacon is where Demarest's people will find them. Outfitted them with a strobe so even they can't miss them in the dark. And in a most compromising position, too." Roger smiled. "I had to have a *little* fun."

Hicks zoomed in on the beacon's signal and got a live satellite feed. "You left them in a park?"

"You didn't expect me to drop them off in front of Langley, did you?"

"Jesus, Roger. It's thirty degrees outside!"

"All the more reason for Demarest and his fellow Barnyard dwellers to make haste." He proceeded to bleat like a goat.

He clicked on the bio feed from the beacon Roger had placed on Tessmer and Yeung. The German was barely alive, and Yeung was in only slightly better condition.

He should've been furious with Roger for this. Maybe it was the residual effects of the painkillers still in his system, but Hicks managed to keep his temper under control.

Roger had technically followed orders. Unfortunately, he'd put his own spin on obedience. Getting angry about it wouldn't accomplish much. Besides, he needed Roger for bigger things.

As he typed out a text message with the coordinates

to Demarest, Hicks told Roger, "I need you back in the air and on your way to Chicago immediately. Scott's delivering another package I need you to open."

"That so?" Roger brightened. "What's inside?"

Although OMNI was a secure, closed network, Hicks didn't feel comfortable telling him too much over the phone. More people knew about the University than ever before. Any number of agencies could be looking for ways the group's people contacted each other. Best to play it safe until additional safeguards could be put in place.

"Your device will download a full briefing report as soon as you get on the plane. The package has information we need before we can take our next step."

"Ah, yes," Roger said. "The ever-important next step. And in what direction will that step take us, James? Or, more importantly, where will it take you? Do you even know anymore? Do you care?"

But Hicks knew exactly where this was leading. Each step he had taken since the moment Tali hit the pavement had been in one direction.

"James," Roger said, snapping Hicks out of his fog. "Are you still there?"

"I'm here." Hicks shook the cobwebs from his mind. "We'll find out together when we get there. In the meantime, get to the safe house in Chicago and get to work."

"Of course," Roger said. "But may I ask why Chicago?"

"Because that's where Scott is bringing the package I need you to unwrap. It's all—"

"Part of the plan," Roger completed the sentence

for him. "Fine, but I need to ask a favor of you before I leave."

Hicks wasn't in the mood for another one of his sermons. "I'm taking my medication and getting plenty of rest."

"That's not the favor," Roger said. "Good God, man. Do you think this is some kind of sappy After-school Special? It's your own ass if you don't take your medication."

Hicks cursed himself for trying to anticipate what Roger was saying. "What is it?"

"I want Mary Foster with me in Chicago."

Hicks felt his head began to ache, though not from his surgery. It ached in the way it usually did when Roger hatched one of his plans. "We don't have much room for creativity on this one. I'm sure Scott or one of his people can provide any support you need."

"I appreciate the offer, but I watched some of the footage of how she handled herself at that market in San Francisco. I think Mary has a certain set of skills neither Scott nor any of his goons can replicate."

"She's played her part in this," Hicks said. "She got pretty banged up at the market. A couple of cracked ribs and a concussion. I planned on letting her rest until the Moscow Protocol is lifted and we can get back to work."

"A great waste of talent," Roger said. "Mary's been to the River, James. I'd like to begin grooming her as a Panelist."

Roger usually took great pride in his contempt for using proper University terms. Now, he had used two in the same sentence. The River was the University term for Assets who had received University training. A

Panelist was the formal title Roger held in the organization. The other was interrogator. "You looking for a sidekick, Batman? Or a pet."

"An heir of sorts," Roger said. "Given all that has happened lately, I think redundancy is a good thing, don't you?"

"We have other Panelists," Hicks said.

"But none with my panache. Mary shows promise."

Hicks sent the text to Demarest and considered Roger's request. He'd heard Roger's methods described in many ways, though panache had never been one of them.

But he was the best Panelist in the University system. And two people with his set of skills would come in handy in the future fight against The Vanguard.

"I think she's got a lot of untapped potential," Roger pushed. "I'd like to find out what's there. What do you say?"

Hicks's face began to ache. Since it would be hours until the next phase in his plans took place, he grabbed the bottle of painkillers and popped the top. "Fine. Do whatever you want. Have Jonathan set it up. Just remember she can be reckless and you're responsible for her."

"Recklessness is my specialty. I'll call after I've touched down in Chicago."

Hicks was about to kill the connection when Roger said, "I'm worried about you, James."

Hicks swallowed the horse pill and downed it with half a cup of stale water. "I'm fine."

"No, you're not. You're all alone, recovering from

major surgery in some Godforsaken corner of the world with no one to care for you."

"I'm fine."

"You need to find a way to end this, James. You need to end this quickly before you go out of your mind. You need time to heal your body and your soul. We've both seen what vengeance can do to good people. We've seen how consuming the fires of rage can be. Too many people are relying on you now, including me."

Hicks's anger burned through the ache. "Call me after you've found something in Chicago."

This time, Hicks killed the connection before Roger had a chance to keep him talking. To keep him thinking.

CHAPTER 13

ARLINGTON, VIRGINIA

CHARLES DEMAREST HADN'T CELEBRATED his birthday in years.

That night had been no exception. The Director of National Intelligence had decided to celebrate the anniversary of his birth at home reading a good book in front of a roaring fire.

He considered the home his sanctuary, his only refuge from the constant demands of a life spent keeping his country safe. Another secret in a life built on secrets.

His father had bought the country home years ago when he had moved his family to Washington. Charles had been proud to be able to keep the property in the family. With several grandchildren to his credit, there was an excellent chance the home would remain in his family long after he was dead. None of his children had followed him into the intelligence field, thank God, and he hoped they would enjoy the solitude this place had given him long after his passing.

He was enjoying a guilty pleasure – reading the latest crime novel by Joe Clifford – beside the fire when his cellphone alerted him to a text message. It was not his official phone. Not even the secure phone only the president had.

He imagined it must be one of his close friends wishing him a happy birthday. Only a special few had this number.

He was surprised to see that it was from an unknown number. He thought it might be spam at first, but the text was titled 'A Present for You'.

He tapped on it to see a map with a pin on it, followed by a set of coordinates.

The text beneath it read:

Christmas came early. You'll find your presents under a tree.

Demarest knew only two men were capable of sending an untraceable message to his private phone. One was Meager, but he didn't have a sense of humor.

That meant it had to be that bastard Hicks.

He took a screenshot of the text and forwarded it to Holloway, the head of his security detail parked right outside his door.

He followed up the text with a phone call. Holloway answered on the first ring. "I have your text, sir," she said. "I've already dispatched units to investigate."

"Make sure they proceed with extreme caution,"

Demarest told her. "They could be walking into anything."

"They're aware, sir," Holloway assured him. "The location is less than a mile from here. I'll call when we know more."

Demarest ended the call and began to respond to the text from Hicks.

How did you get my number?

He didn't have to wait long for a reply.

Ask me a serious question.

Demarest closed his eyes and took a deep breath. Hicks was especially insolent in writing.

His phone began to vibrate. It was from Holloway.

Before he answered it, he received another text from Hicks.

Take the call. I'll wait.

Demarest answered the call.

"Sir, I think someone might be playing a joke on you."

Demarest gritted his teeth. "And why is that?"

"Because our people are at the location you sent us and have found two adult males. Older adult males. They're...naked and handcuffed together. One's missing the bottom part of his leg. Looks like we've interrupted some—"

"Have your people take a picture and send it to me immediately."

"Already have. Sending now, sir."

He tapped on the image and saw a man who looked like Tessmer handcuffed behind a man who was Colonel Yeung. Unfortunately, the picture showed they were quite naked and cold.

Damn Hicks.

He got back on the line with Holloway. "Those men are high priority targets. Cover them up and have them brought to a secure location immediately for interrogation."

"Understood, sir."

"Contact our counterparts at the FBI to take them into custody. I want to know where they bring them so I can be there for the interrogation personally. Have I made myself clear?"

"Quite clear, sir. I'll keep you apprised, and we'll be ready to roll whenever you say."

He could've sworn he heard her laugh as he ended the call.

He tapped out a hasty response to Hicks.

I found your presents. Unwrapped. You're a sick son of a bitch.

Hicks's reply was immediate.

Some people call it panache. Happy birthday, Charles. I'll be in touch.

CHAPTER 14

CHICAGO, ILLINOIS

FOLLOWING the attack on his facility in New York, Hicks used a corrupt financial advisor named Vincent Russo to purchase the safe house in the outskirts of Chicago

From the outside, the building looked just like any other quaint home in the area. Inside, it was a fortress.

Hicks had kept the secure contractors busy. In addition to installing an array of external security cameras, every window and door had been replaced with antiballistic material strong enough to stop a fifty-caliber round. Two-inch steel shutters would automatically drop if OMNI detected an approaching threat. A well-armed SWAT team or an especially heavy truck rumbling through the neighborhood would be enough to trigger the system. The only entrance was through a hatch armed with a biometric sensor in the garage. Steel plating blocked every other entrance.

Hicks watched the inside of the safe house on his

monitor thousands of miles away. Scott and his team were lounging in various places, watching television or playing video games.

It was the calm before the storm.

Victor Resnick was on a hospital bed in the basement, shivering away as the alcohol and other drugs left his system. Resnick was still crashing hard from his overdose, but the IV drip of fluids had kept him stable. Dom had hooked up Resnick to OMNI's sensors so that Roger could analyze his vital signs remotely.

Hicks ran through a mental image while he waited for Roger Cobb and Mary Foster to show up at the safe house. A fair number of dominos had already fallen.

Domino One: Tessmer had fallen and led them to:

Domino Two: Colonel Yeung, who had fallen and led them to:

Domino Three: Colonel Pak and The Vanguard's Los Angeles safe house had fallen and led them to:

Domino Four: Victor Resnick who fallen and led them to:

Domino Five: Veronica Holt. Resnick's boss and the person who ran the bulk of The Vanguard's operations in the United States. Interrogating her would be nice, but only if it led them to the second to last domino in the set up. Holt's boss in The Vanguard. He doubted it would be General Zhou. He'd be smart enough to have a middleman between him and the day-to-day activities. Zhou would have a stop gap to buy time for him in an emergency. Once Hicks had that name, he'd have Zhou.

But he wouldn't get that name unless he had

Veronica Holt in custody. And that would depend on what Roger Cobb did when he reached the safe house.

Hicks heard OMNI's proximity alert and toggled to outside cameras to watch Roger's gray Ford Explorer come into view. The automatic garage door opened, and the SUV pulled inside. The steel-reinforced door quickly lowered behind it. Street side tranquility had been restored.

But Hicks knew there was a good chance the inside of the townhouse wouldn't remain so peaceful.

Hicks toggled to the interior view of the safe house. The next few minutes would decide the fate of the rest of his operation. All Hicks could do was sit and watch.

He watched Thomas greet them in the garage before the large black man led Roger and Mary Foster through the garage and into the facility.

Scott was in the kitchen, wearing the same black tactical gear he'd been wearing in Los Angeles. He was suited up and ready to go to war.

Roger was wearing a cream-colored suit, white shirt open. A paisley red pocket square added a dash of color. He looked like he was ready for a cocktail party.

Scott looked up from his handheld when the three of them entered the kitchen. He ignored Roger but nodded toward Mary. "Who's she?"

"This is Ms. Foster," Roger said. "She got you the address of the LA safe house."

"That market that went up in smoke?" Dom asked from the living room. "You did that?"

"The bodies, not the fire," Mary told him. "But, yeah, I got the address."

"Good work," Thomas said.

Mary didn't look like she appreciated Thomas's

compliment. Hicks thought she might be a good protégé for Roger after all.

Roger asked, "Where's Resnick?"

"Down in the basement, sweating out the dregs of whatever's left in his system," Scott told him. "But you already knew that from the sensors."

"True, but sensors can't tell you everything. What's his condition?"

"Starting to level off," Scott said. "Vitals are stable but just north of critical. The nurse in the LA safe house was treating him for alcohol poisoning, but based on his condition, I'd say he was into some nastier stuff."

"A fair diagnosis, doctor," Roger chided. "I'll look in on him in a bit. In the meantime, I was told you've been planning the next step in our mythic quest."

Hicks leaned in closely to his monitor. They were actually working together.

Scott showed him his tablet on the kitchen table. "Resnick's got a line on every underworld scumbag from here to Hong Kong, but Hicks says Rahul will be handling that part."

"He's just arrived in London," Roger said. "He'll plan his next move based on what we're able to get from Ms. Holt."

"Veronica Holt." Scott threw her image to the television monitor in the kitchen as the rest of his team gathered round. "She's an import-export attorney and according to Resnick, she's The Vanguard's main point of contact in the U.S. If you got the target package from Hicks, you'll know OMNI has already linked Holt to several suspected Vanguard shipments around the world. Resnick claims that Ms. Holt oversees all Vanguard activities within the U.S. and is tied directly to the group's executive leadership committee. I don't know if I believe that, but that's what Mr. Cobb is here to find out."

"Why don't you believe it?" Mary challenged him. "Because she's a woman?"

Scott looked at her. "No, because Resnick's still coming down off something and I don't know how reliable he is. Everything I say has a tactical emphasis, not a personal one. You can't tell the difference, then you might as well get on the next plane back to wherever you're from."

Roger held up his hands. "Let there be peace in the valley, boys and girls. We're all on the same side here."

Hicks was glad to see everyone back off, including Mary.

"See? That was easy, wasn't it?" Roger spoke to Scott, "I agree Ms. Holt might be a blind alley, but she's the best lead we've got now. I trust you've already determined the best place to intercept Ms. Holt?"

Scott handed the tablet to Thomas, who changed the view on the screen to a thermal scan of an apartment building. "She lives less than a block away from her office in the penthouse of a high-rise downtown on the Gold Coast. Word has it Oprah used to live there."

"Marvelous," Roger said as he looked at the screen. Mary looked on beside him. "Nice to know we'll be raising hell in a trendy part of a city for a change. You should've seen the last place they sent me. A real pit. Had a nice pool, though."

Neary took the template and zoomed in on the penthouse. "The build's security is a cakewalk. An elevator opens right into the apartment. Doorman in the lobby is twenty-four-seven, but none of them are heroes. They do their job, but they shouldn't be a problem."

Roger enlarged the screen and changed the angle to look at the layout from above. "Three bedrooms. The master has an en suite bathroom. Very posh. One's for her daughter. She has full custody. Poor thing's been sick the past couple of days. A low-grade fever, according to her pediatrician's records. Her presence will be a complication, but we could use it to our advantage."

Mary agreed.

They both went back to examining the scans. "The third bedroom looks like an office. Nice wrap around terrace. Killer views of the city. That must've set her back a pretty penny."

"She can afford it," Scott said. "Her day job earns her plenty, but it looks like her work for The Vanguard is where she gets the bulk of her money. Even pays taxes on some of it. Just enough to keep the IRS off her trail."

"That's not surprising," Roger said. "The Vanguard doesn't hire stupid people. I take it you want to grab her at her apartment?"

Hicks watched and his men Scott nod. "Two of my guys walk in, grab mom and leave. Simple."

Roger looked at Mary, encouraging her to talk.

"How do you get her out of the building?"

Neary walked up to the television screen and pointed. "Take the elevator down to the garage, then out the side door where the van is waiting and off we go."

Mary followed his finger as it ran the length of the scan. "Just like L.A. How did that turn out for you?"

"Turned out just fine," Dom said. "We're all still here."

"Damned right," Reardon drawled.

His team began high fiving each other but Scott told them to quiet down. "We bring Ms. Holt back here for Roger to work his charms. Preferably with as little blood as possible."

Roger looked at Mary to continue to speak for him. "And what happens with the little girl? We can't just take her mother and leave her there."

Neary shrugged. "Not our problem."

Thomas added. "Just another complication we don't need."

"The child is most certainly our problem, or at least a concern." Roger crossed his arms. "Ms. Holt is a mother. The little girl's presence in the apartment at the time we raid it gives us leverage to ensure Ms. Holt's cooperation." He smiled at Thomas. "Don't look at her as a complication. Look at her as a gift to this mission."

Hicks groaned as he watched Scott slowly get to his feet. "You sick bastard. You want to pull apart guys like Resnick, I'm all for it. Maybe even Ms. Holt if you must. They're adults. They knew what they were getting into. But I'll be damned before I sit by and let you threaten a kid."

Hicks caught a blur of motion before Roger was holding a knife to Scott's throat.

Dom, Thomas, Neary and Reardon pulled their pistols and aimed them at Roger.

Mary aimed her pistol at them.

Roger didn't move and neither did Scott. Hicks didn't blame him. He had a knife against his jugular.

Hicks was glad to see Mike Rivas come out of his

room in the back and wheel down the hallway. When he saw the commotion, he yelled, "What the hell is the matter with you people? Put your guns down."

Reardon spoke for the group. "Not until the creep stows that knife. And he's got five seconds to do it."

Roger tilted the blade against Scott's throat. "If you ever imply that I'd harm a hair on a child again, I'll kill you where you stand. Are we absolutely clear on that?"

Hicks knew Scott had never seen this side of Roger before. Someone else in a similar situation might be bluffing. But Scott could clearly tell that was not the case with Roger.

"I understand," Scott said. "Now put the knife away before someone gets killed."

"Good boy." Roger withdrew the blade as quickly as he'd produced it. He held up his right arm and pushed a button beneath his coat that retracted the knife up his sleeve. "You ought to get yourself one of these, you know. Comes in awful handy sometimes."

Mary, and Scott's team lowered their pistols at the same time and tucked them away.

Rivas cursed as he turned his wheelchair around and rolled back into his room.

Hicks began to breathe again. *Fucking Roger.*

Roger flashed a smile again. "Now that we've all marked our territory like the good apex predators we are, let's talk about how we're going to win Ms. Holt's heart and mind."

Scott resumed his seat and the rest of his men stood easy. "What are you going to do? Invite her to tea?"

Roger looked down at him. "I plan on inviting myself over for tea."

WHILE ROGER and Mary were in route to Veronica Holt's penthouse, Hicks directed OMNI to hack the building's security system. In a matter of moments, he had access to live feeds from every camera in the complex. He even had full control of all the elevators in the building, but only cared about the one that led up to the penthouse.

He opened another window and watched OMNI's thermal scan of the Holt apartment. Only two heat signatures still registered. One at a laptop in the third bedroom that served as the home office. The other in little Jane's bedroom. Nothing had changed since Roger and his people had begun to roll on the penthouse.

HICKS CHECKED OMNI's analysis of Veronica Holt's cellphone and laptop for signs of Vanguard business. None of her devices had detected the hack and the information flowed.

Hicks noticed the penthouse was alarmed, but there were no security cameras inside the apartment. *Smart.*

But that didn't mean he couldn't get a look inside. Hicks directed OMNI to access the camera and microphone on Veronica's laptop. He watched her scowl as she pounded out an email to a cranky client.

He knew from her records that she was forty-five, but a judicious mixture of Botox and makeup made her appear much younger. She was work-stress skinny and moved with furtive, jerky movements. Pale skin and blonde highlights in her long brown hair completed the look. She was wearing a Harvard sweatshirt and drank from a coffee tumbler as she typed with one hand. She looked like a busy single mom. Highly educated, motivated and smart. Perhaps a bit tired but more than capable. She had years of experience and hadn't peaked yet. She still had a decade or two to make her mark.

She didn't look like a traitor, but the best ones never did. She didn't look like the type of person who would sell out her country's interest to the highest bidder, but she had. She'd helped The Vanguard spread its poison throughout the hemisphere. She'd been part of the network that had financed a biological attack in New York and was responsible for deaths and corruption throughout the world. OMNI's scan of her records would show the extent of the damage she had done, but he expected it to be quite a bit.

And he expected Roger to get her to tell him about her boss at The Vanguard.

The domino that would cause General Zhou to fall.

While he waited for Roger and Mary to reach the penthouse, Hicks directed OMNI to narrow its search of her records to interactions with Victor Resnick. She had personally approved every international transaction with The Vanguard arms dealer and financier. She'd set up dummy corporations to move cargo from one port to another, making it virtually impossible for customs officials to track which company was responsible for what cargo. Such information might help Roger with his interrogation of her. The quicker he broke her, the better. The Vanguard was on alert. Hicks had left a trail. It was only a matter of time before they knew Holt was a possible target if they didn't know already.

Holt was Hicks's first solid link to The Vanguard's

infrastructure. Its cash flow. She might not be able to lead him directly to General Zhou, but she could lead him to her boss.

Hicks had no doubt that Roger could get Veronica to talk. The only question was how far he'd have to go before she told them everything.

Hicks forwarded the summary OMNI had prepared on her ties to Resnick to Roger's handheld. He was only a few minutes away from the penthouse, but it was plenty of time for him to devise a list of questions to ask her.

But getting him and Mary into the Holt penthouse was another story.

It was time for Hicks to introduce himself.

———

HICKS WATCHED Veronica Holt's stern expression turn into rage as her screen went black.

She angrily pounded the keyboard and maneuvered her mouse, clicking wildly as she whispered, "What the hell?"

Hicks could have spoken to her over her computer but decided typing would be more unsettling. The capital letters would convey the desired effect:

**STOP TYPING AND PAY ATTENTION.
DO NOT TOUCH YOUR PHONE.
DO NOT MOVE AWAY FROM THE
COMPUTER UNTIL I TELL YOU TO
DO SO.**

**RESPOND TO ME VERBALLY SO I KNOW
YOU UNDERSTAND.**

She pushed herself away from the desk as if she'd
been shot. She brought her hands up to her mouth.

Hicks typed:

DO YOU UNDERSTAND?

"Yes," she whispered. She looked in the direction of
her daughter's room and tried to keep the panic out of
her voice. "Who is this?"

A FRIEND WHO CAN HELP IF YOU LET ME.

"But I don't need any help. I'm not in any trouble.
This is all just a big misunderstanding."

Hicks decided to let her in on the game.

VICTOR RESNICK SAYS OTHERWISE.

He watched her bring her eyes wider as she ran her
hands over her face. She looked like she might be sick.
"Oh my God. Who is this? How do you know Victor?"

Hicks replied:

HOW DO <u>YOU</u> KNOW VICTOR, MS. HOLT?

"He's a client, so I can't answer that question. Who
are you? The FBI?"

Hicks was giving orders, not answer questions.

IN A FEW MOMENTS, YOUR DOORMAN WILL CALL.
THERE ARE TWO PEOPLE WHO WISH TO COME UP.
YOU WILL LET THEM IN.
THEY WILL NOT HURT YOU.
TELL ME YOU UNDERSTAND.

Hicks watched her hands disappear from view. Her upper body was still, too still, as she said, "Yes, I understand. Just please don't hurt my daughter, do you hear me?"

Hicks checked his screen. OMNI's hack on her cell showed him she was typing out a text message on her cell phone to a contact named Eric. The message: '911'.

She hit send without looking away from her computer screen. She hadn't seen that message hadn't been sent. OMNI had already blocked the signal.

Hicks typed:

NO ONE WILL GET HURT.
NOT YOU.
NOT YOUR DAUGHTER.

"Please," she wept without tears. "Don't hurt us. I don't know anything."

Hicks knew that was a lie, but that was up to Roger to handle.

REMAIN SEATED IN FRONT OF THE COMPUTER.
DO NOT TOUCH ANYTHING.

**DO NOT GET UP UNTIL THE DOORMAN
CALLS.
YOU WILL ANSWER ALL OF MY
ASSOCIATES' QUESTIONS.
YOU WILL NOT BE HARMED.
DO YOU UNDERSTAND?**

Veronica read what Hicks had typed and said, "Why do you keep asking me if I understand? I'm not an idiot. Of course I understand. And I'll do everything you say."

**GOOD.
BY THE WAY, ERIC ISN'T COMING.**

Veronica closed her eyes and mouthed 'Fuck'.
Hicks smiled.

CHAPTER 15

CHICAGO, ILLINIOS

THOMAS CONTACTED HICKS from a spot in front of the building. "Base, I've dropped off the packages and they are at the elevator now. Where do you want me?"

"Stay in the car but keep the engine running. Be ready to get out of there in a hurry. Holt tried to contact someone while I was talking to her. OMNI blocked the call, but she might have someone watching her. Watch for any goons who show up, but do not intervene. Report anything suspicious."

"Copy that."

Hicks watched the elevator camera as Roger and Mary rode up to the penthouse. Mary kept her head down away from the view of the camera. Roger looked up and waved at Hicks. *Fucking Roger.*

Hicks toggled back to the view from the television in Veronica's living room. He hadn't seen her answer the doorman's call, but since all her signals were blocked, it wasn't a big deal.

He watched her now, sitting in an overstuffed chair facing the elevator. Arms crossed and her leg bouncing impatiently. The initial shock of the situation had faded and was becoming belligerent. She worked for The Vanguard, after all. They were not to be trifled with.

She'd be a tough nut to crack. He wondered how long it would take Roger to win her cooperation.

The elevator doors opened, and he watched Roger come in with Mary a few deliberate steps behind him. She was casual, but cautious.

Roger gasped and clasped his hands as he walked into the apartment. "My God, Veronica, you have exquisite taste. Would you just look at that view? Rows and rows of Mies van der Rohes. Isn't that what they say on all the tours?" He gasped again as he got closer to the window. "And you can see the lake from here, too? It must be beautiful here in the summer. All seasons, actually."

Veronica kept her arms folded and her leg continued to bounce impatiently. She'd drawn her face into a scowl. "Are you here to play realtor or rough me up?"

Mary took a couple of steps toward her, but Roger held her back.

Roger frowned at Veronica. "You look exhausted, Veronica. I don't blame you. How's Jane feeling? The poor little thing's down with a bug, isn't she? Swollen glands. High fever."

Veronica's leg stopped bouncing. "You keep my daughter out of this. Do you hear me?"

"I'm afraid you brought her into this the moment you decided to work for The Vanguard." Roger looked at Mary and lowered his voice. "Take a look around.

Make sure the girl is comfortable. If she's asleep, don't wake her. If she wakes up, do your best to keep her calm and entertained. Mommy and I have some business to discuss out here."

Mary grumbled, "I don't even like kids," as she headed toward Jane's room.

Veronica practically leapt from her chair. "Don't you touch my baby!"

Mary stopped and drew back her right hand to strike.

Roger's voice cracked the air like a whip and froze Veronica cold. "Sit. Down. Now."

Hicks watched Veronica sit back in the overstuffed chair.

Mary continued into Jane's room, leaving Roger and Veronica alone in the living room.

Roger approached her with his arms clasped behind him. "If you answer my questions, there's no reason why this can't be relatively painless. The sooner you cooperate, the sooner my friend and I will be on our way."

Veronica folded her arms again as she sank back into the chair. "Who the hell are you people?"

Roger ignored the question. "Victor Resnick. Tell me about him."

"Like I told your friend who highjacked my computer, he's a client. That's all I can tell you under attorney-client privilege."

"More like an employer-employee relationship to hear him tell it," Roger said. "With you playing the role of employer."

"That's ridiculous. I have evidence—"

"We have everything you have, Ms. Holt," Roger

said. "All of the records on all of the hard drives of all your devices both here and at your office. It'll take time to rummage through all of it, but we'll find the truth eventually. Do yourself and your daughter a lot of good by giving up the charade and telling me all about The Vanguard. What you do for them and for whom you do it. Be specific and don't make me ask the same question twice."

"Or what?" She raised her chin at him. "You'll hit me? Go ahead. Hurt my daughter? I don't think so. You'd already have her out here at gunpoint if you had that in mind." She sneered. "Don't look so surprised. This isn't my first time in this situation."

Hicks didn't like the way Roger was smiling. She'd challenged him. He liked his subjects to challenge him. It gave him an excuse for being cruel.

"I make it a practice to hit neither women nor children, Ms. Holt," he said. "Call me old fashioned that way. But I understand that The Vanguard has quite a modern view of such things. And once we have all your records, we'll simply let it be known that you handed them over to us. That you've been working with us for years."

Her sneer faded as Roger bent closer to her. "And who's this 'we' I keep referring to? This 'us'? All you need to know is that we won't have to work very hard to convince them of your cooperation. And we won't be there to stop them when they come for you."

Veronica unfolded her arms and sank even deeper into the chair. Her expression told him that she believed him.

"You know what they'll do when they come for you, don't you?" Roger added for good measure. "I know you've heard the stories, but have you seen the pictures?" He pulled out his handheld. "They're actually quite beautiful in a horrifying sort of way."

Her left hand shot out and she placed it over Roger's device. "You wouldn't do that."

"Yes, I would." He put his handheld back in his pocket. "Tell me about The Vanguard. The names of the people you work for. Where they are and what you do for them."

Hicks could see tears begin to stream down Veronica's face. She wasn't sobbing. It was simply the result of the pressure Roger was applying. She was caught and there was no point in denying it anymore.

"My orders come in anonymously," she said. "They always have. I don't know where I'm given a set of shipments that need to be arranged and I work with Resnick to make sure they're carried out. The money is deposited in an offshore account, and I use it to pay Resnick his share. The amounts vary according to what they want shipped. Drugs, weapons, equipment. Sometimes it's people." She did her best to sound sincere when she added, "I don't always know the details and I never know who's giving the orders. I don't ask questions and cash the checks. And since you say you're downloading my records, soon you'll know as much as I do."

"Hardly," Roger sighed. "Tell me about your boss in Hong Kong, Veronica. And Shanghai."

Her eyes flashed for a second. "Resnick told you a lot, didn't he?"

"He knows more than you thought. Last chance to come clean before you become The Vanguard's least favorite person in the whole wide world."

Her sneer returned. "If you knew how to contact them, you wouldn't need me."

"I can always use the North Koreans," Roger said. "They're always a good conduit to reach your friends. Who knows? Maybe you'll get lucky, and the Americans will intercept it first. A federal supermax prison's not exactly Majorca, but it's better than whatever butcher The Vanguard sends after you. And little Jane."

She clearly hadn't expected him to know so much. Her hand trembled as she tucked a strand of hair behind her ear. She brought her knees up and hugged them close to her chest as she finally began to sob. She had no more cards to play. No alleys to duck down. All escape routes blocked.

Her only salvation, a stranger in a cream-colored suit who knew too much.

"You have to swear you'll protect us," Veronica said. Her voice a whisper. "Swear it! Look at me when you say it."

Roger surprised Hicks by resting his hand on her shoulder as he looked her in the eye. "I'll protect you with my life if necessary."

Veronica took a ragged breath as the last of her defenses crumbled. "His name is Tamir Bat-Erdene. He's the one who recruited me. He's the one I answer to."

Hicks already had OMNI working on running down the name.

Veronica continued. "He was born in Mongolia, but spent a lot of time in Africa, particularly Somalia. He uses a lot of aliases and I swear I don't know them all, but that's his real name. He's the one I work for, but I don't know where he is. Now please protect us. Please protect my daughter." She ducked her head against her arms. "Oh God, please protect us."

She began to shake uncontrollably now.

Roger remained as he was and gently gripped her hand. "You did well, Veronica. You held out for as long as you could, and you made the right choice for you and Jane. But we still have work to do."

She weakly raised her head. "For God's sake. What now?"

"Don't worry." Roger smiled warmly. "This part is easy. In order for me to live up to my promise to protect you, I need you to pack a bag. Only one. Quickly now. Then pack one for Jane. We'll get you two settled into your new life."

Veronica grabbed Roger's arm and buried her face in it. She broke down completely now and clung to him as if it was her only lifeline. Maybe because he was.

He watched Roger back away from her and lower his head.

"Happy?" he asked Hicks.

"Good job. Pack them up and move them out. I'll check with Thomas to make sure the street is clear."

"Understood. Give us fifteen minutes."

Hicks killed the connection and contacted Thomas in the car down front. "Everything good on your end?"

"Nothing out of the ordinary."

"Let's hope it stays that way. They'll be coming out with two guests in fifteen minutes. Take them back to the safe house. I'll reach out to Scott and tell him you're coming with guests."

"Copy that."

Hicks checked OMNI's search of Tamir Bat-

Erdene but toggled back to the living room feed when he heard Roger's voice grow sharp. "What did you say? I didn't hear you clearly. Repeat what you said."

Veronica was still curled into a fetal position on the couch. Her tears flowed freely. "We don't have fifteen minutes. We don't even have five."

Roger ducked his head and spoke to Hicks. "We may have to carry her out of here. I think she's suffering a breakdown."

"Do what you have to do. Forget about her shit. Just get her and the kid out of there now."

Roger tried to soothe her. "Calm down. We have people monitoring the area and you're quite safe. No one is near the building. We'd know it if they were."

Veronica pounded the cushion of her sofa as she screamed in Roger's face. "No one's coming because they're already here, goddamn it! Don't you understand? The Vanguard owns the entire building!"

HICKS FELT as if he'd been punched in the gut but shook it off. He'd have to work fast to save the op.

He accessed the building's elevator controls and had the elevator brought up to the penthouse level before locking it in place.

Roger practically had to carry Veronica off the couch as he called out, "Mary! Bundle up Jane and let's go. Now!"

Veronica kept babbling as she held onto Roger. "You don't understand. They have men right downstairs. In the apartment right beneath us."

Roger kept dragging her. "How do you know that?"

"They came here late last night. Told me I might be in danger. Said they'd be watching somehow."

Roger ducked his head again as he spoke to Hicks. "Keep that elevator locked in place and give us an express ride to the lobby."

"Copy." Hicks worked his keyboard. "That elevator's not going anywhere."

Veronica kept talking. "There's a button by the phone to the lobby. I pressed it when I told the doorman to let you up."

Roger stopped and took her by the shoulders. "You what?" How many are there?"

"Five at least," she sobbed. "There's no way we can get out of here alive. Don't you understand?"

Hicks had already blocked all signals into and out of the penthouse, so if they were watching her wirelessly, they hadn't heard anything. But not even OMNI could do much against a buzzer wired to another apartment.

He remembered the text she had tried to send out. A 911 to 'Eric'. To Roger he said, "Ask her if that's the Eric she tried to contact."

Roger kept her propped up. "Is Eric one of them?"

She quickly nodded. "That's the name I was given. Please, we have to hide. Put something in front of the elevator door, anything. They'll be here any second and they'll kill all of us."

Roger's head snapped around when the elevator door began to close.

Hicks switched screens and saw the electronic lock he had placed on the elevator was still in place. It shouldn't be going anywhere.

To Roger, he yelled, "Don't let those doors close!"

Roger shoved Veronica out of the way and sprinted

toward the closing doors. He jammed his foot between them just in time to send the door automatically back open. He pulled the KA Bar knife from his sleeve and jammed it into the base of the elevator door, wedging it open.

The elevator rocked in place for a moment before it gradually began to lower. "Looks like they've found a way to override the system, James. Are you sure you can control it?"

Hicks felt sweat break out across his back. He checked the screen again. "The block on the system is holding. The elevator shouldn't be going anywhere."

Mary came into the living room holding Jane bundled in blankets. "What's wrong?"

Roger jumped back when the elevator shook and began to descend, despite having jammed the doors opens.

Veronica screamed as the elevator sank out of view.

"Damn it," Mary yelled over her. "What's wrong?"

Roger placed his hands on the open doors and leaned out to look down the shaft. "We're about to have company."

Mary pulled Veronica to her feet and handed the child to her. "Get into your bedroom and lock the door. Now!"

Veronica took her child and ran back to her bedroom. She slammed and locked the door behind her.

Hicks saw Roger look back at Mary. "I don't know how they've overridden OMNI."

"Firefighter's key," she said. "Overrides the controls physically."

Hicks hadn't thought of that.

Mary drew her Glock from her belt. "Glad I came prepared."

Roger looked down the shaft when the cables started to shake. "Who's inside the elevator?"

Hicks toggled to the elevator camera and saw five men rush inside from a few floors below. All of them in vests. All of them armed with automatic weapons. AK-47s. He knew nothing in the apartment could stop that much firepower.

He watched one of them turn a key on the control panel and the elevator began to make its ascent.

"You've got five hostiles on their way up. Looks like you're going to have to take cover."

"I've got a better idea." To Mary, he pointed at the couch, "Take cover and open up on them as soon as you have something to shoot at. The earlier the better."

As she backed into position, she asked, "Where will you be?"

Hicks watched Roger look down into the shaft and wait.

"What the hell are you doing?" Hicks asked.

The elevator gears rattled as the car continued its flight upward.

Roger pulled his nine-millimeter Beretta from its shoulder holster beneath his jacket and dropped to a crouch.

As the top of the car rose above the lip of the floor, Hicks watched Roger step lightly out onto the roof of the elevator.

Less than a foot of the elevator cleared the floor when Mary began firing into it. He heard automatic gunfire come from the elevator as the heads of five men came into view.

They were trapped in a confined space and coming under fire.

Mary's shots sent two of them backward into the other three. The remaining men inside the elevator returned fire. Automatic weapons tore into the walls of the living room.

Mary went flat as another long burst shredded the couch, filling the air with stuffing.

The elevator was almost level with the floor when Hicks saw the men jerking as they were struck by gunfire from above. A smoke grenade rolled out of the elevator and detonated, obstructing Hicks's view.

All Hicks knew was that he couldn't see what was going on.

He could hear even less. An eerie quiet settled over the scene as white smoke filled his screen.

As the smoke gradually began to thin out, he saw Mary on her feet, sweeping the room with her Glock.

Mary coughed as she called out, "All hostiles are down. I repeat, all hostiles down. Roger, where are you?"

No response.

"Roger," she repeated, "I say again, where are you?"

The smoke in front of the elevator had cleared enough for Hicks to see a ceiling panel open as Roger's feet came into view.

He dropped onto one of the bodies of the gunmen on the elevator floor.

The man grunted.

Roger aimed down at the man's head and fired.

Roger waved the smoke away from his face as he tucked the empty gun back into his shoulder holster.

Mary firing into the elevator and Roger firing from above, all five gunmen were down.

Roger ejected a clip from his Beretta and slapped in a new one. "Help me clear out the elevator so we can get the mother and child out of here."

While Mary and Roger made quick work of clearing out the elevator, Hicks contacted Thomas. "How are things from the street?"

"No new targets," Thomas reported. "But the doorman is looking nervous as hell all of a sudden. Keeps looking at the elevators and texting something."

"Secure him and cover Roger's exit from the elevator," Hicks ordered. "The Vanguard controls the entire building. Things might get hot in there."

"Copy that."

From the lobby cam, Hicks watched Thomas grab his MP5 from the back before he got out of the SUV and held it against his leg as he pushed through the revolving doors.

He approached the doorman's desk, but the older man ignored him while he tapped out a text on a cellphone just below the desk.

Thomas's rifle in his face got his attention.

The Varsity man snatched the phone from the doorman before he had a chance to lock it. "Hands where I can see them, or you die."

Thomas moved back out of the doorman's reach as he checked the phone. "He's texting someone named Eric, asking him if he needs any help."

"Keep an eye on him," Hicks cautioned as he toggled back to the split screen between the elevator and the apartment.

Mary and Roger had just cleared the last body from

the elevator. He used a throw rug from the couch to mask the sight of the five men they had just killed. He imagined that was for young Jane's benefit. He couldn't do anything about the blood, and Hicks hoped the girl didn't notice.

He gestured to Mary to retrieve their guests while he worked his blade free from the door.

"Lobby clear?" he asked Hicks.

"Thomas has it under control. If there's a firefighter lock key in the elevator, I'd use it."

"There is and I have every intention of using it," Roger said. "We'll be a bad memory in five minutes."

Hicks knew not everyone in the building could be Vanguard personnel. Some of them were bound to be regular civilians who had heard the shots from the penthouse and decided to contact the police. OMNI had only been blocking calls from the penthouse. He hadn't expected a gunfight to ensue.

There hadn't been time.

That word again. *Time.*

Hicks watched Mary practically shove Veronica and her blanket-bound daughter into the elevator. Veronica yelped when she almost lost her footing on some of the gore. Mary kept her upright.

When all four of them were inside, Roger turned the key, and they made their descent to the lobby.

Hicks split the screen between them and Thomas keeping the doorman covered. Both of them watched the elevator make its descent from the penthouse.

"No way they make it, brother," he heard the doorman say to Thomas. "We know who they are. And now, we know who you are, too. Pretty soon, we'll know where, and—"

Hicks saw Thomas thrust his assault rifle's barrel in his face.

"He's bluffing," Hicks said. "I've got the cameras on a loop and blocked his cellphone. They don't have eyes on us."

Thomas pressed the barrel against the side of the doorman's face. "He's seen us, though."

Hicks knew he had a point. "Don't kill him yet. You may need him as a hostage to get out of there."

Thomas looked disappointed but kept his finger off the trigger.

As soon as the elevator doors opened and Roger led his party into the lobby, Thomas asked, "Now?"

Hicks said, "Yeah."

Thomas shot the guard in the head. The Holt girl screamed at the noise and buried her face in her mother's neck as Mary and Roger pushed them through the lobby.

"Was that necessary?" Roger asked as he passed Thomas before he pushed through the revolving doors."

"Yeah," Thomas said as he covered them during the exit.

Hicks was glad they had gotten out of the building alive. He checked OMNI's tactical view, and saw no other vehicles were in bound. "Get back to the safe house ASAP. I'll do my best to keep any police out of your way. Drive smart, but don't speed. You don't want to get pulled over."

"I've done this before, Base," Thomas said.

He was the last one through the revolving doors but scrambled to the car and began to drive them back to the safe house.

CHAPTER 16

SOMEWHERE IN THE VIETNAMESE JUNGLE

Zhou lost patience with his son's stammering. "Say what you came to say or get out of my sight."

The young man steeled himself and delivered the bad news. "Father, our Chicago facility has been compromised. Veronica Holt has been taken. So has her daughter."

"Impossible," Zhou said more for his benefit than for that of his son. "We constructed the building from the ground up decades ago. We can monitor every inch of the structure inside and out. How could she have been taken without our knowledge."

"Our systems discovered a disruption in our data feeds, father. We have since successfully rebooted the system and have regained full control of the facility. However, the cameras reveal the carnage left inside."

"Impossible." Zhou felt like an imbecile repeating himself, but it was the only word that came to mind.

"You told me you had forces in place to prevent such a thing from happening."

"She forbade them from remaining in her apartment, father. Her child was sick, and she didn't want her distressed by the presence of guards. They were on the floor below but had to take the elevator up to her apartment. They were ambushed in the elevator by an unknown number of forces. Our people judge them to be about two. One firing from the apartment and another atop the elevator itself."

Zhou spat. Two was all it would take to kill an elevator crammed with men. The stupidity of it all was radiant.

"But why was she still there? I directed her to be moved immediately."

"She ordered it to be delayed by a day," his son said, "due to her sick child."

Zhou closed his eyes. Competent men thwarted by the whims of a hysterical mother. He was about to ask his son how Hicks could have discovered her location but remembered Hicks had taken Resnick. He was not supposed to know where Holt lived, but apparently did. He had told Hicks, who ordered her abduction.

Zhou had expected Hicks would likely make a play for Holt eventually, but he did not think he could do it so quickly. He had underestimated his enemy and paid accordingly. He would not make the same mistake again.

"Why haven't you told me about the police response?"

"Because there was none," his son reported. "As soon as we detected our systems were compromised, we called other assets to the scene. They confirm all that I have just told you. All of the building's residents sheltered in place when they heard the gunfire and awaited further instructions."

Zhou was glad the occupants of the building had been astute enough to avoid calling the authorities.

Their discretion may have given him a way to turn this disaster to his advantage.

"Do you have a possible location of the Holt woman's whereabouts?"

His son cringed again. "Unfortunately, we do not, father, but our people are quietly scouring the area. We had hoped the traffic camera footage would reveal some clue, but they were compromised as well. The University covers its tracks well, father."

Zhou happened to agree with his son. This was Hicks's doing. It may also be his undoing.

The Holt woman was a cornerstone of their operations in the Western Hemisphere. Vanguard business would certainly continue without her, but her knowledge of their operations was as extensive as it was dangerous.

If she had been taken by the FBI, Zhou would have been able to use the inherent weaknesses in the American justice system to secure her silence.

But she had been taken by Hicks. Zhou knew the Holt woman to be strong and capable, but Hicks had broken Tessmer and Yeung. He would undoubtedly use Holt's daughter against her to secure her cooperation. Hicks was unencumbered by the law.

Zhou smiled. Unencumbered, perhaps, but not entirely immune from it. He had chosen the ground on which to fight. It was time for Zhou to use his choice against him.

He looked at his son, who appeared ready to be struck by his father. "Have our people secured the building? Taken enough pictures to understand what happened?"

"They have completed a thorough investigation for your review, father."

"Then have one of them alert the local authorities as to what happened," Zhou said. "Make sure it is an Anglo who makes the call and remains the face of this. No need to expose our interests more than we already have."

His son looked at him strangely. "The police, father?"

But Zhou was still giving instructions. "Shut your mouth and pay attention! Contact our people in the FBI, too. Tell them what happened and have them make the Holt kidnapping as public as possible. The American media love a good kidnapping. I want her face on every news website and front page immediately. They are to make sure the media focuses on the missing girl. I want it to be the lead story on all their tedious morning news programs. The sight of an innocent child is certain to tug on the heartstrings of every parent in America. I want news of this carnage to sweep the nation."

Zhou watched a light appear in his son's eyes. "You will use the Americans to hunt Hicks, father."

Although his son's understanding was not necessary, he was encouraged by it. "Share our information on Mr. Hicks with our FBI friends. Allude that there is a connection between Ms. Holt's disappearance and the attack on the Korean market in San Francisco. And the rather public display of violence in Los Angeles yesterday."

His son bowed as his father stood to stretch his legs. "A wise plan, father. Americans love a straight line. It's easier to believe. Connecting all these incidents together will seal Hicks's fate within his own country. A most brilliant strategy indeed, father."

Zhou frowned. He wished to encourage his son's enthusiasm without allowing him to become too familiar. He could not allow him to think his praise had too much value, lest he become conceited. "Secure all of the Holt woman's records and erase anything that can lead back to us, then contact the FBI. Keep me apprised of your progress. But act quickly. Time is of the essence."

His son bowed again as he began to leave the tent. "Of course, father. Immediately."

"And make sure Tamir is aware of what has happened with the Holt woman. There is an excellent chance she will lead Hicks to him next. He must do everything he can to improve his security immediately."

"A prudent move as always, father," his son said. "The logical step is for him to go into hiding, but as you know, he is working on several important projects that are vital to our cause, especially since we have lost Tessmer."

Zhou was glad his son had asked an important question. "He is to continue his dealings, but he must be vigilant, especially where new business is concerned. Our enemy is crafty, and I believe his lightning strikes of armed conflict has passed. His next attack will be far more subtle. Tamir is closely linked to the Holt woman.

Tell him he must curb his usual flamboyance until this threat has passed."

"Very wise, father."

Zhou was in no mood to accept compliments from his son. "You should have thought about that already. Now get out of my sight."

His son bowed and left his father alone.

Zhou waited until he was sure his son had gone before he brought a shaking hand to his desktop mouse and toggled his monitor to the photo he had kept in the background for months. The photo of the disheveled man crossing a busy street in Manhattan. James Hicks.

Could such a man truly be responsible for picking apart his operation piece by piece? Taken Tessmer and now the Holt woman? Destroyed his operations in the West Coast? Threaten the lifeblood of the organization. Its Hong Kong operation. Its money.

Each step they had taken in the past few days had brought them one step closer to crippling the Asian side of The Vanguard. One step closer to Zhou himself. Losing Tessmer, Yeung and now Holt were mere inconveniences.

Losing Tamir before the finances he controlled were secure would be devastating. It would take the organization months to recover from his capture, if ever.

But he knew the old pirate was still as crafty as ever. He was more obsessed with security than Zhou, if that was possible. Hicks would no sooner be able to lure Tamir into the open than he could Zhou.

Zhou may have underestimated Hicks, but Hicks had shown his strategy too early. And now that Zhou knew his traps, he would only spring them when they were convenient for him.

The next trap Hicks laid for him would be his last.

WHEN HAI RONG ZHOU returned to his desk with what little pride his father had allowed him to keep, he hid his emotions well. He knew the other clerks in the hut always watched him closely to gauge the general's mood. If Hai Rong returned from his father's hut down-trodden, as was often the case, they knew he was in a bad mood. But if he came back happy, it meant the general was in good spirits.

Which was why Hai Rong worked hard now to keep his emotions from showing. He was bursting with pride and excitement. Proud that he had earned praise, no matter how begrudging, from his father.

Excited that he had chosen this moment to show the old man his true worth. He had played the fool for his father long enough. It was time to show the tyrant who he really was.

Knowing none of the other clerks could see his screen, he clicked on an email he had received a few days before from an old friend from school he had not heard from in years. Li Ming Chen. It had been a brief email that had struck him from out of the blue. It contained only a few words in Mandarin, but they had great impact on him.

'The enemy of my enemy, no matter how vile, may be a friend.'

The nature of the email was curious.

For he and Li Ming Chen had never been close.

And Li Ming Chen had been dead for over twenty years. A training accident in the army had taken his life.

Hai Rong Zhou had pondered the email for hours. He wondered who had sent it and why.

But as the conflict with the University unfolded, the words became ever more important to him. They had soothed the scars his father's words had left on his soul.

They had reminded him that perhaps it was time for a change after all.

He clicked on the message and typed out a reply.

'Wise words, old friend.'

He sent the message without knowing who would read it. He could only hope they would understand it.

CHAPTER 17

SOMEWHERE

Now that most of the swelling had gone down, Hicks began to remove the first layer of bandages from his face.

The pain from his surgery had finally begun to subside enough for him to cut back his meds to once a day. His skin had begun to itch; something his surgeon had told him would be a sign of healing.

Removing the bandages took his mind off the unexpected attention that the American media had paid to the Holt Kidnapping.

He'd known going after the attorney in her apartment was a calculated risk. He hadn't known the building had been built and operated by The Vanguard. He would've found another way to grab her. Another place.

He hadn't thought to check the building thoroughly because he didn't have time.

Time had become his constant enemy the moment

Rahul Patel had grabbed Colonel Yeung. Speed had been essential, and his team had delivered. The dominos had fallen in order.

Domino One: Tessmer, who'd led to:
Domino Two: Yeung, who'd led to:
Domino Three: Resnick, who'd led to:
Domino Four: Veronica Holt, who would hopefully lead them to:
Domino Five: Tamir Bat-Erdene and,
Domino Six: General Zhou.

Tamir Bat-Erdene was the next domino in line to fall. The last domino before Zhou.

Tamir also happened to be the most difficult domino he'd tried to bring down yet.

Avenging Tali was worth the effort.

Hicks stood in front of a long bank of mirrors in the bathroom of the abandoned floor, cutting off his bandages, when his handheld began to buzz on the counter. He let it go to voicemail. He had ignored Roger's repeated texts and calls, asking if Hicks was angry with him about the Holt mess.

Hicks was too busy with planning his Tamir strategy to soothe Roger's concerns. Roger, Mary and the Holts were back at the safe house. Hicks had given Scott operational authority to keep a lid on things while Hicks figured out what to do next. He knew Roger and Scott didn't like each other, but when it came to situations like this, Scott knew what he was doing.

Hicks didn't blame Roger for what had happened at the penthouse. The Vanguard had used the event to strike back at the University. Using his own country's FBI to hunt him had been a clever move on Zhou's part.

Hicks's name and face hadn't appeared in the media yet, but OMNI was tracking the FBI's internal progress on the case. The agency was beginning to zero in on him as their number one suspect but weren't comfortable going public yet.

The narrative was already taking shape within the bureau. James Hicks was a home-grown radical rumored to be behind a failed biological attack on New York. He was a wild card with an unknown agenda looking to destabilize the government of the United States. General Zhou's allies had been busy.

He checked the buzzing handheld and, for once, was glad to see it was Jonathan.

He tapped the icon with his free hand and continued to cut away his bandages.

"What's the situation?"

"Not good, sir," Jonathan said. "The Chicago police are leaking like a sieve. Every news outlet in the country is covering the kidnapping, calling it one of the most blatant abductions in recent history. Her name and face are everywhere. The daughter's, too. They're running a glamour shot of Veronica at a cocktail party on one side and little Jane's first grade school portrait on the other."

Hicks was not surprised the media had taken the bait. He thought of his country's industrial media complex as a Tyrannosaurus Rex. Big with a tiny brain and attracted to movement. Right now, the Holt kidnapping story was moving fast. "How's the FBI taking this?"

"They're furious about the leaks," Jonathan reported, "but they're treating it as a kidnapping. You're coming under a lot of internal scrutiny, but Demarest is deflecting. He's making the case that the capture of Colonel Yeung is the real reason behind the violence. That there's a power grab in Yeung's organization and they're cleaning house. It's been most effective, sir. I think it's the only reason why you haven't been named Public Enemy Number One already."

Hicks removed another bandage. "Looks like we handed over Yeung and Tessmer to Demarest at just the right time."

"Yes, sir," Jonathan said. "They still don't have footage of the kidnapping, which means Roger, Mary and Thomas are safe. All traffic camera footage from the time of the abduction is useless."

Hicks was glad to hear it, but far from confident. "Let's not push our luck. Reach out to Scott and ask him to work out an exit strategy. I want him and his team out of Chicago as soon as possible, but I want it done smart. Tell him I'm open to any ideas he has."

"I'll get right on it," Jonathan assured him, "but I have the Trustee on the other line. She wants an update directly from you. She won't take no for an answer this time."

Although Hicks was the Dean of the University, he answered to a Board of Trustees who oversaw his actions on behalf of the greater good of the organization. It was a stopgap measure to ensure one person couldn't use the organization for his or her own purposes.

Avenging Tali was a main goal in his fight against The Vanguard, but so was defeating an organization that had conducted a proxy war against the West. That's what he'd told the board, anyway.

He was in no mood to explain himself to the trustee or anyone else. But given the attention the Holt kidnapping was generating he needed all the allies he could get. He told Jonathan to put the call through.

He was about to change strategies against The Vanguard and now was as good a time as any to clue her in.

Her voice came over the handheld. "Hello, James. It's been too long. I'm glad you're well."

"That's a relative term." Hicks picked up his scissors and resumed cutting his bandages. His voice was stronger that day and didn't need electronic enhancement. "Sorry about all of the publicity lately. It was necessary, I assure you."

"But not entirely unexpected," she said. "You gave us the worst-case scenario of each step of the way. You've managed to avoid that in all instances so far. It's a miracle no civilians have been hurt, though the Holt situation is distressing."

"She's not a civilian," Hicks reminded her. "She's the head of The Vanguard in the United States, or at least it's financial head, anyway. Just because she's pretty and makes good copy doesn't mean she's America's sweetheart."

"Perhaps, but this Holt kidnapping has brought the board to the brink of asking for your dismissal and I'm beginning to agree with them."

Hicks dropped the scissors in the sink before he accidentally gouged out an eye. "It wasn't a kidnapping, damn it. They took her and the girl to protect them from The Vanguard. Zhou sent a hit squad to kill them both. The board knows that if they've been reading our reports instead of clutching their pearls."

"Some have argued they were sent to defend them," the trustee pointed out.

"With AK-47s that can punch through drywall like paper? Don't buy it, Sarah. They were there to spray and pray. If Holt survived, fine, but if not, they'd have pinned it on Roger and Mary and called it a day. Fortunately, we have them now."

"I know. The question is what are we doing with them?"

"Roger's questioning Veronica about Tamir Bat-Erdene," Hicks said. "He's the heart of The Vanguard's finances. He keeps the gears greased and the coffers full. OMNI's been able to track about half a dozen locations for him, but we're hoping Veronica can help us narrow those down a bit."

"What about this Resnick character?" the trustee asked. "Can anything more be gained from him?"

Hicks winced. He'd hoped she would have forgotten about him. "His heart gave out an hour ago. It was natural causes from whatever junk he'd taken before we got him. We threatened him, but never touched him, so don't yell at me."

The trustee was quiet. "I may be losing my mind, but I actually believe you."

Hicks was glad because it happened to be the truth. "Holt's the real prize here. When the Board gets anxious, remind them of all the records we took from her. It's almost as good as the intel Jabbar fed us in Toronto. Maybe even better."

"And what of Ms. Holt?" the trustee asked. "I hope her heart won't conveniently give out, too. Her daughter, not to mention the public scrutiny, complicates things."

Hicks didn't like telling her of his plan before he'd considered it, but he was long on enemies and short on options. "I plan on handing her over to Demarest's people today or tomorrow."

The trustee grew silent. "How progressive of you, James. I'd called to order you to do that very thing."

Hicks laughed. "You can give me all the orders you want. Whether or not I follow them is a different story. Given how public she's become, the sooner we can hand her back, the better. And you can tell your friends on the board to calm down. We're about to move into the covert phase of the plan."

"Meaning?"

"Sorry, Ma. What you don't know can't hurt my operation." But Hicks knew he had to feed her something if he wanted her continued good will. "Tamir Bat-Erdene will require a gentler touch. I'll have Jonathan send you everything we have on him. Once we find out where he is, Rahul and I will come up with a plan to take him down. Carefully," he added. "I promise."

"Sending it now, ma'am," Jonathan said.

The trustee sounded guardedly impressed. "And you're confident this Tamir can lead you to Zhou."

"Unless The Vanguard has made some drastic changes," Hicks said, "I know he can. It's just a matter of making him want to. That's my problem, not yours."

"Make sure it stays that way," she cautioned. "Charles has done a good job running interference for you with the FBI, James, but one more public event and even his hands will be tied."

Hicks was glad he had already considered that. "If all goes to plan, none of this will ever be public."

He decided he'd already told her more than he

was comfortable saying. "I'll keep you apprised of our next steps, including the handoff of the Holts. Hicks out."

He killed the connection, knowing the trustee was likely outraged. She was usually the one who ended their calls. Let her be angry. He still had an op to finalize.

Hicks stood silent and alone in the office bathroom, looking at his half-bandaged face in the mirror.

At the man he was and the man he used to be all at the same time.

He hadn't removed enough of the bandages to tell how well the surgery had gone. Even after the bandages came off, his face would remain swollen for several days before he had an idea of what he would look like. He had told the doctor what he wanted, but as he knew all too well, wishes weren't always reality.

Time told all truths. About his face. About his war against The Vanguard. About everything.

He picked up the scissors again and resumed cutting away the bandages. His voice echoed in the empty bathroom as he said aloud, "Come on, Roger. Get something from Holt before we have to hand her over."

Then it would be up to Rahul Patel to push the next domino over. Tamir Bat-Erdene.

"I JUST SPOKE TO HIM," Sarah told Demarest when she called him a few minutes later. "I judged him to be in control of his faculties and even tempered."

"I thought you were going to connect me when you

got him," Demarest said. "I have a lot to say to that sick bastard."

"Don't be so dramatic, Charles," Sarah chided. "It doesn't suit you."

"Dramatic?" Demarest yelled. "He's the one who handcuffed two of the most wanted men in the world together, naked, and left them in a park. Tessmer's left leg is gone below the knee, for Christ's sake. God only knows what they did to him."

She knew he had lost the leg during the shootout in the Berlin cemetery but saw no reason to waste time reminding him of that. "I never knew you to be so compassionate toward your enemies."

But Demarest was clearly too worked up to hear her. "Do you know we have to keep Tessmer and Yeung in darkness because they scream whenever we turn on a light? My men have to interrogate them wearing night-vision goggles."

"That's thanks to Roger's methods, not Hicks's," Sarah reminded him. "And James lived up to his word. He handed them over to you alive, if not well."

"Which is the only reason why his face isn't plastered on the front page of every newspaper in the world," Demarest said. "What is he doing with this Holt person and her daughter?"

"Using them for information," she said. "He told me he'll hand them over to your people in the next day or two. It'll be handled through your office, so you'll have complete control of the narrative. You can take as much or as little credit for their recovery as you wish."

Sarah thought Demarest didn't sound like he believed it but was happy to move on to another topic. "It was that easy?"

She smiled. "Yes, Charles. He's in a reasonable mood today. This whole mess will blow over in forty-eight hours, so you'd better get busy on how you want to handle it."

"That depends on what he's planning next. An assault on The Vatican?"

"His next move will be like all those that have preceded it," she said. "He'll attack The Vanguard's operations in Asia. He assures me it will be more covert in nature, and I happen to believe him."

"You might believe him," Demarest said. "I don't. I don't think he's in his right mind. He's hiding out there and, so far, Meager can't find him. He got an old ghost of an email from Savannah and a sighting in Istanbul about two months ago. That's it."

"Meager." Sarah did a poor job of hiding her disappointment. "I told you to keep that old fossil in the museum where he belongs."

Demarest ignored the reprimand. "He's located some questionable feeds to a location in Maryland, also, but I think it's a ruse."

Sarah knew that's where Jonathan lived, not Hicks. Savannah had been where the previous Dean, Al Clay had lived, and was careless with his technology at the end of his life. Meager might be ancient, but he obviously still had skills. "The Maryland and Savannah addresses are server farms. Dead ends. I don't think he's even in the country."

She heard his voice change. "I don't care where he is, just where the Holts are. And if I don't have an arrangement to pick them up soon, I won't be able to keep the FBI at bay. They don't report to me, Sarah, and I only have so much influence over them. You know that."

"And I know how charming you can be when you want to be, Charles," she said. "Be charming now. It'll be worth it in the long run. I promise you."

CHAPTER 18

CHICAGO, ILLINOIS

ROGER SMILED as he inhaled the aromas of his own cooking. The smell of eggs and bacon and fresh coffee made him feel wonderful, perhaps even a bit nostalgic. It reminded him of the lazy mornings of his boyhood, when the world was a much simpler place and his troubles confined to the small town of his youth.

These were smells of better days. Contentment. Blissful ignorance and peace, even though he was cooking for a house full of killers and a woman who had betrayed her own country countless times over.

He didn't remember growing up with a dead drunk in his basement, either. That detail tended to knock the Rockwellian sheen off his memories.

But the thought of young Jane Holt asleep down the hall brightened his spirits. A child as innocent as he had once been. An innocence that had already begun to be stripped away from her while she recovered from a cold. Thomas's shooting of the doorman the night before had scared her. Such memories had a habit of burying themselves deep in a child's mind, flowering only later in life. He hoped she would forget about it as a bad dream. He hoped but was not hopeful.

The world could be a cruel place for the young. He wished there was something he could do to spare her from it, if only for a little while longer.

For her sake. And for the sake of that young boy Roger Cobb had once been.

Roger turned when he felt someone staring at him. Nostalgia could only blur his training so much.

He was surprised to see little Jane Holt peering around the corner of the dining room doorway. Her brown hair was a tangled mess. Her pink pajamas even more so. Her colorful blanket trailed behind her like an afterthought.

Roger smiled down at the six-year-old. "Good morning, young lady. And just who might you be?"

The child tried to blink the sleep away from her eyes. "Where am I? Mommy's still asleep."

Roger wasn't surprised the little girl's mother was still asleep. He had given her something to quell her anxiety after all that had happened in the penthouse. He hated her treason but needed her reasonably conscious if he hoped to get anything out of her.

He had also given little Jane something for the fever and was glad to see her up and about. "Your mommy's very tired, little one. She was worried about you. We all were. How are you feeling?"

She rubbed her tummy. "I'm hungry. Who are you? Where are we?"

"I'm a friend," he smiled. "My name is Roger. And we're in a nice, safe place. You don't have to worry about a thing. I'm making you breakfast right now. Do you like eggs? Bacon?"

She clutched her blanket tighter and nodded. "Grandma gives me bacon when I'm with her, but mommy doesn't like it. My daddy doesn't like it, either. They say it's bad for you, but I think it tastes good."

Roger's smile widened. *The seeds of the forbidden already sewn in a mind so young.* He patted one of the chairs at the counter. "Hop up here, little one, and I'll give as much bacon as you wish. It'll be our secret, I promise."

Jane paddled barefoot over to the stool, trailing her blanket behind her. Roger kept an eye on her attempt to climb up into the chair but didn't help her. He knew children took pride in their independence and he had no desire to rob her of it.

Given what faced her and her mother, she was bound to need it in the days to come.

Once little Jane had wiggled her way onto the chair, Roger plated the bacon and eggs and placed them in front of her with great flair. She giggled at his exaggerated presentation. *"Por vous, mademoiselle."*

"Merci, monsieur."

Her response caught him off-guard. "Your French is excellent, little one."

She delicately set her blanket on the chair next to her as she selected a piece of bacon. "Mommy taught me. She says it's a good way to talk with Papa."

"Papa?" Roger was intrigued. He remembered reading Veronica Holt's file. He didn't remember seeing she had been married or in a relationship with any French men. Or French women for that matter. The record hadn't referenced a father. He could always access OMNI and search, but why use technology when he had an adorable – and hungry – font of information right in front of him?

He was careful to not ask too much too soon. No sense in risking her getting nervous and causing her to withdraw. "Do you see Papa often?"

"No," she said as she chewed her bacon. "He doesn't live with us. He lives far away. He's not much fun, though. Even when I see him, he doesn't like to play with me."

"That's silly," Roger said. "Who wouldn't want to play with a lovely girl like you?"

"Mommy says it doesn't mean he doesn't love me. She says it's because he's old."

Roger knew a six-year-old's perception of age wasn't always accurate. They thought thirty was ancient. He'd circle back to that in due time. Best to keep things light for now. Keep her talking. "The bacon good?"

She brightened again. "Delicious. Can I have some juice?"

Of course. Juice. Roger went to the refrigerator. "Let's see if Scott and his merry band of mongoloids thought to buy juice."

"What's a 'mong-oid'?" she repeated.

He forgot that kids were better than OMNI's most sophisticated recording devices. They heard everything.

"I'll show you an example of one when he wakes up," Roger said as he began exploring the fridge. Bottled water and energy drinks were all he found. He cursed himself for remembering to buy everything except juice. The energy drinks would make the little thing bounce off the walls for hours, which wouldn't do any of them any good. "I don't have juice, my love, but how about some nice, cold water."

She looked disappointed, but slowly nodded.

Roger took a bottle from the fridge and poured her a glass. "Look at how clear and cold that is. You'll love it."

"Cold water hurts my teeth."

"Well, how about I hold the glass in my hand and warm it up a little for you?"

She nodded her approval and Roger held on to the glass. It gave him the chance to get his first real good look at her blanket.

He had seen the pattern before. Long ago. It brought back some unpleasant memories and answered a lot of questions.

"I love your blanket," he said. "Did mommy give it to you?"

Jane shook her head as she struggled to shovel a spoonful of eggs into her tiny mouth. "Daddy gave it to me."

"Ah, yes," Roger smiled. "Daddy. Of course. It's very nice."

He looked up and saw Veronica in the same spot where her daughter had stood only a few minutes before. He had no idea how long she'd been standing there but, judging by the look on her face, long enough to hear what her daughter had just told him.

And the significance of it.

Jane saw her, too. Roger had expected her to run to her mother, but instead she stayed where in her chair and slowly pushed the plate away from her. "I'm sorry, mommy. I was hungry."

"It's okay, sweetheart." Veronica came to her and stroked her daughter's hair. "You can have it this once."

Little Jane eagerly pulled the plate toward her and began eating again.

Roger grabbed his tablet from the kitchen counter and spoke to her in French, "My love, what cartoons do you like to watch?"

He saw Veronica bristle when her daughter responded in French, "Olivia's my favorite."

"She is?" Roger had no idea who Olivia was, but a quick search of the internet revealed no shortage of Olivia cartoons. He downloaded several and took headphones from the security post off the kitchen and plugged it into his tablet. "I'm going to put these on you so you can enjoy Olivia while you eat. How does that sound?"

She eagerly nodded and Roger slipped the headphones over her tiny ears. She pawed mindlessly at the bacon while she immediately became absorbed in the animated exploits of an adventurous child.

He smiled as he gently placed the side of his hand against her cheek and she giggled, ticklish. Her fever was gone.

He had never spent much time around children, but Jane seemed like an exceptionally cheerful little girl.

Except when Mommy was around.

But when Roger looked at Veronica, he was no longer smiling. He lifted the corner of the blanket and showed it to her. "Her father is in Thailand. You didn't mention that."

For an educated woman, Veronica Holt was a lousy liar. "He's not. She didn't tell you that. She doesn't even know where Thailand is."

"But her blanket is from there and she said her

father gave it to her the last time she saw him." He placed his hand on top of Jane's head, but the child was too involved in the cartoon to notice. "Her French is excellent. Guess she had a lot of practice speaking it when conversing with Daddy. N'est-ce pas?"

Veronica took several steps away from him. "You said you wouldn't hurt us."

"Isn't that quaint?" Roger glided between her and Jane. "You don't want me to hurt her, but you have no problems hurting her, do you?"

She began to protest, but Roger stopped her by raising a single finger. "I know a bit about fear, Veronica, and that precious little girl is afraid of you. Why? You make her pay for your indiscretion with her father, don't you? It's Tamir, isn't it?"

She folded her arms across her flat stomach. "That's none of your business."

"We'll see about that." He motioned toward a door off the kitchen. "Come. There's something I want to show you downstairs."

Reluctantly, Veronica opened the door that led down to the cellar. She stopped to look back at her daughter, as if it was for the last time.

Roger moved to block her view. "She'll be fine and so will you as long as you do exactly as I say. Downstairs. Now."

Veronica began walking down the narrow wooden staircase. Roger looked at Jane before closing the door. She was too taken with the animated antics of Olivia to notice.

Watching her completely lost in a cartoon while sitting in a house filled with armed and dead men,

Roger witnessed an innocence he hadn't remembered since his own childhood.

He envied the little girl and vowed, in that moment, that he would do anything he could to keep her that way for as long as possible. For once innocence was lost, it was gone forever and quickly forgotten, only to be mourned when it was too late.

He quietly closed the door before descending to show Veronica his prisoner in the basement.

VERONICA GASPED when she saw Victor Resnick lying slack in a hospital bed.

Roger gently took her by the arm to prevent her from running back upstairs. He guided her further down into the cellar.

"You remember old Victor here, don't you? Helped you betray your country a couple of hundred times?"

She brought her hands to her face. "Oh my God."

Roger gave her arm a slight squeeze. "God has no place down here with us devils. You and me and Victor. This is a place for information. Facts. And Victor here has been quite helpful to us. After all, he led us to you."

Veronica looked away from the man in the bed. "Please. I've told you everything. Just let me go."

"So, it's 'me' now, not 'us' anymore? Willing to leave poor little Jane behind?" Roger frowned. "Yes, I'm afraid that fits. That's why you backed away from her just now upstairs. Another mother would've thrown herself between me and her child, but not you. Not Veronica Holt. You're good at protecting yourself, aren't you?"

"Please. I've given you everything. I've told you about Tamir."

"You told me about him," Roger agreed, "but not where he is. He's not only your boss in The Vanguard. He's also Jane's father, isn't he?"

She quickly nodded.

"See? That wasn't so hard." His eyes flicked upstairs. "She was an accident, wasn't she?"

Veronica shook and nodded her head at the same time before burying her face in her hands. "He insisted on sleeping with me before he trusted me. Said it was the only way he could be certain I wasn't a spy. Jane was the result."

"A blessing then," Roger said. "At least something wonderful came from your debasement." His eyes narrowed. "You resent her, don't you? That's why she's afraid of you."

She began to deny it but the look on Roger's face made her change her mind. "I never intended on being a mother. Kids were never part of my career path. I guess I'm not as maternal as I should be."

Roger thanked her for her honesty. "I know the feeling. I've always liked kids but never thought of having one. They're a lot of responsibility and I've always had more than my share." He nodded toward Resnick. "Questioning people like him is how I make my living. You could say the truth is my stock and trade. So is knowing who's useful to me and who isn't."

His smile made Veronica flinch. "What about you, Veronica? Will you be useful to me now and tell me where he is?"

"Please," she said. "I can't do that. He won't hurt Jane, but—"

Roger drew his Glock from under his shirt and fired a single shot into Resnick's corpse. The impact of the bullet sent the man's dead limbs flopping.

Veronica screamed and stumbled back onto the stairs.

Roger lowered the gun and faced her. "He told me everything he knew, which made him expendable. You've just seen what I do to people who are no longer useful to me. And unless you tell me everything you know about Tamir, and I do mean everything, I'm afraid you're not much use to anyone. Not to me. Certainly not to poor Victor over there. Not even little Jane upstairs. Oh, she'll miss you at first, the way she might miss a lost puppy or dead goldfish, but she'll get used to it. Children at that age are much tougher than we think."

Veronica looked back up the stairs. "You say you care about her? That gunshot must've terrified her."

"She's lost in her cartoon." Roger grinned. "The headphones helped. She's frightened of you and, were you to disappear, I'd simply tell her that mommy went on another business trip. She'd be relieved, wouldn't she?"

Roger held the pistol against his leg as his grin faded away. "I recognized that look she gave you. I had the very same look whenever my father would walk into a room. I didn't like him very much. I'm beginning to not like you, too."

She dropped her head in her hands and began to weep. Last night on her couch, he had seen the last of her defenses crumble before she told him about Tamir. Now, he watched the floor disintegrate beneath her and she fell into the blackness below. Only the truth would break her fall.

Roger decided the pistol had served its purpose and tucked it away. "You have nothing to fear from me if you tell me the truth, and everything to fear from me if you lie."

He gently lowered Veronica's hands away from her face. "Now, tell me everything. Tell me where I can find Tamir."

CHAPTER 19

RAHUL PATEL PULLED up his collar against the biting autumn wind as he walked along Coventry Street toward Shaftesbury Memorial Fountain.

He tapped the handheld in his pocket and checked his comm link to Hicks.

"Base, this is Rook." Patel didn't like his call sign, but he hadn't been given a choice. "I am approaching the meeting point now. Do you copy?"

A voice he barely recognized as Hicks's sounded in his ear. "Base reads you loud and clear, Rook. OMNI has eyes on your position. Make sure you keep your handheld active during the meeting so we can listen in."

Rahul was disturbed by the quality of Hicks's voice. "Base, you sound different. What's wrong with your voice?"

"New filters, Rook," Hicks told him. "It makes everything sound tinny."

But Rahul didn't think Hicks's voice sounded tinny.

It sounded enhanced, filtered and altered. Why would Hicks be using voice-altering software with him? Why would he be dishonest about it? Hadn't Rahul proven his worth to the University at the seaport in Harwich? In Berlin? In China and, more recently, in Russia?

Rahul remembered Hicks had been hesitant about recruiting him after he had been put out to pasture by India's National Investigation Agency as he grieved the execution of his sister. But that had more been over a year ago. A lifetime in clandestine work.

Much had happened since then. Rahul was different. So was Hicks. The events in Berlin had changed them both. Hicks had lost a lover and an agent. Rahul had lost a colleague and a friend. He'd also lost the self-doubt that had crippled him for more than a year.

Rahul decided it wasn't his place to pry. If The Life had taught him anything, it was that some things were best left in the shadows.

"OMNI shows your contact is already on site," Hicks told him. "At least I didn't have to zoom in to see him. I think he's gotten even fatter since the last time I saw him."

"Now, now," Rahul chided. "Be nice, Base. After you played him for a fool, we're lucky he's agreed to meet us at all."

"He got what he wanted," Hicks said. "He's got no reason to complain. Just don't offer him more than we've discussed. He can help us cut a lot of corners, but he's not the only game in town. And don't tell him we already know where the target is." Rahul knew the target was Tamir. "Let him share that with you. Build up his trust."

Rahul laughed. "I've worked with the man for more

than ten years. I've built up all the trust I need. Listen in and learn, Base."

"Copy, Rook. Just keep my name out of it. That fat bastard doesn't like me very much."

Rahul used an old University saying. "That puts him in excellent company, doesn't it?"

"Keep your eyes on the prize, Rook. Base going dark."

Rahul knew Hicks would be listening in on his meeting. In fact, he was counting on it. If Hicks didn't agree to the terms, the meeting was for nothing.

He spotted Bruce Clarke amid the throng of tourists armed with selfie sticks flocking around the fountain.

Clarke's impressive obesity and slovenly appearance made it nearly impossible to miss him. Rahul knew his colleague well enough to be sure he took quiet delight in ruining more than one tourist photo.

Tufts of unruly reddish hair turning an unsightly gray fluttered in the wind. One may have been forgiven for mistaking his fleshy face as being reddened from the cold air, but Rahul knew ruddy was the spy's natural color.

Among the gaggle of eager tourists flocking around the fountain, Clarke, ever the dour native Londoner, was by far the worst dressed. His white shirt was untucked, and his open collar looked as if it had never been starched. His half-hearted attempt at knotting a tie was tugged well below the double chins beneath his open collar. Rahul gave him high marks for tying a Full Windsor and knew he'd probably tied it without the benefit of a mirror. A relic of Clarke's days at Eton, then Cambridge.

Clarke's red Arsenal jacket and khakis were both in need of a good scrubbing. The Salvation Army would have thrown them away had Clarke donated them, which Rahul doubted he would do. He came from a long line of Gunners' supporters and wasn't known to give up on something just because its best days were behind it.

Rahul was glad of it. Clarke's support had helped Patel keep his job when he'd hit that rough patch following his sister's murder.

No one could accuse Clarke of being a fashion plate, but people discounted him at their peril. Clarke had once been Rahul's point of contact whenever Her Majesty's governmental interests coincided with those of The Republic of India. The two nations had maintained a cordial, but wary relationship following independence. A relationship that had benefited both men many times throughout the years.

While Rahul had risen to be considered one of his country's best counter-terrorism operatives, Clarke had secured a sleepy posting to The Club's office in New York. The Club was England's counterpart to the University.

An assignment to the Club was something of a reward to agents in good standing close to retirement looking to run out their string before their pensions kicked in. Good, loyal men and women who had been put out to pasture for a bit before hanging up the old cloak and dagger for good.

Clarke had scored high marks for his apprehension of the terrorist Djebar and was brought back into the MI6 fold in London. He had been elevated to position of Chairman of The Club as a result.

The fat man barely gave Rahul a glance as the Indian man approached him. The lit cigarette tucked in the corner of Clarke's narrow mouth bobbed up and down as he said, "Nice to see you, Paki. It's been ages."

Rahul smiled. The Brit had mistaken him for a Pakistani agent the first time they'd met more than a decade before. As an Indian, Patel normally would have taken offense to being referred to as a Pakistani, but when two men had been through as much as they had, Rahul had come to see it as a term of endearment.

"Good to see you, Bruce. You're looking as prosperous as ever. Must've lost five ounces since I saw you last."

"Fuck off." The fat man's dull eyes never stopped moving over the tourists mingling around them. "Mind telling me why we're meeting in the middle of the bloody Circus in broad daylight. Sounds like that Yank's idea to me."

Rahul knew he was referring to Hicks. "He thought you might be more comfortable meeting in an open surrounding."

"Damned Yanks," Clarke spat. "They're all the same. No imagination. No appreciation for the craft. I'm surprised he didn't want us meeting on a foggy night in Whitehall with Big Ben gonging in the distance."

Rahul laughed. "He probably would've done except we haven't got that kind of time."

"Always a rush with him." Clarke flicked the lapel of Rahul's leather coat to check for a microphone. "He listening now?"

Rahul saw no reason to lie. Clarke would only sense

it and it would risk making him suspicious. "I believe he is."

Clarke leaned toward his lapel. "Fuck off, Hicks. Thanks for nothing."

In Rahul's ear, Hicks said, "Tell him to kiss my colonial ass."

Rahul translated. "He sends his regards."

Clarke's natural frown grew deeper. "Have you got any idea what that lousy bastard did to me?" Clarke looked around to make sure he hadn't spoken loud enough to catch the attention of any of the tourists gawking at the fountain before continuing. "Promised to hand over Djebar to us in good condition." Clarke laughed without humor. "Good condition my arse. Took us a fortnight to get the punk to stop screaming every time we went near him."

Rahul had already read the briefing on the Djebar handover. "All they did was give him a local and took out his appendix." Another one of Roger Cobb's master strokes. "It's not our fault he thought he was being disemboweled."

Clarke still wasn't happy. "I'm not one for coddling terrorists, but your new boss is a sick one."

"Made your career, didn't it?" Rahul countered. "Got you off the bench and back onto the pitch, as it were. You're the new chairman of the Club, from what I hear. Congratulations are in order."

Clarke puffed on his cigarette. "Plucked from comfortable obscurity is more like it. I had a nice thing going in New York until your man made me an offer I couldn't refuse like some goddamned *Mafiosi*. Bringing in Djebar went and made a respectable man out of me again."

Rahul knew Clarke well enough to see through the act. "You're having the time of your life and don't bother denying it."

Clarke looked away. "Damn your eyes. You were always too smart for your own good."

Rahul watched his old friend flick away his dying cigarette. He glanced at Patel before his eyes went back to scanning the crowd of tourists. He hadn't looked at him long, but a man with Clarke's training saw more in a glance than most people saw in a lifetime.

"You look better than ever. India's Cary Grant we always used to say. Still off the piss, I hope."

Rahul stiffened at the mention of his year-long drinking binge following his sister's murder. He thought his superiors in Mumbai had been able to keep his alcoholism under wraps, but a spy's livelihood was gossip and secrets. "I am. One day at a time."

"Save that shite for the drunks in the church basement. You either drink or you don't. And I'm glad you don't." Clarke pulled a crumpled pack of cigarettes from his jacket pocket, shook one loose and tucked one into his mouth. "Now that we've got the pleasantries out of the way, let's skip to the point where you tell me what we're doing here." He glowered over at a group of teenagers flashing peace signs in front of the fountain while someone took their picture. "I hate bloody tourists."

"The name Tamir mean anything to you?"

"Fella who owns the kebab joint around the corner from the Clubhouse. Good food, even the takeaway. Never too greasy. Generous with an extra spoonful of rice when the mood strikes him. Turk, I think, though I've never looked into his background properly. Guess I should. Bastard could've been poisoning me slowly all these years."

Rahul ignored his old friend's sarcasm. "You know who I mean."

Clarke lit his cigarette with a cheap lighter. "Of course, I know him. So does every intelligence officer in the world worth his salt. The only question is, what's he to you, besides the obvious?"

"We need to find him."

"You and everyone else in the Community." Clarke stopped looking at the tourists and looked at Rahul instead. "And in the off chance that you do find him, what do you plan to do with him?"

"Something that'll benefit everyone involved." Rahul gently poked a finger at the Arsenal crest on Clarke's jacket. "Especially you."

Clarke caught on quick. "So, the Yank's planning something big, is he? Another smash-and-grab job like you boys pulled in Berlin?" He seemed to enjoy the look of surprise on Rahul's face. "Yeah, I heard about that one. Most figure it was just mobsters having it out, but our people know better. That mess at the cemetery had Hicks's name written all over it."

Rahul wasn't surprised Clarke knew about Berlin. Clarke had always had good ties to the Germans. But Rahul knew the topic was likely to upset Hicks, and since he was listening in, he steered the conversation back on course.

"Do you know where Tamir is or not?"

"What makes you think I'd know something like that?"

"Because you were station chief for Hong Kong for years," Rahul said. "You moved your base around

Southeast Asia, and you've managed to keep your network largely intact." It was time to appeal to his friend's vanity. "If anyone knows how to find Tamir, I'd wager it's you."

"Cheeky bastard." A long stream of smoke trailed behind him. "Shining me on like this when you already know I've got a lock on him. That's why we're talking, isn't it?"

"Don't confirm that!" Hicks yelled in Rahul's ear. "If you tell him we've cross-referenced Holt's contacts with his known assets, we'll lose him."

Rahul ignored him. "Let's concentrate on generalities before specifics, shall we? Let's start with something easy. Narrow it down to a country, perhaps?"

Clarke scratched the side of his fleshy face as he thought it over. "Tamir's been running his operation out of a compound in Bangkok for the past five years or so. Locals and visiting businessmen call it Three Floors of Whores for good reason. It's a strip club, brothel and drug den all rolled up in one, but that's just knockaround money for our boy Tamir. His real operation is a drug processing plant in the back of the compound. Heroin, mostly, last we checked. Has a warehouse, too, for other items he traffics in. Weapons and the like."

Rahul was glad Veronica Holt's information had proven to be right. Bangkok made sense as Tamir's base of operations. From there, it was a quick flight to anywhere in Southeast Asia. "We don't care about the drugs unless we can use it as a way to get to him."

"We've known where he is since the beginning," Clarke told him. "The Yanks, too. The location isn't the problem. Getting to him is the problem. The place looks like a good wind would blow it over, but that's by design. The place is a fortress. Believe me, we've done our homework on it. It' not just a bunch of local goons with guns I'm talking about. He's got top-of-the-line security equipment all over the place. Scanners, jammers and cameras that would put GCHQ to shame. And he hires people who know how to use them, too. The bastard even has a SAM battery to take out any plane that gets too close. He's also got an electronic blanket over the place that'll knock down any drone that tries to fly over it."

Clarke paused to take another puff on his cigarette. "He's a careful one, our boy Tamir. No one can get near the place without his say so. That's why he's managed to be around for so long. And what his boys don't do, the local cops and military do for him. Every one of them is on the teat. So, if your man Hicks is thinking of grabbing him, tell him to keep thinking. Finding him is easy. Getting to him is tough. Capturing him is impossible. Has a standing order with all his men to shoot him if he's ever taken captive during a raid. Says he'd rather die by his own men than be taken in alive."

Rahul had already suspected as much. "From what I hear, he's not a hermit. He gets around a good deal. There must be some way to grab him in transit."

"Gee, why didn't I think of that?" Clarke sneered. "He has a helicopter, armored and armed to the teeth, of course, that lands at the compound and take him anywhere he wants to go. Even has a jet escort if he wants it." The Brit spread out his hands. "Sorry to disappoint you and the Yank, but like I told you, the man's untouchable. We've run the numbers and figure it'd take a battalion with plenty of air support to put a dent in the place, but he'd be long gone by the time they got there. Grabbing him is out of the question, so get that thought right out of that handsome head of yours."

Rahul believed him. He was glad that grabbing Tamir wasn't part of Hicks's plan.

"Let's say I didn't want to grab him. In fact, let's say I want him to remain as free as a bird."

Clarke flicked his cigarette into the street. "Drop the metaphors and tell me what you're planning."

Rahul looked at him. "I understand you might have someone who does business with Tamir. Someone he trusts. Someone who could put me in the same room with him."

Clarke's eyes narrowed. "Where the hell did you hear that?"

OMNI had already cross-referenced the records they had pulled from Veronica Holt's computers with various assets European intelligence agencies had used in the past. The information didn't give them a name or address of an asset, but OMNI had narrowed it down to a likely source Clarke had used before.

Rahul said, "A man in my position knows things, Bruce. Hears things. Important things that can be kept between friends should the need arise."

Clarke's fleshy hands balled up into fists. Rahul had seen those fists connect too often to discount their power. He'd seen what they could do to flesh and bone. "Details, old friend. I'll need some before I confirm anything. Something for something is still the coin of the realm, old boy."

"Be careful," Hicks said in Rahul's ear. "Don't give him a name. Let him tell us on his own."

But Rahul already knew how to handle the situation. "We think Tamir handles operations for a clandestine organization known as The Vanguard."

Clarke stood there, as if he was waiting for Rahul to say more.

When the silence lasted too long, he said, "I'm sorry. Was that supposed to be the grand revelation that bowls me over?" Clarke laughed. "We've known about that lot for years. But we only knew what they were really up to when your people started knocking things over. We figured The Vanguard must be up to a hell of a lot more than running guns and drugs. Not exactly a subtle man, your Hicks."

Rahul felt a surge of defensiveness for his new employer. "I can rattle off a few dozen recent public missteps of British intelligence if you'd like."

"Rattle all you'd like. None of them were my ops, mate. My ops don't go sideways. So, if you want me to use my resources to help you try to get next to Tamir – and I did say try – then it comes with a price."

"Name it," Rahul said a little too quickly for his own liking.

"I run the op. Me. Not Hicks. No one from his damned University. My people, my operation or no deal."

In his ear, Rahul heard Hicks say, "No way. Out of the question."

But Rahul let Clarke talk. "My asset is your only way of getting anywhere near Tamir. I'm risking my only link to one of the most wanted men in the world, so I run the op, understand? Tamir might live a posh lifestyle now, but he's Russian trained and deadly as hell. I know him better than you ever will, so I run the show from start to finish. You and the Yank can spitball

all you'd like, but I have final say over what happens, how and when. None of that cowboy nonsense Hicks has been pulling lately. That business in California was a bit too public for my taste. My bosses, too. Either you agree to my terms, or we've got nothing to talk about."

Rahul wasn't surprised by his old colleague's demands. A lot of people had written off Clarke as a lazy slob. Most of them had been run out of the Game by now, while Clarke was still very much at it.

Rahul knew Hicks wouldn't like it, but he wasn't risking his life. Rahul was and he trusted Bruce Clarke with it. "Agreed."

Clarke looked about as content as he was capable of looking. "Good. Now you can tell me why you want to get next to him."

Rahul was glad he already knew the motive for this next part of Hicks's plan. "We want to influence Tamir's actions to damage The Vanguard's ability to operate. Without him knowing it, of course."

Clarke's fleshy eyes narrowed. "You don't want to kill him. You want to manipulate him."

Rahul nodded.

Clarke let out a long breath as he looked up at the sky. There wasn't much to see. Just another gray cloudy day in old London town.

If Rahul didn't know any better, he would have thought his friend was looking to the heavens for guidance. But men like Clarke didn't believe in gods above or demons below. They had spent their lives too concerned about the uncertainties of this world to worry about what might be waiting for them in the next.

Clarke's expression softened. "It might work.

Tamir's ego certainly makes him susceptible to manipulation, especially if you play to his vanity. But if he so much as thinks you're up to something, he'll cut your throat just to be sure. He's killed men for less and that's no exaggeration."

"That part of the plan depends entirely on your asset." Rahul knew OMNI had already narrowed down the possible Tamir assets in Clarke's employ to one of ten men. But telling the Brit that would only put him on the defensive.

Clarke rubbed his fleshy face again, obviously struggling with how much he should let on. "I do have one asset who comes to mind. He keeps me updated on Tamir's moves, which is why we've let Tamir go for so long. He tells me Tamir is working on retaliating against the Chinese for attacking a facility he had near Mongolia. He's planning on taking out some infrastructure assets China has in Central America. Send a message back to Beijing that The Vanguard still has teeth in its head."

Rahul knew that was something OMNI hadn't picked up. "Interesting."

Clarke went on. "That's why Tamir reached out to my man. He wants a meeting to discuss moving some funds around to help pay for this attack. Money, men, things of that sort."

He looked at Rahul. "My asset could be your way in. Your only way to get close to Tamir."

Once again, Rahul was impressed with OMNI's reach. "What kind of leverage do you have on this asset of yours?"

"He's a civilian and as crooked as a dog's hind leg. Fear of prison is how we've been able to compel him to feed us information on Tamir's activities from time to time." He held up a stubby finger. "But we don't ask too much of him and we never act directly on anything he tells us. We don't want to risk exposing him. We watch the stone hit the water and see where the ripples spread."

Rahul knew they had just entered a delicate part of the conversation. "Think you can make him help us?"

"It'll take some convincing to make him go through with it," Clarke admitted, "but I can definitely get him to meet with you. Convincing him will be your job."

Rahul flashed his best smile. "Lucky for me I can be quite charming when the need arises. How quickly can you arrange it?"

"A few days," Clarke said. "Tamir's anxious to meet him, but my man's been stalling. He's waiting for me to give him some direction on the matter. I'll contact him today and find out if he's open to talking to you."

Rahul didn't like the sound of that. "Make him be open to it, Bruce. Please."

"Doesn't work that way," Clarke told him. "But I'll be sure to stress the point. Don't worry, Paki. I'll do my best to get you a seat at the table."

Rahul wrapped his arm around his old friend's fleshy shoulders. "I'll not only have a seat at the table, old boy. I'll be at the head of it. And Tamir will even hold my chair for me."

CHAPTER 20

THE ANNEX, NEW YORK CITY

FROM HIS WORKSPACE at the Annex in New York, Mark Stephens made sure he understood what Hicks was asking him to do.

"I'm not an assassin."

"Don't sell yourself short, Ace," Hicks said. "You've killed people before."

"That was different," the black man said. "That was war."

"So is this," Hicks reminded him. "Same sides as before, just a different battlefield. Instead of Afghanistan or Iraq, this war is taking place in a board-room. Don't go growing a conscience on me now that you're a civilian."

Mark Stephens still had trouble thinking of himself as a civilian. The military had been his life. First the Air Force Academy, then a few key postings in intelligence, followed by his dream job with the counter-intelligence unit of the Defense Intelligence Agency (DIA).

THE MOSCOW PROTOCOL / 237

Stephens was a natural. He'd worked hard to become one of the most respected Beekeepers in the DIA. Beekeepers ran abduction and rendition operations on hostile targets overseas. They didn't just grab high-value-targets off the street and beat confessions out of them. They carefully chose their targets and played them for the long haul. They pumped them for information with methods specifically crafted to the target's psychological profile. They nurtured a prisoner and got them as comfortable or as uncomfortable as it took to extract as much information from them as possible. It was a careful process, just like the way a beekeeper gets honey.

It was a tough, tedious job, but Stephens always got the best results from his subjects. It was the kind of job only a few people could do well. Stephens had been proud to be one of them.

His career had come crashing down when he learned that one of the terrorists he'd been tracking for years had been grabbed by a mystery man. On American soil, no less. Stephens hadn't even known Bajjah was in the country. He later discovered the mystery man was James Hicks.

Stephens and his colleagues had let their egos get the better of him and employed unorthodox ways to get Hicks to hand over Bajjah. Stephens had not only failed but had also lost his job thanks to a Congressional investigation spurred by Hicks. He hadn't just shaken the tree. He burned down the forest.

While he was out of commission with a wife and two kids to support, Hicks appeared in his driveway one morning. He offered him a job with the University. The same man who had taken his life away had offered to return it. To give him a second chance to make a difference.

His way, of course.

Stephens had taken the job to learn more about Hicks and the University. He thought about taking revenge for wrecking his life. To destroy it from within just as Hicks had destroyed him.

But all these months later, he not only ran the University's New York office, but had a new appreciation for the University's mission. He understood why Hicks operated the way he did.

That didn't mean he couldn't buck when ordered to put a bullet in an innocent man's head.

"I'm not an assassin," Stephens repeated. "I didn't think you were, either."

"I'm whatever the job needs me to be," Hicks told him. "So are you. Right now, the job calls for you to track a man, draw your weapon and put two in the back of his head."

Stephens understood the mission. He also knew this wasn't the military. He could question orders. And the man giving them to him. "He's a civilian."

"Umar Adibi is a white-collar criminal," Hicks said. "He works for a guy in London who helps The Vanguard finance their war against Western targets. He quit being a civilian the second he started working for the other side. Killing him now will save a lot of lives later. I've compiled a complete target package that I'm sending you now."

Stephens looked at his desktop and saw the file open on his screen. "Where do you want me to hit him?"

"At home. Not on the street. Not in front of his office. In his apartment. Tonight. No witnesses."

"Two shots to the head," Stephens repeated. "I heard you the first two times you said it. Doesn't mean I like it any better."

"Doesn't mean I like ordering you to do it," Hicks admitted, "but it needs to be done and you're the best man for the job. The apartment's a soft target. A loft in SoHo. The lock on his door is digital. Hold your device next to it and OMNI will open it for you. There's no doorman to worry about. No alarm in the apartment. Not even a pet goldfish to get in your way."

Stephens heard something familiar in Hicks's voice. "There's a 'but' somewhere, isn't there?"

"But," Hicks added, "Adibi might be under surveillance by The Vanguard, so keep an eye out for any devices in the apartment. OMNI will alert you to any unusual frequencies, of course, but you know that's not foolproof. Make sure you keep your head on a swivel on your way out. Your mission doesn't end until you're back at the Annex."

"Great," Stephens laughed. "As if a black man breaking into an apartment in SoHo isn't tough enough, I've got to worry about The Vanguard nailing my ass."

"All the more reason to be careful," Hicks said.

Stephens still didn't like the assignment. He'd never hesitated to kill a man before, but it helped to have a reason. "Seems like a lot of effort for a lousy money man. Why don't you just have the feds pick him up?"

He heard Hicks hesitate. "You're still pretty new here, so just accomplish the mission as I've laid out. I'll be monitoring the situation remotely. My call sign is

'Base'. Yours will be 'Vulture'. Keep the chatter to a minimum and accomplish your mission."

Based on their past history, Stephens shouldn't have been surprised by how casual Hicks was about ordering him to kill a man, but he was. "You're a real bastard, you know that?"

"Tell me something I don't already know," Hicks said. "Lobby traffic in the building is lowest at four o'clock. The target package I just sent you has a complete set of OMNI commands to put all cameras in the area on a one-minute loop as you approach. Anyone who tries to search security footage afterwards won't find any trace of you while you're on the premises. Wait in the apartment until the target comes home and do the deed. I'll be watching. Happy hunting, Vulture. Base out."

Hicks killed the connection. Stephens pushed the handheld away from him.

It was already two o'clock on the dot.

He had two hours to get in place.

And the target only had a few hours left to live.

Stephens opened the bottom drawer of his metal desk, took his Glock and tucked it in his shoulder holster.

Time to move.

WEARING a black hooded sweatshirt and baseball cap, Stephens watched Umar Adibi's building from the window of the coffee shop across the street.

SoHo might be a trendy part of the city, but a black man standing on the street in that part of town would draw attention. Black lives mattered, but preferably not in their neighborhood.

Stephens didn't mind. At least no one was shooting at him.

Yet.

He sipped his cup of dark roast and began reading the target package Hicks had sent to his handheld. The screen was polarized, so he didn't worry about anyone looking over his shoulder while he read it.

According to OMNI, Umar Adibi had lived a painfully normal life. The thirty-five-year-old Pakistani immigrant had attended Columbia Business School on a full scholarship and graduated near the top of his class. He had decided to stay in New York after school, taking a job with the same bank where he had interned in college. A Pakistani-owned bank with a branch in midtown Manhattan. A red flag? Maybe.

On the surface, Adibi was a model citizen. He'd never been arrested. He'd never owned a car, so he'd never received a speeding ticket or been late on a payment. He'd been born a Muslim but didn't practice his faith. His social media profile was devoid of politics. He was a finance geek who streamed videos after work and didn't go out much. He liked Anime and trashy horror flicks. He dated off and on, but his longest relationship had lasted three months. There was no evidence of radicalization.

He spent his days getting to work early, working late and his weekends sleeping in. Occasionally, he even went to brunch with friends on Sunday. He had a cleaning lady who came in once a week to do the laundry and clean up a bit. He visited his folks and sister in Paramus every other weekend. No radical ties there, either. None of his relatives or known associates were particularly religious, either.

He'd travelled extensively for business – Southeast Asia, mostly – and even then, seemed to behave himself. His credit cards showed no sign of jiggle joints or wild nights on the town.

The guy was boring as hell. The last guy in the world you'd peg for an ally for terrorism. He knew from experience those were the best kind.

Stephens's experiences also told him Adibi's death wouldn't stop anything. His co-workers would mourn his loss, but his portfolio would be reassigned to other people well before lunch.

He decided to quit trying to justify his orders. He'd been given a mission and no chance to opt out. Best to get it done and move on. He hoped that would be enough to allow him to look his wife and kids in the eye when he got home that night.

His handheld alarm buzzed on the countertop. Four o'clock on the nose. He took a final look across the street. The foot traffic in and out of the building was as quiet as Hicks had told him it would be.

The few kids who lived in the building were already home from school. The stay-at-home parents and nannies were inside with their charges and the working-class stiffs were still at their offices.

Time to go.

Stephens pocketed his handheld and drained his coffee as he stood to leave. He drew a few looks from the customers as he threw out his cup and pulled his hat closer over his eyes. Some of the customers gave him a quick, awkward smile. *See? I'm not racist. I smiled at a black guy today.*

A tweaker in the corner sniffed and looked away as Stephens passed.

Stephens knew why. The druggie thought he was a cop or some kind of military man. He still had that air of authority that he knew he'd never shake. He didn't want to shake it. It was why he'd never be good at undercover work, but it had helped him excel at interrogation.

He left the coffee shop and crossed at the corner, then walked back up the block on the same side of the street as Adibi's building.

He was prepared to pick the front door lock when he caught a break. A mother pulling a stroller was backing out while trying to corral her toddler to follow.

Stephens stepped in to hold the outer and inner door open for her while she struggled through. He was more than tall enough to do this easily.

The woman looked tired, but grateful. "Thank you very much. Noah, come on. We don't have time for this!"

The little boy darted out of the lobby and into to the street, bringing another fresh set of admonishments from mom.

Stephens stepped inside the lobby and let the door shut behind him. When the cops ultimately asked the residents if they had seen anyone strange in the building around the time Adibi had been murdered, the mother-of-two would reluctantly tell them about the nice black man who'd held the door for her. White guilt would make her feel bad about it, but she'd tell them just the same.

Fortunately, when she tried to give them a description, she would most likely hedge and say he looked like a tall Kanye West. She hadn't looked at him long enough to give the cops a good description and even if she had, witness memories were unreliable. And she'd been too preoccupied with her kids to pay him much notice.

Stephens hit the elevator call button and spotted the security camera in the lobby. He checked his handheld to make sure the feed was on a loop. He was glad it showed an empty lobby, not him.

The elevator opened. Empty.

He decided to call it in. "Base, this Vulture. I'm in the lobby."

"Copy, Vulture," Hicks said in his ear. "Let me know when you're in position."

Stephens rode the elevator to the fourth floor and got out. There were five apartments on that level, lettered A through E. Adibi's apartment was 4C.

Stephens looked around the hall and spotted several cameras at the corners. A quick check of his handheld showed they were on a loop, too.

Knowing he had some time before Adibi got home, he closed his eyes and listened to the sounds coming from the apartments. He wanted to get a sense of his surroundings.

Someone in 4A was listening to cartoons too loud. A woman in 4E sounded like she was on a video call with a bad connection. She'd be too distracted to hear him enter 4C.

No sounds came from the other three apartments. *Good.*

Stephens checked Adibi's door and saw it was a biometric lock just as Hicks had described. He saw Adibi had also installed a remote viewing doorbell so he could see who was ringing his door from his phone anywhere in the world. Unless he happened to be looking at the phone at that exact moment, he wouldn't even notice the signal was being blocked by OMNI.

Stephens took out his handheld and held it against the door. After little more than a second, the screen turned green, and the door clicked open.

Stephens smiled. He loved technology.

He stepped into the apartment and slowly closed the door behind him. Again, he remained still and focused on his surroundings.

The loft apartment was autumn dark and quiet. He allowed his eyes to adjust to the dull light while he listened for the natural sounds of the place before he went exploring.

Even in the weak light, Stephens could tell this was a bachelor pad. The kitchen was off to his left, a marble counter separating it from the rest of the space. He knew from the layout Hicks had sent him in advance that the bathroom was off to his right. The rest of the loft was an open layout.

Exposed brick ran down the left side of the wall to the windows. A sixty-inch flat screen television, cable box and gaming console in a cabinet stood along that wall. A leather couch set and coffee table were right in front of it. A bedroom setup was off to the left and the bed was unmade.

Adibi wasn't home, unless he was in the bathroom. The door was closed.

That didn't feel right. Who closed their bathroom door when they left?

Stephens stood quietly and continued to listen, just to make sure he was alone.

That's when he heard it. A sound that didn't belong in an empty apartment.

A muffled electronic voice. Like something from an earbud.

But it wasn't *his* earbud.

Shit.

He drew his Glock just as a man popped up from around the kitchen counter and pushed him against the brick wall. The man had gone for Stephens's gun hand, trying to pin it against the wall.

Stephens used his left hand to grab the left man by the neck as he drove a knee into his groin. The first attempt hit the man's thigh. The man backed off a bit and tried to bring his forearm into Stephens's throat.

Stephens continued to hold him off by the throat and brought up his knee again. This time, he caught his attacker in the stomach.

The blow was enough to make his attacker take another step back. The third knee strike hit the jackpot and the man buckled, losing his grip on his arm.

Stephens grabbed a handful of his attacker's hair and slammed the man's face into the brick wall once, then twice, then a third time. Stephens pushed the dizzy man to the right, tripping him as he stumbled and sent him sprawling onto the floor.

Stephens was about to kick him when a pistol barked from the bathroom, striking the brickwork next to his head.

Stephens dropped behind the kitchen counter. His Glock up and ready.

A silencer had muffled the shot. It wasn't a gentle puff like in the movies, but it wasn't loud enough to alert the neighbors.

Two more shots struck the side of the counter where the shooter judged Stephens's head would be.

Stephens shifted deeper into the kitchen, keeping his head low beneath the counter.

Listening.

The man on the floor was groaning, but still down.

Then, a rustle of fabric. The gunman was still in the bathroom but had moved to get a better angle on his target.

Knowing there was no light behind him, Stephens slowly popped his head up above the counter. He saw the gunman just inside the bathroom door. Standing as he peered into the kitchen.

Stephens brought up his Glock and fired once, striking the gunman in the left arm, sending him backward against the sink.

Realizing the neighbors must have heard his shot, Stephens hopped the counter and charged the gunman before he could recover. He wanted to avoid shooting again if he could.

The wounded man was slumped against the sink, but still upright. His arm wound had only begun to bleed.

His gun was still in his right hand.

Stephens knocked it out of his hand, sending it falling into the tub. He shoved his left hand under the man's chin, smashing it backward into the mirror. The glass shattered and Stephens placed his Glock against the man's cheek, holding him in place.

He saw the man was big. Asian.

Stephens pressed the barrel of his gun hard against the man's face, pushing his head even further into the broken mirror. "Who sent you?"

248 / TERRENCE MCCAULEY

He realized too late that the man's right hand was free. He caught Stephens with a hard right to the temple that rocked him backward and out of the bathroom. The man followed up with a flat hand aimed for his throat but caught his collar bone instead. The impact of the blow was still strong enough to knock him off balance and send him to the floor.

But his grip on the Glock held.

The man dove at him, but not before Stephens had been able to bring up his knees. He caught the man by the throat with his left, buried his pistol in his assailant's side and fired three times.

Stephens pushed the man off him and rolled into a crouching position. His last three shots had been muffled by the man's body, but one of the neighbors may have heard the first shot.

He'd almost forgotten about his first attacker as Stephens's head snapped back as the man let loose with a kick that connected with Stephens's chin.

The blow sent him flat on his back. His mind filled with pain and stars. He felt the fight begin to go out of him as the world started to swim.

He saw the blurry outline of two men standing above him. Both of them drawing a pistol at the same time.

He raised his Glock and fired into the middle of them. Both men melded into one as they fell over on their side together.

Stephens shook off his dizziness as he forced himself to sit up. His stomach lurched as he used the couch to help pull himself to his feet without taking his eyes off the man he had just shot.

The man was still alive. All of Stephens's shots had

hit him center mass in the vest. He was winded, but that wouldn't last.

Stephens staggered as he looked around and saw a rumpled blanket across the arm of the couch.

He balled it up with his left hand and kicked the gunman's pistol away before dropping to a crouch and placing the blanket over the man's face.

He thought about shooting him through the blanket. The sound would be muffled, but he couldn't risk it. It would be a miracle if someone hadn't already heard the gunshots and called the cops, but another shot would leave no doubt.

He tucked his Glock away and decided smothering the man was his best and quietest option.

Sometimes, the old ways were best.

The wounded man's legs thrashed as Stephens applied pressure, but Stephens adjusted his weight to pin them down. He leaned forward and pushed the blanket down on the man's face as hard as he could.

The dying man's hands found Stephens's face and frantically sought something to grab on to. He pulled his head back while maintaining pressure on the blanket.

Fists flailed and hit nothing. Outstretched fingers sought out eyes to gouge, a throat to grab, anything that would give him just one gasp of air to continue the fight.

Stephens dodged them all and kept on pressing.

Then the man feebly tried to pry Stephens's hands loose from the blanket.

But Stephens wouldn't be moved. The struggles only made him hold on tighter, ever tighter until the man's grip weakened, and his arms fell to his sides.

Stephens knew it could be a ploy to feign unconsciousness. He remained in place for another minute until he knew the deed was done.

When he shoved the blanket aside, he knew the man wasn't faking anything. His bulging eyes stared into the infinity of death.

Stephens quickly got to his feet and backed away from the man. He stumbled against a desk, and he almost fell over. He grabbed onto the chair to keep his balance.

Those blows to the head had made him dizzy, but he kept his feet. He remained still until he was sure he wouldn't fall over.

He brought his hand up to his nose and found it was bleeding. Broken. He grabbed the blanket he had used to smother the man and held it to his face. He didn't want to risk leaving DNA behind when the police eventually showed up.

He felt the room begin to spin when Hicks's voice in his ear snapped him out of it. "Vulture, this is Base. Sit rep."

Stephens removed the blanket from his nose and gasped, "Two targets down. Not the main target. Repeat, not the main target."

"Copy, Vulture. Are you hurt?"

"Got my bell rung and a broken nose, but I'm operational."

"Apply pressure to the wound and proceed with a new objective."

Stephens knew his vision was blurry, but was his hearing going, too? "New objective."

"Take pictures of the targets and their fingerprints," Hicks told him. "Then place your device next to the laptop and follow the instructions on the screen. Do you copy, Vulture?"

"Copy, Base," Stephens said, and went about carrying out his new objectives. It was good to have something to focus on to keep the dizziness at bay.

He pulled out his handheld, took pictures of the men he'd just killed and scanned their fingerprints on the screen. All of it was automatically uploaded to OMNI for identification.

"Well done, Vulture," Hicks said. "Now place your handheld next to Adibi's laptop and follow the directions on the screen. Do it now."

Stephens stepped over the dead men and did what Hicks had told him to do. His screen automatically switched to black, and a gray bar slowly began to grow longer at the bottom of it.

While he watched the device copy the hard drive, he knew he might've taken a couple of good shots, but he hadn't lost his common sense. "Base, this is Vulture. Download is a go. Are police on the way?"

"Negative," Hicks said, "but be careful when you leave the building. Your friends probably aren't alone."

Stephens blinked his eyes clear. "Adibi was never the target, was he?"

"We'll have time to talk about that later, Vulture. For now, get that hard drive uploaded and prepare to move out."

Stephens knew he couldn't walk around the street holding the blanket up to his nose. He went into the bathroom and saw the medicine cabinet's contents had fallen into the sink when the dead man's head destroyed it. He picked up a box of cotton balls and jammed a couple into his nostrils. The pain almost made him black out.

Again, Hicks's voice kept him aware. "Download is complete, Vulture. Grab your device and get moving. No police inbound but watch for more targets."

"Copy, Base." He pushed himself out of the bathroom and saw his device's screen was blinking green. The upload had been completed.

He pocketed the handheld and folded the bloody blanket before heading for the door. "Vulture is on the move."

Stephens tucked the blanket under his arm and paused at the door before stepping into the hallway. If the dead men had friends, they might be waiting for him on the other side. Hearing nothing, he opened the door a crack before taking a quick look. The hallway was clear.

He hit the hallway. Adibi's door automatically locked behind him.

He decided waiting for the elevator would be pushing his luck. He took the stairs down to the lobby and checked the street before going outside. No one seemed to be watching the building.

"Base, this is Vulture. Confirm the street is clear."

Hicks responded, "No abnormal signals detected, Vulture. Nothing on visual, either. Proceed with caution."

Stephens thought of something. "Did you detect any signals in the apartment before I went in?"

"You are clear to proceed with caution, Vulture."

Hicks's response told him all he needed to know.

Stephens took a deep breath as he opened the front door. "Copy that."

Once on the street, he looked around as he pulled his hood over his cap and wiped at the thin trickle of blood that had pooled above his upper lip. "Base, this is Vulture. I'm clear and proceeding to the Annex."

"Copy that, Vulture. Good job in there. Mission accomplished. See Dr. Carter when you get back to the Annex. She'll give you something for the bleeding and the pain. You'll be good as new before you head back home to the wife and kids tonight."

Stephens continued to eye the street as he walked. The men in the apartment had been talking to someone before he walked in there. He forgot about the comms protocol bullshit and said, "You knew I was walking into a trap, didn't you?"

"You were apprised of the danger before you entered," Hicks said. "You'd questioned my orders. You don't get to do that. Ever. Not under Moscow Protocol. Do you copy, Vulture?"

Stephens would've told him what he really thought of him if he wasn't in public. "I copy, Base. I copy that you're an asshole. Don't do that again."

"Don't question orders again and I won't have to," Hicks said. "The targets who hit you were a three-man team. The third was a driver and he's long gone from the area. You're in the clear."

Stephens felt his anger rise like bile in his throat. "But you and I are way far from clear."

Hicks surprised him by laughing. "We're not in the clear business, Ace. I'll call ahead to have Dr. Carter ready to take care of you. Maybe she can give you something for your bruised ego. Just remember the lessons that stick are the ones that hurt. Take care, Vulture. You did good work today. Base out."

Stephens heard Hicks kill the connection. He dumped the blanket in a trash bin at the corner as he crossed the street.

Just because he'd questioned an order didn't mean he deserved to walk into a trap. But as he walked, he remembered Hicks had told him there could be trouble. Stephens had been informed. And he probably wouldn't have handled the situation any different than he had.

That was the damnable part about working for Hicks. Even when the man was wrong, he was usually right.

Stephens thought about taking a cab, but the more he walked, the clearer he felt. He decided to walk to The Annex if possible.

He could use all the clarity he could get.

CHAPTER 21

SOMEWHERE

HICKS WINCED as he removed the last of his bandages and examined his new face in the mirror. The swelling was going down and the pain had become more than manageable. He did not take the horse pills anymore. He was finally getting an idea of what he would look like when he healed.

He liked what he saw. The man looking back at him was a total stranger, but that had been the case for most of his adult life. He had lost any idea of who he was a long time ago. Only the present mattered. He was only as good as the mission in front of him. The rest was just noise.

He picked up his handheld from the sink and saw Stephens was more than five blocks away from Adibi's place. The neighbors either hadn't heard the shots or had decided to not get involved. Either way worked for Hicks.

It was time to put the next phase of his plan in motion.

He checked OMNI's locator on Adibi's phone and saw he was still at his office. He could have accessed his computer to see what he was working on, but decided it wasn't worth the risk. OMNI could hack his company's firewall, but financial institutions were tricky. Layers of security made it difficult to access and there was always a chance they could be tracked. That was why he'd sent Stephens to download the contents of his laptop. He often worked from home and the personal laptop was easier to access.

OMNI had confirmed that the men in his apartment had been working for The Vanguard. Tamir's men, most likely. They had been there to conduct a security sweep of Adibi's place ahead of his meeting with Tamir. Stephens had killed them, thus pushing Adibi out of the way and allowing Rahul to take his place at the meeting with Clarke's asset.

Hicks stopped examining his swollen face.

Time to throw Demarest a bone and help his plan in the process.

Hicks contacted the DNI directly. He picked up on the second ring. "Where's Veronica Holt and her daughter? I need them and I need them right now or we've got nothing to talk about."

Hicks had been ready for that. "Do you have people in Chicago?"

"Don't be a smartass, Hicks. I've had it up to here with your bullshit. Just hand them over and don't get cute about it like you did with Tessmer and Young."

"You wanted them back alive and that's how you

got them," Hicks reminded him. "As for Holt, she and her daughter are still in the Chicago area. Text me a contact number for one of your people and I'll arrange the handoff within the hour. But you'd better come correct, Charles. No rough stuff and no attempts to grab my team or I won't be responsible for the consequences."

"You have my word," Demarest said. "This will go a long way to getting this story off the front pages and the FBI off your back. I've already got a good cover story in place that'll put all the talk about you to rest."

But Hicks wasn't worried about the FBI. He had bigger concerns. "You think your heart can stand another gift today?"

Demarest hesitated. "Depends on what it is."

"Tamir Bat-Erdene."

Hicks couldn't swear to it, but he thought he heard the Director of National Intelligence gasp. "You have him."

"Not yet," Hicks admitted, "but I'm working on it. You can help me stop him if you're willing."

"Of course, I'm willing," Demarest said. "How?"

Hicks kept it plain and specific. "One of my guys just killed two of Tamir's heavies doing a final security sweep on a finance geek's place. Said finance geek was scheduled to meet Tamir to review Vanguard finances in a couple of days. I need your people to take the heat for the hit and bring said geek into custody. A civilian named Umar Adibi in New York."

He heard Demarest write that down. "Sounds Pakistani. He a radical?"

"No, just a civilian with some nasty clients. I need

you to have your men pick him up as he leaves his office in a little while. I'd also appreciate it if you could get rid of the bodies my man left behind."

"You want me to clean up your mess? Again? You're out of your mind."

"It'll burn Adibi forever with Tamir," Hicks explained. "Tamir will think part of his finance operation has been compromised by the FBI. My man will show up as the white knight who saves the day. I get close to Tamir and you not only get the finance guy, but his laptop, too. But you'd better move fast. He's due home in an hour."

He heard Demarest tapping his pen against a pad as he thought it over. "Why do I think there's a catch to this?"

"No catch," Hicks said. "Just let it leak that you've got Adibi and he's one of yours. You'll have to put him into Witness Protection, but he's worth the effort."

"If he talks."

"He's a millennial nerd who likes Anime," Hicks said. "I think even your people can crack him. Once he sees your feds in windbreakers, you'll have to beg him to shut up."

Demarest swore under his breath. "The time frame isn't a problem, and I can have people at his place in fifteen minutes. But before I agree to anything, I want the particulars on the meeting with Tamir."

Even if Hicks hadn't already promised that part of the operation to Clarke, he wouldn't have told Demarest about it. OMNI confirmed that The Barnyard only suspected that Tamir was in Bangkok. They had several other locations listed as more likely places.

Hicks wanted it to stay that way. He needed Tamir alive, not blown to bits by a cruise missile.

"I don't have the particulars yet," Hicks admitted. "My people are pushing for a meeting this week and, if you play your part, there's a good chance we'll get it."

"I doubt it," Demarest said. "Once Tamir finds out we've grabbed his finance guy, he'll go underground and pull the hole in after him."

Hicks had already thought of that. "Tamir doesn't have that kind of time. Adibi only handles a small part of his finances. The asset setting up the meeting is the shot caller here. He's solid. And no, I'm not going to give you his name yet. Not until we have the meeting in place and things are set in motion."

"Hold on." Demarest muted the phone for a minute before he came back on the line. "I have people rolling on Adibi now. We'll have him in custody as soon as he leaves his office. It'll be more of a spectacle that way. Better chance for word to get back to Tamir that his boy's been picked up. We'll let it leak through back channels over the next few days. I already have a separate team heading straight for Adibi's apartment now."

Hicks would've handled it another way, but Demarest's strategy was sound. "Just don't let them search the place for DNA. My guy got hurt in there and I don't want him getting caught up in this."

Demarest laughed. "I thought you boys knew how to cover your tracks. You must be slipping, Hicks."

"His tracks are covered. Just wanted to save your people from wasting their time chasing a blind lead. Happy hunting. I'll be in touch. Hicks out."

Hicks killed the connection before Demarest made any more demands.

He rested his hands on the sink and looked closely at the stranger he saw. The eyes were still the same. Contacts would change the color, but not what they had seen. Not what they were or who they belonged to.

He had done his part. Now it was up to Rahul and Clarke to go to work.

CHAPTER 22

ZHOU SIPPED his ginger tea to soothe his aching belly.

He tried to focus on his breathing to control his heart rate as Tamir tried to convince him The Vanguard's operation in America was still functional.

Zhou was glad Tamir was on the phone and not here in his hut. Rage may have surpassed logic. He might have shot the man where he sat. To do so may have been justified, but it would have been a miscalculation of the highest order.

Emotion was a selfish, capitalist disease that poisoned everything it touched. He had succeeded in keeping The Vanguard healthy for decades by managing the emotional inclinations of others. He did not intend on being the man who introduced the virus to the Asian aspect of the organization.

Zhou knew there was a time for anger and a time for action. Now was a time for action. The luxuries of anger and vengeance could come later, if at all.

The general waited until he had a firm grip on his rage before he spoke. He never showed emotion in front of his people. Emotion betrayed weakness and men like Tamir Bat-Erdene thrived on the weaknesses of their betters.

Zhou needed Tamir to fear him now more than ever.

"Our operation in America is paralyzed," Zhou said in Russian, for he found Tamir's Mandarin beyond deplorable. "You not only lost our foothold in California, but Veronica Holt and the man who reported to her. All within a twenty-four-hour period. An impressive feat of incompetence, comrade, even for you."

"A gross but understandable overreaction, comrade," Tamir responded in Russian. "The losses in California are due to our over-reliance on North Korean efficiency. I have already begun to use my influence with the Americans that the California facilities were entirely under North Korean control. The result will be a further escalation of tensions between the two countries. Of course, we will be in a position to take full advantage of their weakness."

Zhou's temper abated, but only a little. "And what of the overall strength of our operations in America?"

"An overwhelming majority of our assets remain in place," Tamir assured him. "The damage Holt's capture caused is being mitigated as we speak. The Americans think they have dealt us a death blow, but it is little more than a paper cut. They will soon find they are punching at clouds."

Zhou did not share is comrade's confidence. "And the arrest of your clerk by the FBI? Is that North Korean incompetence too or yours?"

"Neither," Tamir said. "My sources tell me he was arrested on an entirely different matter. As we were able to corrupt him, it only stands to reason he was greedy in other aspects of his job. He knows but a fraction of a tiny percentage of our holdings. And he knows nothing about our organization, only me. He can only add to a list of charges against me that is already quite long."

Zhou rubbed the palms of his hands along the top of his desk. Tamir's arrogance was proving to be more of an annoyance than even the insects that plagued him in this humid jungle.

Calm. Calm.

"The clerk's arrest was not a coincidence, comrade. It is another strike against us from James Hicks and his University. The information this clerk can provide them, no matter how small, can only bring Hicks closer to us. This is clearly part of a greater plan."

"All the more reason for my call," Tamir said. "For I, too, have a greater plan. A contingency plan I would like to implement with your permission. A plan that will safeguard our assets even further."

Zhou was glad that Tamir already had a plan in place. The old pirate was nothing if not crafty. His dedication to the Cause aside, he also had a remarkable capacity for self-preservation. He knew all the measures he had taken to fortify his Bangkok compound would be worthless if Zhou gave the order to have him removed. Most of Tamir's guards were also on Zhou's payroll.

"I am most anxious to hear it, comrade."

Tamir sounded all too happy to tell him. "The first part of the plan involves Ms. Holt. My sources report that she and her child are currently in the hands of the

NSA. Not the FBI, which is strange given how news of her abduction has dominated the news. The Americans have quietly urged the media to stop covering the story. Media outlets appear to be complying."

Zhou had not been aware of this. "What does this tell us?"

"That the Americans are not fools," Tamir said. "They never would have allowed news of the Holt kidnapping to spread if they had taken her. And if Hicks had taken her, why hand her over to the federal authorities so quickly? Your earlier assumption of a broader plan is correct, comrade."

Zhou's eyes narrowed. "Flattery is lost on me, Tamir, and I have already determined that her abduction is part of a greater plan to destroy us. Our inability to get our sources to publicly blame Hicks for their kidnapping could be seen as another failure on your part."

"I do not seek to flatter, merely remark on your wisdom, General. The loss of our clerk in New York poses a minimal risk. Veronica, on the other hand, can provide them with information on our broader methods of operation."

"Veronica, is it?" Zhou repeated. "Do you always become so familiar with your assets, Tamir?"

The smuggler attempted to recover quickly. "Please forgive my familiarity, comrade. She has worked for our cause for so long, I will confess to seeing her as a colleague rather than mere cogs in the machinery of the Cause."

Zhou did not believe it but saw no benefit in pursuing it further. The Holt woman was in the hands of the Americans. Vanguard technicians had assured him they had wiped all traces of her dealings from her computer. But technicians had a habit of telling Zhou what they thought he wanted to hear. The Americans were excellent at retrieving information once thought to be lost.

"What are you doing to mitigate the damage she could do to us?"

Tamir explained, "Methods are already being changed. Facilities are being relocated. More importantly, assets have already been moved to hide them from the Americans and their allies. I will provide you with a complete report on my efforts after this call. But I'm afraid the bulk of our finances are still exposed to a degree."

Zhou may have had a contempt of capitalism, but he understood how it worked. It was why he had insisted on certain security measures being in place to keep Vanguard resources safe from the greed of men like Tessmer, Tamir and others who may seek to enrich themselves financially at the expense of the Cause.

"We have taken steps to ensure they cannot be moved," Zhou reminded him. "I had Tessmer see to it personally more than ten years ago."

"I am aware of that, comrade," Tamir said, "but those accounts can still be seized or frozen by the Americans should they learn about them from Ver..., I mean, the Holt woman or her records."

Zhou exhaled heavily. His own cleverness so long ago seems to be posing a problem for them now. "How do you suggest we protect them further?"

"I would like your permission to meet with my London banker to make other, more permanent arrangements to relocate our holdings. The meeting would not take place in London. It would take place here in my compound in Bangkok to ensure my safety."

Zhou opened his mouth and breathed in deeply. He continued to glide his hands across his desk.

Calm. Calm.

But despite his best efforts, his calm evaporated. "Have you lost your mind? You wish to meet with a westerner now, in the wake of all that has just happened?"

"Comrade, please. Our situation requires—"

But no amount of pleading could contain the general's bounding wrath. "You wish to meet with a man who may, himself, already be compromised by his clerk's capture? How do you know the Americans, or the British have not already gotten to him? How do you know that it wasn't he who betrayed his clerk to the Americans in the first place?"

Zhou quickly remembered that emotions were weakness and he dared not show such weakness to Tamir now. He lowered his voice as he regained his composure. "I question your strategy, comrade, not your goal, which I know is for the betterment of our organization and the Cause."

Zhou detected a tremor in Tamir's voice as he said, "I am honored to still have your confidence, comrade. Rest assured that my London banker is under constant surveillance by my people in England. He has not been compromised and grows rich from doing business with us. He cannot afford to risk that relationship. I vouch for his integrity personally."

Zhou grew very still. "With your life, comrade?"

"If necessary," Tamir said. "Yes, I would pledge my life on his discretion and loyalty. Holt's capture requires us to reallocate the bulk of our funds. Unfortunately, this necessary step will expose both of us to some small degree of risk."

Zhou knew what Tamir was referring to and their implications. "Employing those safeguards would require both of us to go to our bank in Shanghai to personally give authority for the transfer to take place. That is clearly impossible given the current threats we face. Have your banker make other arrangements. Surely they can be changed so they can be done remotely and online."

Tamir's nervous laugh gave Zhou cold comfort. "I'm afraid that is impossible, comrade. We can change those safeguards later if you wish, but under the current arrangement, there is no other way. Our biometric readings are required on bank property to grant authority to move the funds. As you remember, you insisted on such strict protocols."

Zhou's temper flared again. "I do not require you to remind me of the very protocols I devised and ordered to be implemented, comrade. I'm not some senile old fool who needs his orders read back to him. I am aware of the safeguards and why they were in place. I am ordering you to have your banker make other arrangements for the transfer."

"Yes, comrade," Tamir said. "I will tell him of our concerns. Any accommodation that can be made will be made."

Zhou was growing tired of the conversation and sought to end it to prevent his temper from being taxed any further. "Please proceed with your meeting as planned, comrade. I trust you will have good news to report in the coming days. That is all."

Zhou disconnected the call and closed his eyes. He focused on his breathing, his calm, choosing to ignore the fly that had landed on his nose.

He needed to recenter himself. To concentrate on the well-being of his mind. Too much had happened to distract him. Too much had gone wrong to make him lose sight of the true path.

Everything was for the Cause and the Cause was everything. A perfect circle that no man could break. Not even him. And certainly not the barbarian James Hicks.

The American had chased him long enough. It was time to swat him like the fly he was.

"Boy," he called out to his son.

His son appeared in the doorway. "Yes, father."

"I want you to closely monitor Tamir's plans about consolidating our assets. Analyze everything he does, especially this ridiculous, outdated notion that I must personally provide biometric approval of the transfer of funds at our bank in Shanghai. I will rely on your counsel before I offer my approval. Do you understand?"

His son bowed. "I am honored by your faith in me, father."

Zhou looked at his son. He detected a change in him. Was it pride or simply a self-assurance that had not been there before? He decided it did not matter. "I do not need you to be honored. Just be effective. And correct."

"And I will be, father. However, may I be permitted to offer a suggestion that may bring you ease of mind?"

The boy had never shown such motivation before.

It was a welcomed distraction following the taxing conversation with Tamir. "You may."

"You appear to be concerned about being present to authorize the transfer of funds," his son said. "Your concerns are well-founded. But comrade Tamir was placating you when he said he could have the protocols changed. This was undoubtedly done out of an abundance of respect for you. The protocols cannot be changed and must be done on bank property. The biometric safeguards are hardwired to your account and cannot be changed."

Zhou was quickly losing patients. "Why do you tell me what I already know?"

"To put your mind at ease, father. You are understandably concerned about going to the bank's offices in Shanghai. Tessmer made the arrangements and may have told Hicks of this. As always, your prudence is wise. But the bank has another, smaller branch that can accommodate such measures. In Singapore."

Zhou slowly raised his head. "It does?"

"What's more, the branch is accessible by helicopter, thus further securing your safety. You can land a few feet outside the office, go inside, authorize the transfer and be back on the helicopter within a few minutes. I'm sure they will be willing to accommodate you at any hour of the day or night, and I respectfully suggest a later time would be better."

Zhou sat back in his chair and looked at his son. Yes, he had grown more confident in recent days. And smart. Perhaps these troubles with the University had changed him. Often, a man's true character did not reveal itself until it faced adversity.

"Monitor Tamir's progress as I ordered. If this

banker is unable to make other arrangements, perhaps I will consider your proposal. Now leave. I have much work to do."

His son bowed again and left.

Zhou remained looking at the spot where his son had just stood. Perhaps he was growing into a clever man after all?

AT HIS COMPOUND IN BANGKOK, Tamir's hand shook as he grabbed the bottle of vodka and poured more than three fingers' worth into a glass. He downed it in two swallows, welcoming the burn at the back of his throat.

The pain meant he was still alive, a privilege he may not enjoy for much longer.

The old bastard knows about Veronica. He knows about Jane being his child. He knows but does nothing. He just sits there like a spider, waiting for a mistake to fall into his web before he crawls over to devour it.

Tamir reached for the bottle again, almost knocking it over, and poured more vodka into his glass.

Part of him wondered why he bothered pouring it at all. He should cut out the middleman and just drink from the bottle. But he would not do that. He would not allow his rising fear to lower himself to such a state.

Zhou's disappointment reminded him of his childhood in the rancid slums of Sabah. He had spent his entire life trying to scrub away all traces of his past, but no amount of money or women or children could quell the stench of the gutter he knew would follow him to the grave.

And in those rare moments when he thought he

had left his humble beginnings behind him, General Zhou would enter his life and resurrect old ghosts.

Tamir's fear of returning to Sabah had grown with each passing year, always lingering in the back of his mind. That fear had served him well over the years. It had given him the drive he needed to make his fortune.

But now that he was an old man with more money than he could spend, his fear of returning to that place only grew. He knew Zhou could take everything away from him with a flick of his little finger. He would relish sending Tamir back to the slums from which he had come. Old men did not have much to look forward to in Sabah. Only disease and a slow, agonizing death.

Tamir had no intention of allowing that to happen.

Tamir's hand was steadier now as he poured more vodka in his glass. Zhou had shown him much in their brief conversation. Something he had never seen in the old general in all the years of their association. Fear.

Zhou was a mighty and powerful man, but he wasn't indestructible. He wasn't irreplaceable, either. He remembered a saying one of his American customers had told him after a night of too much whiskey and not enough food. 'Cemeteries are filled with irreplaceable men.'

Tamir had spent his life feeding off zealots like the general. He loved Communists most of all as money was only a necessary evil to them. A tool to attain a higher good for their beloved Cause.

But to a man born to the slums like Tamir, money meant everything. Money helped the poor fill their bowls, not high words from a manifesto. He had made a sizable fortune off The Vanguard's war against the West. Profiting from Communist expansionism was too rich of an irony for Tamir to avoid. In his heart, he despised the Communists as much as he hated the Capitalists.

Zhou's only advantage, in Tamir's mind, was that he was a fellow Asian. They had always had a bond The Vanguard's barbarian partners in Russia and Germany could never have.

But Tamir knew his life would not last long if Zhou had found out about the men he had lost at Adibi's apartment. It would have taken too long to explain Adibi's complicated role in the Vanguard's financial security of cutout men and accountants working blind. Zhou might have concluded that Tamir had put the lifeblood of the Vanguard at risk – its money – and as a result, Zhou would put a significant price on Tamir's head.

Yes, Tamir had his own small army guarding his fortified compound, but Zhou *was* an army. Tamir could not withstand an assault from a vengeful, paranoid madman determined to destroy him. His men could keep a single assassin away from him, but no one could defend his base against a barrage of guided missile fired from one of Zhou's former commanders.

Evasion was the only thing Tamir could rely on now. Skills he had learned in a life spent evading the law for more than sixty years now. He knew his dalliance with Veronica Holt had been a mistake. They had become lovers while she was working for the Vanguard in Laos six years before. As fate would have it, their brief interlude had produced a child, something he thought would be impossible given his advanced age and lifestyle. He had other children, twenty or more by his last count, but Jane was special for he knew she would be his last.

Veronica and Jane were in Zhou's crosshairs. Tamir knew her concern for the wellbeing of the child would prevent her from telling the Americans about Tamir. She would fear that Tamir would harm the child, but Tamir could never hurt his own blood. The number of his own bastards he kept in his employ was proof of that.

Zhou, on the other hand, was not a sentimental man. He had lost many sons in his conflicts with the West. He would not hesitate to kill Veronica and Jane, as a reminder to the rest of The Vanguard that his power over the organization was absolute. Punishment for failure to protect the organization was swift.

Tamir had never been a religious man, but he found himself praying to any gods inclined to listen that Zhou would let Veronica and Jane live, even at the cost of his own life.

He had served Zhou for years but knew his loyalty would be easily forgotten in the fog of war. Men like Zhou waxed poetically about the Cause and the future, but their feet were firmly planted in the present. And Tamir's feet were planted next to his. Their destinies were intertwined and had been for decades. He had never thought otherwise.

He had to find a way to make this transaction successful or his life would be in forfeit. So would the life of the woman he had loved, however briefly, and of his last child.

Zhou's words about the wisdom of bringing a westerner into their affairs still rang in his ears, but Tamir had no choice. The longer they delayed the transfer, the greater the possibility that the Americans or their allies would locate and freeze their assets. He could successfully hide some of it, but the bulk of it was still vulnerable.

And if one cent was garnished by the Americans, Zhou would have his head on a pike.

He pulled out his satellite phone and decided to call his London banker before he got too drunk. He had already requested a meeting for some time soon, but now he needed to meet him immediately. Time was of the essence. He hoped the banker could work his magic once again, for more than just his life depended on it now.

CHAPTER 23

LONDON, ENGLAND

RAHUL PATEL FOUND the neon lights of Piccadilly Circus especially gaudy that night as he drank his scotch on the rooftop bar of The Gilded Cage and listened to Vasha Pomeru fret over his plan. At least the view was nice, and the outdoor heaters effective against the London chill.

Rahul knew he shouldn't be drinking, but it was necessary for the sake of his cover. He told himself he had it under control.

"What you ask is not as simple as you think," Pomeru protested in passable Hindi. Though Romanian by birth, the banker had a knack for picking up languages.

He looked around to see if anyone was listening, but the large Thursday night crowd was too busy flirting to pay attention to their conversation. Rahul doubted any of them understood their dialect. Hindi had an almost countless variety of them.

"It simply cannot be done," Pomeru continued. "The danger to both of us is far too great."

"You worry too much, Vasha." Rahul set his drink on the table and regarded the banker for a moment. A round little man whose expensive clothes and manicured nails did little to lend him the respectability he obviously sought. His hair was slicked back and dyed a ridiculous shade for a man Patel knew to be almost seventy.

"You've already cleared the highest hurdle," Rahul went on, careful to avoid mentioning names. "Our client is under great pressure to meet us from his betters. You've put my name forward as your assistant's replacement after his unfortunate arrest and our client agreed. Any goal can be achieved with the proper incentive. And I understand our mutual friend has provided you with plenty of that."

Pomeru's dark eyes narrowed at the mention of Bruce Clarke. "There are limits to even his kind of persuasion, Mr. Sawaya," Pomeru said, using Rahul's cover name, "especially where our client is involved. How the devil did the Americans know about my assistant in the first place?"

Rahul, in his role of the suave banker, shrugged easily. "Who knows? Who cares? He was probably careless and greedy. He *is* a Pakistani, after all."

The Romanian waved off the ancient animosity between Indians and Pakistanis.

Rahul laughed at his discomfort, more for the benefit of whomever was undoubtedly watching them. He was operating under the assumption that Tamir always had eyes on Pomeru. "Maybe the Americans got lucky. They're known for that. The reasons don't matter. Your assistant is gone in a puff of scandal and I'm a more than suitable replacement."

"Yes, how convenient." Pomeru frowned. "And our client is not a man who believes in the charm of coincidence. He may not know about my connection to our mutual friend, but he may kill both of us as a precautionary measure."

Rahul took his drink. "If he were in a position to be cautious, he wouldn't have called you this morning practically begging for a meeting. All you have to do is get me in the same room with him. It'll be my show after that."

Pomeru continued to look at Rahul as he drank his scotch. Pomeru's own martini hadn't been touched since the server laid it on the table. The twist of lemon floated sadly near the brim of the glass. "I'll bet your real name isn't even Athar Sawaya, is it?"

"It most certainly is," Patel lied, willing Pomeru to stay on script. "I've worked at your bank for more than three years. The performance evaluations and hiring papers and payment records that have been placed in your company's system prove it. Those same records show I was at two other larger banks in the years preceding that. I'm a steady, competent banker who knows his place in the discreet world of high finance. I'd advise you to remember that. Both of our lives depend on it now."

He watched the banker take a cocktail napkin from the table and dab the sweat from his head. "I don't like this. It took me over a year to get him to trust your predecessor. I may just call the whole thing off."

"You'll do nothing of the sort," Rahul said harsher than he'd intended. But his words snapped Pomeru to attention. He tried softening the blow by adding, "Look, all you have to do is remember my name and my length of employment at the bank. Three years is a solid, easy number to remember. He's already reviewed my credentials and has allowed me into the meeting. The hard part is over." He gestured at the martini. "Now relax and enjoy yourself. This pensive bit isn't doing either of us any good. We're probably being watched, remember?"

"Remember?" Pomeru finished dabbing his head and tossed the balled-up napkin on the table. "How could I forget?"

Rahul laughed again before finishing his scotch and flagging down a passing waitress. He thickened his British accent as he spoke to her in English. "Another round for me and my nervous friend here. He's trying to snatch victory from the jaws of defeat."

Her eyes lingered on him a little longer than normal before she giggled and walked away.

"You're too cute for your own good, Mr. Sawaya," Pomeru observed in Hindi. "Perhaps for both our good."

"I had to think of some way to explain your behavior," Rahul said. "Now, if one of Tamir's spies asks her about us, she'll have an answer for them."

"Oh, God. You're right." Pomeru grabbed his martini and drank it down in two gulps.

"That's the spirit," Rahul said in English. "You've got some catching up to do, old sport. Might as well get at it."

But Pomeru was not in a jovial mood. He leaned forward and tapped the table as he returned to the Hindi dialect. "My agreement with our friend means I don't have to do anything I'm not comfortable doing."

"Agreements are amended all the time," Rahul said. "I'd expect a banker above all people to understand that."

"What I understand, better than you, is what our client does to people he even suspects of betraying him. You haven't seen what he's capable of. I have. He's a lunatic. An absolute madman who guards his privacy jealously, especially now that he burned the North Koreans in America."

"Keep your voice down and a smile on your face," Rahul cautioned.

Pomeru remembered himself. "Do you know he barbecued the last man who betrayed him? Alive. I was there. He made me watch the entire thing. The screams. The smells." He shuddered and dabbed his forehead again with the cocktail napkin. "This is the measure of the man you think we have fooled."

They stopped speaking when the waitress returned with their drinks. She kept her eyes on Rahul as she removed the empty glasses.

"You're an angel of mercy," Patel charmed in English. "Let's hope this next one makes my friend here feel better."

The waitress giggled again, her eyes lingering on Rahul longer this time. His tan skin and brown eyes. His thick black hair and clean jawline. She offered a smile before moving away.

"I think she wants to sleep with you," Pomeru observed.

"I know she does." He knew how women looked at him. There was no point in being modest. He looked at Pomeru and winked. "Perhaps I'll make a pass at her. Could be good for my cover."

Pomeru sagged again and reached for his martini. "I might as well get drunk. I'll be dead in a couple of days."

Rahul made a show of laughing it off. If they couldn't understand what they were saying, Tamir's spies could read their body language.

"Don't be so gloomy." Rahul checked his handheld and brought up the feed from the concealed camera in his University flat. "If it makes you feel any better, our client has people searching my place as we speak." He turned the device so Pomeru could see it.

The Romanian's reaction could've been to a picture of a beautiful girl or an angry e-mail he had fired off to a colleague.

Rahul continued. "As you can see, they're going over everything I own with a fine-toothed comb, including my work records for you on my laptop."

He tucked the handheld in the inside pocket of his suit jacket. "Once they're done, my cover is as solid as it can be. And if you don't trust me, you can trust our mutual friend."

Pomeru's expression soured at the mention of Clarke. "Our friend isn't sticking his neck out and neither are you. I am."

Rahul leaned forward. "That's where you're wrong, old boy. My neck is stuck out just as far as your own, if not further."

He slapped Pomeru on the shoulder and laughed. "Cheer up. If we're both alive this time tomorrow, we'll be laughing about this over a bottle of champagne. My treat."

Pomeru looked down at his martini. "And if not?"

Rahul shrugged. "Then our troubles will be over."

He raised his glass and waited for Pomeru to toast him. "Come," he said in English. "A drink before the war."

Pomeru reluctantly clinked glasses and sipped his martini. "Perhaps the torture won't hurt if I'm hungover."

"A hangover makes everything worse, old boy. I speak from experience."

CHAPTER 24

SOMEWHERE

HICKS WAS glad the tech company that had inhabited this space before him had put in a full bathroom in the executive office. The shower felt good. Necessary. The warm water felt even better against his face.

It had been a couple of days since he'd removed the bandages and although his skin was still sensitive, it was healing nicely. The pain was almost entirely gone, save for a few pulls, aches and twinges. The swelling was minimal.

Hicks turned off the shower and began toweling off in the windowless bathroom. He kept a rolled-up towel at the base of the door to prevent light from escaping beneath it. It was better to be safe than sorry.

He had come too far to allow a simple mistake like errant light ruin his journey.

The face he saw in the mirror was still a stranger. His appearance had always been unremarkable. Dark hair, pale skin, eyes that were closer to gray. No distinguishing marks or features to make him memorable.

Now his hair was as close to the skull as Scott's. Implants gave him more definition in his brow, cheek-bones and chin. His nose had been reshaped to be narrower and sit lower. He looked like an aging celebrity who'd had too much work done. He looked completely different, which had been the point of the operation.

Every datapoint used by facial recognition software had been changed except for his eyes. His retina scans for OMNI remained the same. Uploading a new facial scan to his device profile would be easy.

Eventually, his new face would wind up in a data-base somewhere. These days, no one could escape cameras. But it would take a fair amount of luck for a program or an analyst to discover his true identity.

James Hicks had been given a fresh chance at life. He intended to make the most of it.

He switched off the light and wrapped a towel around his waist as he walked through the abandoned office. The ambient glow from the surrounding build-ings gave him enough light to navigate through the maze of discarded cubicles. He knew there was a chance he could be spotted by a guard from across the street scanning the floor with night vision goggles, but the risk was minimal.

He had spent the past several weeks observing the patterns of the guards. Inactivity had made them soft. They hadn't paid attention to the abandoned floor since he'd gotten there. They hadn't even glanced at it except in passing as they took smoke breaks out on the deck.

Hicks was glad. They had forgotten about the

space. They would only remember it when it was too late.

Hicks stopped when he heard the fire stair door at the far end of the space rattle in the darkness.

Naked, save for a towel, he crouched behind an old cubicle and remained still. He was too far from his workspace to hide. He had no weapon, either.

But the rattling stopped, and he listened as the night watchman went on with his rounds, satisfied all was well.

Hicks went back to his interior office and dressed as if he was about to undertake the final part of his mission. As if the final domino was set to fall.

Domino One: Tessmer, who'd led to:
Domino Two: Yeung, who'd led to:
Domino Three: Resnick, who'd led to:
Domino Four: Veronica Holt, who'd let to:
Domino Five: Tamir Bat-Erdene who would lead them to:
Domino Six: General Zhou.

The fifth domino was teetering, but far from falling over. It was up to Rahul and Clarke to knock it over and send Zhou his way.

And Hicks knew he'd have to be ready when he came. He began to practice for that eventuality. *No time like the present.*

He laid out his gear on the makeshift bed. The outfit he had packed was simple and practical.

A black, Kevlar-lined hooded sweatshirt, black tactical pants and black side-zip tactical boots. Scott had even given him one of his team's Devtac helmets as a going away present.

He timed himself as he dressed. He shrugged into the black nylon shoulder holster that held his .454 Ruger under his left shoulder and a Mark 3 knife sheathed on his right. Both weapons were easy to reach. He rolled his shoulders until the fit became second nature again. It had been a long time since he'd worn normal clothes.

It had taken him ninety seconds to gear up and hit the door. *Too long. Too sluggish.*

He disrobed again and repeated the action until he got it down to forty-five seconds. He knew he could do better, but that had been enough practice for one night. The effort had left him a bit winded. He'd work on that, too.

With proper planning, he would have plenty of time to get ready before striking his final blow, but The Vanguard had proven to be unpredictable before. He had to be ready for anything.

He decided it was time for the final test.

Hicks raised his handheld and scanned his new face to see if OMNI could identify him. In seconds, the system came back with a fifty percent match on one hundred men, most of them regular civilians.

He scrolled through the results. None of them were James Hicks.

As Dean, he had the authority to create a new profile photo for himself. He did so but blocked anyone else on the system from seeing his new face. He was anonymous and wanted to remain that way for the time being. Even from Jonathan and Roger. At least until his war against The Vanguard's Asian branch was over.

Only then would he call off the Moscow Protocol and have the vast University network go back to the business of gathering intelligence. It would be up to Hicks to make sure the University was ready to finish The Vanguard once and for all.

He sat at his laptop and opened a secure audio channel via OMNI to Jonathan, who answered right away.

"How are you feeling, sir?"

"Closer to my old self, thanks." He realized he hadn't activated the voice-altering software and decided he didn't need it. His voice was strong. "What's the latest?"

"The NSA took possession of Veronica Holt and her daughter a few hours ago. Roger handled the exchange, and it went off without a hitch. Demarest's office has already begun to quell news stories of her abduction in the media."

Hicks had expected no less from Demarest. "How's he explaining her disappearance?"

"He's allowing it to leak that she fled from one of her clients and is now cooperating with authorities in an ongoing investigation," Jonathan explained. "It's just plausible enough for the media to get bored with it. Right now, the media is absorbed with a rap star who was found shot to death in a nightclub bathroom in Detroit."

"We didn't do that, did we?"

"No, sir," Jonathan confirmed. "An entirely unrelated event. But, the Adibi arrest has made Demarest a happy man. It seems Adibi was involved with other questionable clients and is a fountain of information for

The Barnyard. You've built up a lot of good will with the new DNI, sir."

Hicks was glad he'd thrown Demarest a bone. Let him chew on it while Hicks took care of The Vanguard.

"Convey my thanks to the Chicago team. Tell them to lie low until further notice. They should be able to go home in a couple of days, but don't tell them that."

He was immediately sorry he'd told Jonathan that much. "So, I take it the end is at hand?"

"It's over when it's over," Hicks said. "I'll be in touch with more, soon."

He killed the connection before he made another mistake.

It had been days since he'd taken a pain pill, but he still felt groggy. His brain was just a bit slower than it should've been. He knew being cooped up in the office wasn't helping. He hadn't felt the sun on his face or had a breath of fresh air since after his operation.

Just a little longer. Just until it's over.

He forced himself to forget his mistake with Jonathan and accessed the records on Rahul's activities in London. Clarke's pet, Pomeru, had started to get cold feet, but Rahul had handled him well. He'd applied just the right amount of carrot and stick to keep the banker in line.

Any lingering doubts he may have had about Rahul's abilities began to fade. He didn't like the idea of him drinking, of course, but that was part of his cover. He'd stopped after three scotches and helped Pomeru home, but Hicks would remind him to keep the tiger in its cage. He didn't need old weaknesses rearing their ugly head now that the finish line was in sight.

He read the report Rahul had sent just before he'd

gone to sleep the night before. He confirmed Pomeru was generally terrified of everything but had already crossed the Rubicon. It was too late for regrets and Rahul was using that fear to keep the banker on script.

Hicks tracked Rahul's handheld and was surprised he could still see he was on a private jet to Bangkok. Given Tamir's paranoia about security, Hicks had expected the flight crew to have confiscated his device. So far, he hadn't, but it was only a matter of time. Fortunately, Clarke had outfitted Rahul with glasses that would transmit from Tamir's compound despite Tamir's electronic countermeasures. The range wasn't great, but Clarke said he had a plan for that. Only time would tell.

Hicks hated not being in control of this part of the mission. He didn't like the idea of leaving the fate of Rahul and his plan in Clarke's hands. He didn't like the idea of leaving it in anyone's hands but his own.

So much had already gone wrong, but his team's tactical abilities had gotten him this far.

Rahul was walking into danger unarmed with a nervous banker and a pair of glasses that might not work manned by an out-of-shape British spy who hadn't run a complicated field op in years.

Hicks ran his hands over his new face and willed himself to relax. He was beginning to sound like Pomeru. And like Pomeru, Hicks had already committed himself to the plan. All he could do now is wait to do his part.

He looked over at the crate that had been serving as a bed for the past six weeks.

It was finally time to open it and get ready.

As Jonathan had said, the end was at hand.

CHAPTER 25

SOMEWHERE OVER EUROPE

RAHUL PATEL LOOKED up from his laptop and stretched.

Tamir might be an international terrorist, but he certainly knew how to treat his guests. The leather airline seat was more than comfortable. He had already tested the seat's ability to convert to a full-size bed and knew he'd sleep like a baby before landing in Bangkok. He'd need the rest for what lay ahead of him.

He looked across the aisle at Pomeru, who was rubbing his chin deep in thought as he gazed out the window.

Patel knew the flight crew was undoubtedly watching them, though they were discreet about it. He was sure the flatscreen at his seat had a camera and microphone to record his every move. He had allowed his laptop to be mirrored on the screen, certain that the plane's wireless network was also scanning his hard drive and phone. He hoped OMNI's security programs were as safe as they were rumored to be.

He wanted to tell Pomeru to stop his brooding. His pensive mood would only put Tamir and his people on edge. What's more, he didn't dare speak to him in the Hindi dialect they had used last night at the bar. He was certain the flight attendants wouldn't understand them, but Tamir's people would review the footage if they weren't observing him live. It would be difficult to identify it, much less translate it, but it wasn't impossible for a man of Tamir's means.

He decided to speak in English instead. "Are you always this troubled before a big meeting?"

Pomeru looked at him as if he'd been awakened from a dream but remained in character. "I'm always nervous when I'm about to propose a major shift in strategy to a client, especially one as important as Tamir."

Rahul understood Pomeru wasn't just talking about investment strategy and sought to once again put his mind at ease. "You've known the man for years and made him a lot of money. I've crafted a sound portfolio that will only make him richer and more secure. Relax and enjoy the flight." He picked up the champagne at his elbow and toasted him. "I know I am."

Pomeru frowned. "Ah, the luxury of youth. I wish I could be as relaxed as you, my friend, but our client is a difficult man to please. We may be confident in our plan, but he may not. I hope you're prepared to answer all of his questions, for you may very well find yourself on the hot seat."

"He may have changes," Rahul said, "but we're more than ready to address all of his concerns. I'm the one who devised the strategy, remember? And I haven't let you down yet, have I?"

Pomeru looked out the window rather than confront the lie. "There's a first time for everything. Let's hope this isn't it."

Rahul drank from his glass and felt the champagne hit home. The tingling in his brain awakened something dark in him. Something he had locked away now pounded against the door. The feeling was different from the scotch he had enjoyed the night before. He knew what hard liquor could do to him and he respected it. He'd had his guard up and had remained on-side.

But the champagne made him feel lighter. Uninhibited. Cocky. It reminded him of the tortured oblivion he'd enjoyed in the year following his sister's murder. Tortured, perhaps, but oblivion was still oblivion. It had dulled his feelings. The pain he had felt. It had made the guilt of her loss easier to bear. It had dulled his anger about his inability to avenge her death. It was easier to keep his mind free of such things while constantly running away from a hangover.

It had also allowed him to focus his hatred on the man who had denied him justice. The same man who had later saved him from the abyss. James Hicks.

Old animosities now came to the fore in his mind. The embers of old resentments rekindled. Scars began to hurt anew.

He felt his mind become alive and begin to spin. He caught himself before it went out of control. The champagne, for all its elegance, was having a bad effect on him. It hadn't been tampered with. The flight crew hadn't drugged him. They didn't have to for the poison was already in his system, locked deep within his mind. The old monster that had haunted him was pounding against the door. Hungry and eager to be fed.

He could not afford to let it out. *Not now. Not ever.*

He reluctantly finished the last of the champagne and set the glass aside. It would be his last drink until his meeting with Tamir. He was sure the arms dealer would require him to drink with him. He would need all his strength to keep both demons at bay.

Rahul smiled when the flight attendant glided toward him. She wasn't like their server at The Gilded Cage the night before. She was tan and tall with straight black hair tucked up beneath her cap. Her brown, almond-shaped eyes and accent led him to take her for Pakistani, which oddly enough, made him think of Clarke's nickname for him.

Paki.

The memory helped anchor him in the present.

The attendant lifted the champagne bottle from the standing ice bucket and began to refill his glass. Rahul covered it with his hand. "Any more of that and I won't get any work done." He smiled. "I'll just take some coffee please. Some water, too."

She wrapped the half-empty bottle in a towel and carried it with her to her station at the back of the jet before closing the door behind her.

Part of him regretted allowing such a fine bottle of champagne go to waste, but he knew it was for the best. He'd need to be at the top of his game if he had any hope of completing his mission alive.

After the attendant had brought him a cup of coffee and a glass of water, Rahul decided to look out the window for a bit to help quiet his mind before returning to his laptop. He was no financial genius, but for his meeting with Tamir, he didn't need to be. He simply had to be in the same room with him and allowed to speak. The rest of the plan would unfold naturally.

Rahul became aware his dizziness from the champagne increased while his hostility decreased. He didn't understand how that was possible. A glass of alcohol may have been enough to waken old hungers in him, but not enough to make him so groggy.

His eyes grew heavy, and he blinked them hard in an attempt to clear them, but it was no use. Had he been drugged after all?

He decided that wasn't possible. He had been trained to taste and smell most toxins and the champagne had been fine.

With great effort, he looked up at the air vents above him. The air had grown slightly warmer and had a bitter smell to it.

He hadn't been poisoned. He was being gassed.

He looked over at Pomeru and saw his partner slumped against the window. His mouth slack and beginning to drool.

Rahul looked to the back of the cabin to alert the pretty flight attendant, but the door was closed.

And in his final seconds of consciousness, he realized that it wasn't the regular kind of door he'd seen on other private jets. It resembled an air-tight hatch.

His suspicions had been confirmed. They were being gassed.

His cares soon left him as his eyes closed and the growing darkness enveloped him.

CHAPTER 26

DON MUEANG AIRPORT - BANGKOK, THAILAND

CLARKE STRUGGLED to keep the earbud in place. Hicks and his damned gadgets. How did they communicate with such a tiny thing? Give him an old satellite phone any day.

But he'd traded comfort for technology when Hicks agreed to allow him to run the op from the ground.

He heard Hicks loud and clear when he finally got the earbud situated properly. "King, this is Base. Do you copy?"

"Yes, I copy. Loud and clear." From his Club-issued mobile phone, Clarke read through the list of lingo Hicks had insisted on using for the duration of the operation. "The situation is in hand."

What the devil did that mean? Why couldn't he just say the plane landed. He was at an airport, for God's sake. Even if someone was listening in, it was a perfectly normal thing to say. Americans and their bloody spy craft.

"Copied and confirmed, King," Hicks said. "Do you have a visual?"

He used the laptop on the passenger seat to tap into the internal systems of Don Mueang Airport. He got a lock on the location of Rahul's plane and didn't like what he saw.

He didn't know what bloody code to use, so he spoke plainly. "They're using a hangar on the opposite side of the airport from my position. They've never used that one before." He accessed the airport's camera systems to get a closer look at the hangar. "I'm remaining at my current position. Getting closer might draw attention."

"Copy that, King."

The Club technicians had worked with one of Hicks's people to temporarily share access of each organization's feeds for this mission. Clarke had objected to the idea at first but was glad of it now.

Clarke began to sweat as he scrolled through the options, and it wasn't from the ungodly weather outside. His SUV's air conditioning was cranked to the max. He was worried about Rahul and Pomeru. Tamir had never changed hangars like this. Something was off.

After cycling through all the security camera feeds in that part of the airport, he found one atop the gate closest to the hangar. Knowing Hicks could see what he saw, Clarke said, "That's as close as we can get, Base."

"It's good enough, King. Suggest you remain in place until we know what we're dealing with."

Clarke didn't need Hicks to tell him that. He didn't need to tell him to worry about Rahul, either. Not being able to access the camera network inside the hangar was a bad sign. He didn't know if they were interrogating

Rahul and Pomeru or if they were boarding another plane bound for elsewhere or if Tamir had decided to break protocol and meet them at the airport.

It could all be as innocent as the jet company had moved hangars, though he would've known about it had that been the case.

He tapped his laptop as he watched the camera feed from the gatehouse. He saw cars and trucks stream in after the guard let them through, but none went near the hangar. The large hangar door was open, but shadows made it impossible for him to see inside.

He switched to another window that showed him military satellites in the area that might be able to give him a thermal reading of the hangar, but none were in position. At least none that he could access cleanly.

He looked closely as he watched two Cadillac Escalades glide out of the hangar and approach the gate. They took their time with the guard, showing him some paperwork.

While the guard reviewed them, Clarke attempted to zoom in on the driver, but the windows were tinted, and the camera was static. He couldn't enhance the image.

"Those look interesting, King," Hicks said in his ear. "Be ready to follow."

Clarke knew better. "Negative, base. Too flashy for our boy. I think I'll stick around."

He could practically feel the American's tension in his earpiece. "I repeat, King. I want you to follow those people."

But Clarke remained where he was as the two SUVs were allowed to proceed through the checkpoint.

"That's still a negative, Base. Our boy likes more covert transport. This is a decoy."

Clarke had tracked Tamir for years. He liked to spend money abroad, but at home, he played it humble. Just a simple nightclub owner. He had money but didn't like to flash it around in his own patch. Might make him too appealing a target for some local boys to take a shot at him. He rolled heavy, but all it took was a lucky shot from a .22 to ruin his day. When he travelled, he used something ancient to blend in.

The Cadillacs were a ruse for anyone who might be watching. Clarke knew it in his bones.

"King," Hicks said, "I must insist you follow my directions. They're getting away and we don't have visuals to track them."

Clarke kept his eyes on the guardhouse feed. There was going to be another vehicle. Something beat up. There had to be. Tamir's system had kept him safe this long. He wouldn't change it now with the heat on him.

His patience was rewarded when a faded brown Toyota sedan pulled out of the hangar and moved toward the gate. The undercarriage was lined with rust spots. The door panels were different colors. One of the headlights was busted.

But the passenger and rear windows were tinted. Darker than the windows on the Escalades.

He had seen that car before. It was Tamir's preferred mode of transportation.

And, as if he had any doubt, the guard raised the barrier and let the car through without a stop. *Of course, he did. The Cadillacs made straight your path, didn't it?*

"Contact, Base. I see something interesting." *Just*

like I told you, you damned Yank. "Will advise. Feel free to look over my shoulder."

"Copy that, King. You know I will."

Clarke put his SUV into gear and merged into the heavy traffic around the airport.

Without the benefit of a tracking device or a satellite, he was relying on the Club's technicians back in London to send any traffic camera footage to his laptop. Although he was sure they were bringing Rahul and Pomeru to the nightclub compound, it always paid to be certain.

He spotted the old Toyota in his rearview mirror as the two lanes of traffic merged. He'd track them from the front to avoid being spotted. *I'm here, Paki, old boy. Don't you worry your pretty head. Uncle Bruce is on the job. Just keep up the charm and I'll see you through.*

Hicks interrupted the good wishes he was sending Rahul's way. "King, this is Base. You're sure you'll be able to read him at his final destination, right?"

When dealing with a man like Tamir, Clarke knew only a fool could be sure of anything. "Looks like we'll find out soon enough, Base. King out."

CHAPTER 27

BANGKOK, THAILAND

It was the stench that woke him.

Rahul opened his eyes and realized someone had placed a hood over his head. Not a hood, really. A burlap sack from what little light he could see filtering through it. A sack that had once held the carcass of a dead animal, given how horrible it smelled.

His senses were slow to return, but he had the feeling he was being carried. He tried to move but was still too weak to try. His mouth was incredibly dry, and he was beginning to sense that his arms and legs were bound.

He'd been trained for this. He didn't panic.

He could tell he was fully clothed but felt damp. Not from water, but as if he had sweated through them. The air around his body felt humid, even for Thailand. The air inside the sack was simply horrible.

He felt the sensation of falling, followed by the impact of hitting the floor. It wasn't a dirt floor, and it wasn't metal. A familiar smell reached him through the stench of the burlap.

Damp wood.

Despite the weakness in his joints, Rahul tried to move back and forth, but could not. He sensed confinement around his shoulders, as if he'd been placed in a tight wooden box. Not a coffin, but something narrow.

A crate, perhaps?

His suspicions were confirmed when what little light he could see through the sack slid away and he heard hammering just above his head.

Someone was nailing the lid shut.

He refused to allow himself to panic. *You're still alive. That counts for something.*

More feeling began to return to his arms and legs, but he didn't try to struggle. One of the first lessons he had learned in the trade was how fear had killed more agents than the enemy. He kept himself focused and conserved his strength.

He remembered losing consciousness on the plane. The rest was a blank until now. The future would be revealed to him in time. For now, all he could do is enjoy the ride.

He felt the sensation of being picked up again and heard the squeak of wheels beneath him. He heard a stifled cry from beneath him that sounded like Pomeru.

Rahul guessed they had just been placed on a cart of some kind. The sound of casters straining from the effort confirmed his suspicion.

He smiled at the thought of Pomeru. The poor bastard had probably wet himself by now.

He was jostled by every bump along whatever path they were using to bring him to Tamir. He decided they had probably been placed in crates to conceal their entrance into the compound.

Perhaps Tamir didn't want his men to know with whom he was meeting.

Perhaps The Vanguard's recent setbacks had made him more careful than normal. He wouldn't know for certain until Tamir revealed his plan. For now, all he could do was speculate. It beat dwelling on other things.

The swaying of the cart almost made him nod off again, but the harsh voices around him kept him awake. He couldn't make out what they were saying, but recognized it as a derivation of Thai. He knew any attempt to translate it would be useless. Thailand had almost as many dialects as his native India. It sounded like his escorts were calling to other workers or guards as they rolled by with their cargo. He took the banter as a good sign. They were trying to make his transportation as casual as possible. They wouldn't go through all that effort if they just wanted to kill him.

He continued to keep his body slack as he rocked along the rutted path.

He perked up when he heard a new set of voices and felt the wheels beneath him roll smoother. He had a feeling he was now inside a building. His suspicions were confirmed when he heard a wooden door creak and a metal lock thrown. He was as certain as he could be that he was now inside somewhere. His instinct told him the curtain was about to go up.

As Hicks was fond of saying, 'Showtime.'

His body jerked as the cart came to an abrupt halt. He had the sensation of being lifted again and placed on a floor as more voices mingled with the screech of nails being pried out of the lid.

He could sense more than see a dim light as the lid was cast aside. A rush of humid air confirmed his suspicion. He remained limp as two sets of hands grabbed him under the shoulders, and another grabbed his feet as they lifted him from the crate.

Rahul heard three men chattering away, their voices echoing in the room he was certain he was in. The air was cooler now. Not air conditioned, but more like the natural coolness of a building with thick walls.

Like one of the many buildings he had seen from the footage of Tamir's compound.

The men carrying him stopped and he felt his feet hit the floor. Yes, it was definitely a solid floor. He was sure of that.

The men at his shoulders dragged him a few feet before lowering him into a chair. A wooden chair, given the way it squeaked when his weight landed on it.

His arms were still bound behind him and his legs were still bound beneath him. He pitched forward a little to relieve the ache in his shoulders from the long ride.

The sack was still on his head, and he kept his breathing under control as he used his senses to gauge his environment. He listened to another conversation in yet another unfamiliar dialect.

This one was different; more nasally and harsh. It was two men talking, two different men from the hand cart.

He listened between the unfamiliar words and heard something else. Another set of feet moving. A chair scraping against the floor. Despite the burlap sack, he counted perhaps four people in the room with him. Given Tamir's profile, he knew they were probably men. Pomeru had already mentioned that Tamir refused to discuss business when women were present. No one could accuse the old pirate of being a feminist.

Rahul caught a vague, familiar odor through the rancid sack. It took him a second to recognize it as cologne. An expensive cologne, if his nose was right. He'd smelled it only a few times before.

A deep voice in broken English said, "What is your name?"

"Athar Sawaya." Rahul found his voice raspy from a lack of water. "But my British friends call me Arthur."

"Do I sound British to you?"

"No, I can't say that you do. Feel free to call me Athar if you like. Or Sawaya, if you prefer the Eton tradition. I'm comfortable with either one."

Someone struck him across the left ear. Not hard enough to knock him off the chair, but just hard enough to get his attention. A pro.

The voice said, "I asked you for your name. Your real name. Not the fiction printed on your passport."

Rahul began to wonder if Pomeru had lost his nerve and given him up after all. There was no way of telling, so he decided to maintain the lie until presented with the truth. "I told you my name is Athar Sawaya. I'm sure you must have already done some kind of background check on me, so you know I'm telling the truth. I know you've had people at my house going through my things, my computers. You know who I am, so why are you hitting me?"

The voice was very close now. "How do you know we did this background check?"

"Because I wouldn't be here if you hadn't. My client is a very careful man."

Another backhand, this time from the right side.
Hard enough to almost knock him off the chair. "I want
your name. Your real name."

Rahul shook off the blow and ignored the ringing in
both ears. He knew if they had broken his cover, they
wouldn't be acting like this. He'd already have a bullet
in his belly with the promise of a quick death if he told
them the truth.

He decided the time was right to put some fear in
his voice. "You can hit me all you like but when you're
done, I'll be a bleeding, toothless mess and my name
will still be Athar Sawaya!"

Hands grabbed him around the throat over the
hood. "Who do you work for? Who do you really work
for?"

"I'm a consultant for Mr. Pomeru," Rahul croaked.
"If you don't believe me, ask him. He'll confirm
everything."

"What makes you think we believe that lying,
Romanian piece of shit?"

Rahul gambled with bravado. "Because that lying
piece of shit has made you an awful lot of money, sir.
You're a dangerous and competent man who doesn't
suffer fools lightly and who doesn't allow anyone who
can threaten you to live very long. I know this because I
did a background check on my own, too."

He flinched when he felt the cold steel of a gun
barrel placed against the back of his neck. "You seem to
be taking this well for someone who's supposed to be a
banker."

Rahul had been in this situation too many times
before to get rattled. "You know I'm not just a banker.
I'm a banker who helps people like you remain in

health, wealth and business. I've been through such treatment before, so either cut my throat or cut me loose and let me do what I came here to do. But you don't need another corpse right now. You need my help."

Rahul sensed the air in the room change, but he didn't know how. The tension was still there but changed.

A decision had been made.

The gun barrel pressed hard enough against his skin to make Rahul cry out.

The voice said, "And just what kind of work did you come here to do, Athar Sawaya? To kill me? Betray me?"

This time, Rahul didn't have to fake the pain in his voice. "To prevent you from losing every penny you have!"

The gun barrel lifted from his skin. He braced for another blow or a bullet.

He felt a tug at his feet and the rope give way instead. Another tug at his hands and they were free as well.

The hood was pulled from his head, and he had his first clean breath of air since the plane.

And although his eyes were open, he was in complete darkness.

"Shield your eyes, Athar Sawaya," said the voice. "It is about to get very bright in here."

Rahul slowly brought his hands up to his face and closed his eyes. The room became much brighter, and he allowed himself to look.

The light revealed all.

Rahul found himself on a wooden chair in a room that resembled a concrete bunker. The only light came from the fluorescent bulbs above a long wooden table about ten feet away.

He saw Pomeru sitting at the table looking about as bad as Rahul felt. His suit jacket was on the back of his chair. His shirt was open at the collar and his tie had been pulled down. He was patting at the sweat on his bald head with his pocket square.

But he was smiling proudly, like a father whose son had just kicked the game-winning goal. "I told you he was a cool customer, Tamir. One of my very best people."

In front of the table stood a round, swarthy Thai of about seventy. He wore a white suit with a stark red tie and matching pocket square.

No sweat stains were visible on the jacket despite the cool humidity of the room. A pencil-thin mustache adorned his upper lip. Rahul saw his own reflection in the thick black sunglasses he wore.

The man in the suit said, "I am Tamir."

Rahul's nostrils flared for a final confirmation before he said, "Hardly."

The man took a pistol from the table and aimed it at Rahul.

Pomeru looked on with mild interest.

The man in the suit roared, "How dare you doubt me, you miserable dog!"

Rahul sat back in the chair and crossed his legs. "The suit's a nice touch but I'm afraid the cologne gives it away."

The pistol trembled slightly in his hand as he raged, "Cologne? You speak to me of cologne? What cologne?"

He closed his eyes and raised his nose to the air. "A hint of vanilla, cinnamon, rose de mai and Ylang

ylang." He looked at the man in the suit. "Roja cologne unless I miss my guest. Goes for about three-thousand-pounds a bottle in Harrods last I checked, not that it's ever been a particular favorite of mine. You'd know that if you were wearing it, but you're not. Someone else is, and it's not dear old Pomeru. He's too thrifty for that."

Rahul nodded to a corner of the room. "My guess it's coming from that gentleman standing in the shadows just off to your right." Rahul gave him his best smile. "Feel free to shoot me if I'm wrong."

Rahul flinched as he heard someone begin to clap from the left side of the room. A man of seventy with long white hair and mustaches in loose-fitting smock stepped forward. He was the picture of a simple peasant if there ever was one. His body broad and his stomach flat. His skin lined from years of hard labor and concern.

Exactly what the kind of man who sought to blend in with his surroundings would look like.

"Excellent, Mr. Sawaya," the man said in halting English. "You are the first man who ever saw through my ruse on the first try." He stopped clapping and gestured for the man in the suit to lower his pistol. "Even Pomeru didn't know who I was for the first year."

Rahul bowed his head slightly. Relieved. "A testament to your showmanship, sir."

He watched Tamir pull off the long wig and the long white mustaches, revealing himself to be a bald man with a stringy, gray mustache. He removed his peasant robe to reveal that he was wearing a blue suit and shirt without a tie.

He spoke to the man who had portrayed him and,

while Rahul couldn't understand what he said, it was obvious he had told him to leave.

"Ylang ylang," the man said in English as he handed the pistol to Tamir. "We have a whore who uses that name."

Tamir and Pomeru laughed as the man walked into the shadows and left the room by an unseen door. Rahul joined in the laughter to be polite, though he didn't find anything funny about it. He'd almost lost his life.

Rahul noticed Tamir tossed the elements of his disguise on the floor and a man rushed out of the shadows to pick them up. The smuggler pulled out the chair at the head of the table. "Come take a seat, Mr. Sawaya. You have come far and we have much to discuss. I would apologize for your harsh treatment, but I never apologize about my security. Such steps are necessary in times like these."

"No need to apologize, sir," Rahul stood up, straightened his suit jacket and walked to the chair Tamir had pulled out for him. "A prudent man is always cautious, sir. And a powerful man never has to apologize for anything."

Pomeru was beaming. "What did I tell you, Tamir? He always knows what to say at the right time."

"An improvement over Adibi to be sure," Tamir noted. "He was a strange young man. I always sensed there was something off about him."

"You're as wise as ever," Pomeru said. "But as I said on the phone, you may rest assured that his trouble with the FBI has nothing to do with me or his work for you. And I've already taken steps to isolate you from anything he might tell them. All your accounts are safe and sound. At least those in my power to command, anyway."

Tamir rubbed his hands over his face as he removed the last remnants of the glue that had held his disguise in place. "Perhaps. But Adibi can certainly lead them to you, who can lead them to me."

Pomeru laughed it off. "Impossible, my friend. He has no leverage on either of us. What can he tell them? That he has come here to meet you several times? Your nightclub and compound are open to the world. He cannot tell the Americans anything they don't already know."

"Perhaps," Tamir said. "But you can."

Pomeru was too busy explaining his innocence to see Tamir grab the pistol and fire. A single shot struck him in the temple.

Rahul did not jump at the sound of the gunshot. The sight of Pomeru rocking back before he pitched forward did not make him cry out. Neither did the thin stream of blood that began to run the length of the table in the opposite direction.

Tamir lowered the smoking pistol as he looked at Rahul. Instead of putting it down, he kept it in his right hand but did not aim it at him.

Tamir looked as calm as if he had just finished his morning tea.

Rahul swallowed as he watched Tamir's eyes move over him.

The man's eyes narrowed. "You're a cool customer, Mr. Sawaya. Far too cool to be a simple banker, no matter what you say."

Rahul eyed the gun, aware that Tamir undoubtedly

had more men in the shadows. "As I've already said, sir, I have experience –"

Tamir waved him quiet. "Most of the men in my family never lived past forty. I am about to turn seventy in a week. Do you know what makes me different from all the other men in my family besides money?" He raised the pistol and tapped the side of his head with it. "Instinct. It's kept me alive this long and it'll keep me alive even longer."

He nodded toward Pomeru's head lying on the table. "I killed him on instinct. Not because I thought he was lying to me. My sources confirmed he was being truthful about Adibi's capture by the FBI. They even said there was nothing in his records that could point back to me. No, I didn't shoot him because he was lying. I shot him because Adibi might be able to tell the FBI enough to get him. His liabilities outweighed his usefulness."

"You may rest assured that I offer you only my services." Rahul folded his hands on the table. It was a polite gesture. It also put his hands in play. He knew he could snatch the pistol and kill the old man. Whether or not he could do it before the men in the shadows killed him was the question for which he didn't have an answer.

Rahul continued, "I have no affiliation or connection with Adibi whatsoever. And I have only worked with Pomeru as an occasional consultant."

"That's a lie," Tamir said. "Please don't do that again. Lies annoy me almost as much as coincidences. Your story checks out but only in ways convenient to you. Investors speak well of you, but only those I already suspect of having been corrupted by the authorities. Pomeru quickly finding a replacement for Adibi didn't bother me but finding a man such as you so quickly did. You were obviously more qualified than Adibi. Why didn't he bring you in instead of him in the first place?"

He grinned as he tapped the side of his head with the pistol again. "Instinct, remember? I know you're not a banker. I know Pomeru knew that to. The next words out of your mouth had better be the truth, or I promise that you will spend the next several weeks enduring more degradation than you ever thought possible."

Rahul noted he had said it as calmly as if he'd been discussing the weather. He knew Tamir and Roger Cobb would be fast friends if they met.

He decided the time had come to reveal his true purpose in coming here. "I wish to speak to you in private." He looked at the pistol. "You're armed and I'm not, so there's nothing I can do to you."

He'd expected the old pirate to balk at the idea at first, but he didn't. Tamir's dark eyes searched Rahul's and Rahul didn't look away.

When Tamir had seen enough, he said, "They stay. I trust these men with my life."

"What about the lives of those close to you?" Rahul asked. "What about your future?" He switched to Russian, hoping none of the men understood him. "Some of them serve more than one master."

There comes a time in such situations when inevitability set in. Rahul sat calmly and allowed his words to sink in. He'd done his part. Tamir would either believe him or not. He would either kill him or he would not. It was that simple and the time for considering consequences was long past.

Tamir peered into the darkness and gave an order in a language Rahul didn't recognize. He heard several pairs of shoes leave before a door shut.

Rahul knew this was his chance had finally come, but he could sense something wasn't right.

"Someone's still here," he said.

He received an answer by a long blade placed against his throat.

Tamir's grin widened. "I may be an old man, but I am not an old fool. This man with the blade to your throat is one of my many sons. You may speak freely in front of him. If you tell the truth, we will continue to speak. If you lie?" He glanced at Pomeru's body. The blood had stopped flowing and had begun to congeal on the table. "The rats in our basement will eat twice as well tonight."

The blade at his throat hadn't changed what he planned to say. "My name is Rahul Patel and I work for the Indian government. Counter-terrorism unit."

Rahul's heart skipped a beat when Tamir looked up at his son. He expected him to give the order to kill him, but instead said, "You win."

Tamir enjoyed Rahul's fear as he looked at him again. "We had a bet. I thought you were British. He said you were working for the Indians. My boy is as sharp as his blade. He'll be a fitting replacement for me someday. Now, tell me why are you here? I know it's not to kill me."

Rahul stayed on the script he had worked out with Hicks. Pomeru's execution had complicated matters, but the plan was still sound. "I used Pomeru to get next to you to deliver a message. I ask you to take it as a message and not a threat."

"That depends on what you say and how you say it."

Rahul continued, "My government has learned the Americans have Veronica Holt and your daughter. You probably know that, too. We also have uncovered a plot from General Zhou to kill them to maintain their silence. He has many friends in the FBI. The Americans don't want to see that happen and neither does my government."

Tamir's eyes twitched as they narrowed. Rahul knew he had just hit a nerve. Tamir had the same concerns.

"You and your government know a great deal," Tamir said. "Why the concern about me or my family?"

"Truth be told, we have none, but we are most interested in The Vanguard," Rahul explained. "We know General Zhou is currently in charge of the organization. And since his counterweight in Russia has been removed, he enjoys unbridled control of the organization for the first time in its history. It only stands to reason that he will devote most of his energies to expanding his influence throughout Asia. My government wants to work with you to make sure that doesn't happen."

Tamir's eyebrows rose as he sat back in the chair. The blade remained at Rahul's throat, but he sensed another change in the room. "And how do you propose to do that? Wanting it is one thing. Stopping it from happening is another. The general's reach extends far."

"Some believe too far," Rahul agreed. "He has infiltrated the Americans, India's intelligence community and the Chinese military. His control of North Korea's military is extensive. He even has people in your operation, which I believe is why you insisted on hiding us in boxes as you brought us past your guards."

Again, Tamir looked up at his son. "That Romanian ferret was right about him. He does speak well, doesn't he?"

Rahul couldn't see the son's reaction. He could only feel his blade at his throat.

Tamir looked at Rahul again. "You propose to kill Zhou, don't you? No easy task."

"A nearly impossible task for us," Rahul allowed. "But you could do it easily enough. You would not only save your family and your daughter but take his place as the head of The Vanguard."

Tamir's laughter surprised him. It was more of a high-pitched giggle than a genuine laugh. "You think it will be that simple? To kill a man who has spent the last twenty-five years solidifying his power and gaining allies. You think they will just fall in line behind me simply because I put a bullet in Zhou's brain?"

Tamir shook his head. "He has many sons, my friend. Even more than me. They are spread throughout his operation. They will not simply sit back and allow me to take their legacy from them. And neither the Americans nor your government will allow The Vanguard to remain operational after Zhou is dead. The Chinese will seek to wipe the organization from existence."

He wagged a crooked finger at Rahul. "Like I said, I may be old, but I'm not a fool."

"The Chinese have been hunting Zhou for decades," Rahul said. "They want nothing more than to see him dead but would like to take credit for it. We have already agreed to allow them to do so. You will be allowed ascend as the consensus candidate to replace him. The Chinese, the Americans and my government would allow that to happen and aid in any way we can."

Tamir's eyes moved over him. "How did I become so lucky? They hate me almost as much as they hate Zhou."

"Almost being the key word," Rahul said. "We believe the general is an aging zealot and out of control. We believe you would be someone we could do business with."

Tamir brought his left fist down on the table. "You mean control! I am no one's puppet."

Rahul remained calm. "I mean do business with. We understand there will always be someone willing to traffic in drugs and weapons and money. We are prepared to allow you to continue to do so provided you don't wage a proxy war against the West. We know you're not an idealogue, so this would be a beneficial relationship all around."

Tamir began to drum the fingers of his left hand on the table. The pistol was still in his right but seemed an afterthought.

He was still looking at his fingers as he said, "I don't trust the Chinese. I'm Malaysian by birth. I despise those bastards."

"No one's asking you to work with them," Rahul assured him. "They just want credit for the Zhou kill. They want to purge his influence from their ranks and use him as an example. His death will also allow other countries to clear out his allies there as well. All we want is for him to be dead and for you to succeed."

Tamir looked at him. "It can't be that easy."

Rahul relented and opened his hands in a show of

honesty. "Of course, we would like to seize the occasional shipment now and then, of course, but we'd be willing to work with you on that. Nothing that will damage your finances or your reputation too much. Just enough for a headline once a year or so. Make us look good and perhaps hurt a difficult customer of yours. We're willing to be reasonable. Once Zhou is out of the way, of course."

Tamir stopped drumming his fingers. "I assume there's a timeframe involved."

Conscious of the blade still at his throat, he said, "Only in so far as your family's well-being is concerned. If we take extraordinary steps to protect them, we'll tip our hand to Zhou's plans which won't do either of us any good."

Tamir shook his head. "Killing a man like Zhou is no easy thing. It requires planning. I don't mind losing my life to protect my family, but I won't throw it away on a failed effort. It can't be rushed and will require great planning. He is a difficult man to find. Even now, I have no idea where he is."

Rahul judged that to be true. "Perhaps we could help in that regard."

"I thought you might. How?"

Rahul gestured to the knife at his throat. "Perhaps we could dispense with the blade?"

Tamir shook his head. "Talk."

Rahul stayed on script. "Pomeru already supplied you with a new portfolio to safeguard Vanguard assets. It's a sound plan you can present to Zhou."

"No tricks?" Tamir said. "Zhou may be a Communist, but he understands finances. If you move the money into a government account, I'll be no use to you for I will be dead."

"Pomeru's suggestions are sound," Rahul assured him. "Once the transfer takes place, the money will be entirely in your control."

Tamir looked up at his son, then back at Rahul. "How does any of this help you track Zhou?"

"We understand Zhou has an archaic system to move his money. Both of you need to be present and scanned for any significant movement to take place."

Tamir's eyebrows rose. "Tessmer told you a lot, didn't he? I never trusted that bastard."

Rahul continued. "You're supposed to make the transfer at your bank's Shanghai headquarters. If you use your influence with him to do it at the Singapore branch instead, we'll have resources in place to track him once he leaves. It's a more secure location and easier to guard. He'll be perfectly at ease. We'll be able to track him and provide you with his location. You can carry out your plan to execute him whenever and however you wish. We only ask that you allow the Chinese to take the credit, as we discussed earlier. After your people have cleared out, of course."

"Of course." Tamir stood up and began to walk around the table. Rahul couldn't tell if he was thinking it over or thinking of a way to double cross him.

He stopped in mid-stride. "I take it this agreement is void if you fail to leave here with your life."

Rahul smiled. "I'm afraid that's a dealbreaker for my government. But let's not focus on the negative, shall we?"

Tamir returned to his thoughts as he continued his circuit around the table. By the time he reached Rahul's left side, he stopped. "Here's another dealbreaker for you. You must be my contact. No one else. I like you. You're tough, but also crazy. I don't trust someone who isn't a little crazy. And if you're smart, you'll allow me to make you a rich man."

Rahul felt the blade on his skin as he looked at the pistol Tamir was holding in his right hand. "On one condition. We shake hands on it."

Tamir placed the pistol on the table, well out of Rahul's reach, and held out his hand to him. He looked up at his son and, with a look, ordered him to withdraw the blade.

Rahul slowly stood and shook Tamir's hand. He maintained eye contact the entire time.

"Congratulations," Tamir smiled. "You've just made a deal with the devil."

"No," Rahul said. An image of Hicks flashed in his mind. "I've seen the devil. I look at this as a partnership between businessmen."

Tamir shrugged. "Have it your way."

The two men stood together and Tamir linked his arm through Rahul's. "Let's have a drink to celebrate our new partnership."

Neither of them looked back as Tamir's son tended to Pomeru's body.

Rahul was glad the rats would have one less meal for dinner.

OUT IN THE BAR, Bruce Clarke was just another fat, sweaty *farang* guzzling beer while he drooled over the naked women dancing between the tables to thudding music. His glasses kept fogging up from the humidity.

But he wasn't wearing them for sight.

None of the bouncers noticed him paying attention to the Indian man their boss led out into the VIP section overlooking the bar. Clarke was more interested in who wasn't with them. Pomeru.

A drunk American in a cheap suit elbowed Clarke's fleshy side and pointed at one of the girls who'd begun to dance on a table. "They sure don't have anything like this at home, do they?"

Clarke went along with it for the sake of his cover.

As the man leaned forward to get a closer look at the dancer, Clarke pitched toward him as if they were talking. He kept his voice low beneath the loud music. He couldn't hear himself as he said, "Base, this is King. Are you getting this?"

"I got it all," Hicks said in his ear. "Your relay of his transmission from the glasses was relatively clear. Good work."

Clarke turned his head so Hicks could see the view from his glasses. Tamir and Rahul had just toasted each other with martini glasses as they looked over the crowd below.

"At least one of them did well," Clarke said. *Poor Pomeru.*

"Fortunately, it was the one who counted. We are on plan and ready to go."

Clarke knew Hicks had a reputation for being a cool customer but hadn't expected that. "Anyone ever call you a cold bastard?"

"All the time, Ace. Keep eyes on the prize and report

when he's clear. And make sure you keep your hands to yourself in there. We wouldn't want you bringing home anything to mother. I'm here if you need me. Base out."

The drunk backed into Clarke again as Clarke sat up. He gestured at another naked dancer one table over. "We *definitely* don't have that at home."

"No," Clarke said, still thinking of Hicks. "No, we don't."

He glanced up at the VIP area and saw Rahul tap Tamir on the shoulder and point at a dancer in Clarke's vicinity. Tamir spoke into his ear and Clarke read Rahul's lips.

'She's beautiful. She's yours if you want her. My gift to you.'

Rahul raised his glass to toast her, but Clarke saw him look directly at him. He bowed his head slightly as he held his martini aloft.

Tamir was too busy taking in the sights to see Rahul mouth. 'To Pomeru.'

Clarke lifted his beer an inch from the table. 'To Pomeru.'

He downed his beer and signaled the waitress for another. He'd done his bit. So had Rahul. He might as well drink.

This was the Yank's show now.

CHAPTER 28

SINGAPORE

HICKS HAD FINISHED one final yoga routine before he began to get ready.

He'd spent the last day stretching as often as he could to get as limber as possible. He'd been inactive for weeks. He couldn't afford to be stiff now.

His face had healed. His mind was clear. He was ready.

It was night by then and he'd worked out in the office. He wasn't worried about being spotted. The guards hadn't paid any attention to his building.

What little he was bringing with him had already been stowed away the previous evening. His laptop and tactical gear would be coming with him. All that was left to do was get dressed and wait.

He went back into the interior office that had served as his home for weeks. He eyed his laptop as he began to get ready.

The dressing drills he'd conducted had proven to be

unnecessary but had helped make him sharp. And he'd need to be at his sharpest for what lay ahead.

He watched his laptop as he dressed. OMNI had been tracking Tamir's private jet until it landed in Vietnam, where camera footage from the airport showed he'd picked up General Zhou and his five-man security team.

Tamir had come out to greet the general personally. He enthusiastically shook his hand, all smiles. Hicks knew he had reason to be happy. He was about to become the head of The Vanguard.

Hicks was surprised the general had decided to rough it in the jungles of Vietnam instead of holing up in one of the lavish apartments he kept in Hong Kong or Shanghai. He probably knew those places would've been watched. He'd have been right. If he'd stayed in one of them, Hicks would've ended this weeks ago.

But now, hours later, he watched Tamir's plane make a graceful landing on the runway of a small private airport in Singapore. The jet slowly came to a stop beside two waiting Augusta Westland 119 'Koala' helicopters. The AW119 was one of the most expensive private helicopters in the world.

Hicks was familiar with the brand. It was used by law enforcement as well but could easily be fitted for clients who demanded luxury. Although the flight time between the airport and downtown was less than five minutes, only the best would do for General Zhou and his men.

He watched the feed from the runway closely as the jet's hatch opened, and the stairway unfolded. The guards were out first, forming a line that extended from Tamir's jet to the helicopters.

He felt a trickle of sweat break out on his brow when he saw Zhou and Tamir walk down the stairs and enter one of the helicopters. Just the two of them. Hicks clicked on the helicopter to track it.

The last domino was about to fall. He needed to be precise.

Zhou's helicopter began to lift off from the tarmac as the security team piled into the second helicopter. It rose from the ground and hovered beside the other.

Hicks switched his feed to a satellite that showed the helicopters were flying in formation. The guards first with Zhou and Tamir's helicopter close behind.

They were four minutes out from destiny.

And so was James Hicks.

He slammed the laptop shut, knowing the live feed would automatically be transferred to his handheld. He slid the laptop into a nylon case and placed it on his back. The straps were tight enough to keep it from bouncing as he moved, but not hinder his movement.

He gave the room a final glance to make sure the material he had left scattered around the place. It didn't look staged. It looked like a member of the Thai revolutionary movement had been staying there for days, waiting to launch his attack.

He slid on his tactical helmet and got ready to go to work.

He tossed his mattress aside and opened the lid of the crate that had served as his bed for weeks. He hefted the FIM-92 stinger launcher from its foam container and carried it out into the office.

In his mind, the countdown continued. *Three minutes out.*

He walked around the maze of abandoned cubicles until he reached the stairway door.

He gently rested the launcher against the wall and pulled out his handheld. He toggled to the camera feed from the stairwell and saw three guards were still on the other side of the door, protecting the entrance to the roof. He switched to the cameras he had hidden on the roof. Another four guards were still outside.

Seven targets in all. He'd faced worse odds.

Two minutes out.

The building rumbled as the first helicopter began to make its approach. Hicks checked the satellite feed one final time to make sure they were still in formation. They were. The first helicopter had the guards. The second had Zhou and Tamir.

He pocketed his handheld and drew his Ruger .454. The pistol would be loud, but the whirling blades of the approaching helicopters would be deafening.

That was part of his plan, too.

One minute out.

He heard the first helicopter's engine throttle down as it landed on the rooftop.

Showtime.

Hicks hit the bar on the stairway door, knocking one of the guards off his feet. The other two turned as they sensed – more than heard – the commotion.

Hicks's first shot struck the closest guard in the throat. His second hit the guard closest to the roof door, obliterating the left side of his head.

As the two corpses tumbled down the stairwell, Hicks stepped on the first guard's assault rifle, pinning it to his chest. The man's eyes widened, and he began to scream.

But no one could hear him over the noise of the landing helicopter.

Just as no one heard the final shot that took his life.

Hicks pulled the dead man's rifle from his grip, a compact, Chinese-made QBZ-191, and slung it across his chest. He'd need both hands for the next part of the op.

The roar from the rotor blades of the helicopters shook the building as he reached back into the office and grabbed the rocket launcher.

He hauled it up to the top of the stairs and paused at the door leading to the roof. He listened to the sound change as the first helicopter lifted off and the other approached. The sounds blurred together, but he knew what to listen for.

He took another deep breath and closed his eyes.

He'd been waiting weeks for this moment. Everything he and the rest of his people had done had led up to this.

He no longer cared if he lived or not. This was bigger than him.

Now.

The adrenalin coursing through his system caused time to slow down.

He kicked open the door and stepped onto the roof. The four guards were watching the second helicopter approach the much taller building across the street. They had no idea he was there.

Hicks brought the launcher to his shoulder and activated the guidance system. The image of the landing helicopter filled his screen. The missile had locked on to the helicopter's heat signature.

"For Tali!" he yelled into the rising noise.

He squeezed the trigger and the Stinger missile roared above the sound of the helicopter.

Hicks dropped the launcher as Zhou's helicopter disappeared into an angry orange plume of fire and death.

Death for Tamir.

Death for General Zhou.

The four guards on the roof had already begun to turn when they watched the missile streak overhead.

Hicks dropped to a knee and brought up the assault rifle he had had taken from their dead comrade.

Bullets struck the roof door and plinked off his face shield and helmet as Hicks opened fire in controlled bursts.

Each of the four men was struck in the chest, where Kevlar vests prevented his shots from piercing their skin.

But the impact from each burst was enough to send the men over the side, falling among the flaming debris of the helicopter that now rained down on the empty street below.

He threw off the empty rifle and dropped it on the rooftop as he slowly walked to the helipad on the opposite side of the building where his own AW-119 helicopter sat waiting for him.

He'd selected the building as his safe house not only because of its proximity to the bank Tessmer had chosen for The Vanguard's money, but because its helipad was out of the projected debris field.

Yes, James Hicks had planned this carefully.

He glanced up at the burning rooftop across the street. The entire top floor was still burning hot. Figures he assumed were guards fell from the rooftop, undoubtedly hoping leaping to their death would be better than burning alive.

Hicks didn't care. Zhou was dead. Tamir was a bonus. That's all that mattered now.

He climbed up to the elevated helipad, undid the ties that had kept the landing skids in place for weeks and climbed in behind the stick. He began to flick on the necessary switches that caused the helicopter blades to begin turning and bring the airship to life.

While the rotors came up to speed, he called Jonathan.

The Dutchman's voice came through loud and clear through his helmet's comms. "So, you've been in Singapore this entire time? I wish you'd told me. We have some good people in Singapore who could've helped."

"This was a one man show, Ace. I'm departing for Seletar Airport now. Have the flight crew taxi the G6 for take-off. I want wheels up ASAP. File a flight plan for Turkey."

He could hear Jonathan's fingers going to work. "What's in Turkey?"

"Who cares? I'm not going there. I'm landing in Japan just long enough to refuel and fly back to the States. Tell Demarest that Zhou is dead. Tamir, too. That ought to brighten his day."

"I'll be happy to tell him," Jonathan said. "Anything else?"

In fact, there was something. "Send another email to Zhou's son. Find a cryptic way to thank him for nudging his old man our way."

"It'll be a pleasure," Jonathan said. "And it'll be even better to have you back home where you belong, sir."

Home. He wasn't sure what that was and wondered if he'd ever really know. It meant nothing to him now.

"Alert the rest of the University that the Moscow Protocols have been lifted. It's back to business as usual. I'll check in when I'm back stateside."

"Where will you be, sir?" Jonathan asked.

Hicks worked the levers and pulled back on the stick, bringing the helicopter off the helipad. Nice and even, just like his father had taught him all those years ago.

"We'll see, Ace. Until then, this is Leader. Over and out."

As he rose high above the helipad, he looked down at the burning carnage below him. He knew he might not have ended The Vanguard that night, but he had ended enough of it to give him peace.

'For Tali' he'd yelled before launching the missile. But he knew that wasn't right.

The sight of the flames reaching up into the night sky warmed him.

Not for her. For me.

He pitched the helicopter forward and headed for the airport.

There was still plenty of work to do.

TAKE A LOOK AT GHOSTS OF
WAR: BLAZER BOOK ONE

BY G. C. HARMON

GO BACK IN TIME WITH BLAZER AS THIS HEART-STOPPING ACTION TAKES A CLEVER LOOK AT HISTORY.

Before Steve Blazer was given command of SFPD's Special Forces—before he was a crack Homicide Inspector—he was an elite up and comer on the Vice Squad.

During an Asian drug smuggler bust, two Vice cops are murdered. The killer leaves a signature—one that means something to Blazer's mentor, Captain John Stanson— leading him to believe the smuggler gang is tied to a wealthy Vietnamese businessman who rules San Francisco's Little Saigon district with an iron fist. As Blazer dives deeper into the investigation, he clashes with the Federal Agency providing his protection, and when the Vietnamese businessman is murdered, the feds put Blazer on the top of their suspect list.

While the Vice squad pursues a drug ring from the Golden Triangle and a cop killer, Stanson goes on a perilous journey of his own, reliving parts of his violent past where he was taken as a prisoner of the Vietnam War. Blazer takes notice and sets out to prevent Stanson from crossing a line he can't come back from.

But will Blazer get to him in time? Will the mysterious killer connected to Stanson's perilous past be brought to justice once and for all?

AVAILABLE NOW ON AMAZON

ABOUT THE AUTHOR

Terrence McCauley is an award-winning writer of
Thrillers, Crime Fiction and Westerns. A proud native
of The Bronx, NY, he currently lives in Dutchess
County, NY where he is writing his next work of
fiction.

CPSIA information can be obtained
at www.ICGtesting.com
Printed in the USA
BVHW081701250722
642964BV00026B/422

9 781685 490195